OVER THE
RAINBOW

OVER THE RAINBOW

THE EXILE BOOK OF ANTHOLOGY SERIES
NUMBER SEVENTEEN

EDITED AND WITH AN INTRODUCTION BY
DEREK NEWMAN-STILLE

Publishers of Singular
Fiction, Poetry, Nonfiction, Translation, Drama and Graphic Books

Library and Archives Canada Cataloguing in Publication

Over the rainbow / edited and with an introduction by Derek Newman-Stille.

(The Exile book of anthology series ; number seventeen)
Short stories.
Issued in print and electronic formats.
ISBN 978-1-55096-712-8 (softcover).--ISBN 978-1-55096-713-5 (EPUB).--
ISBN 978-1-55096-714-2 (Kindle).--ISBN 978-1-55096-715-9 (PDF)

1. Marginality, Social--Canada--Fiction. 2. Short stories, Canadian (English).
3. Canadian prose literature (English)--21st century. 4. Fairy tales.
I. Newman-Stille, Derek, 1978-, editor, writer of introduction
II. Series: Exile book of anthology series ; no. 17

PS8323.M35O94 2018   C813'.01089206   C2018-904740-2
                                                C2018-904741-0

Published by Exile Editions Limited ~ www.ExileEditions.com
144483 Southgate Road 14 – GD, Holstein, Ontario, N0G 2A0
Printed and Bound in Canada by Marquis

We gratefully acknowledge the Canada Council for the Arts,
the Government of Canada, the Ontario Arts Council,
and the Ontario Media Development Corporation
for their support toward our publishing activities.

Canadian sales representation:
The Canadian Manda Group, 664 Annette Street,
Toronto ON M6S 2C8   www.mandagroup.com   416 516 0911

North American and international distribution, and U.S. sales:
Independent Publishers Group, 814 North Franklin Street,
Chicago IL 60610   www.ipgbook.com   toll free: 1 800 888 4741

*I dedicate this to book to all of the folks
like myself who grew up loving fairy tales
and wanted to see ourselves in fairy tales.
I dedicate it to the storytellers, the readers,
and the people who love tales of wonder.
This book is for us.*

FAIRY TALE TRANSFORMATIONS

INTRODUCTION

DEREK NEWMAN-STILLE

Born out of oral narrative, fairy tales are themselves magical. They are spoken into existence like a spell, and they make changes in the world as people listen to and read them. They are spells that change the way we think. These spells draw ingredients from mythology and the subconscious, speaking to our innermost thoughts, desires, fears, uncertainties, and needs. Even though they are filled with magical creatures – fairy godmothers, witches, talking frogs, and transforming swans – these are essentially human tales. They are ways to tell us about ourselves, and yet, with each fairy tale we read, we change. We become something different. Maybe not a unicorn or a bear, but we become different, our thoughts spiraling into new possibilities.

Because fairy tales come from oral narratives, they are changeable. They shift and modify themselves depending on who is telling the tale and who is being told the tale. Maybe this is why fairy tales have survived so well...because they can change as our cultures change. Fairy tales take on our cultural baggage, picking it up like magical fruits on a hero's journey. This magical fruit salad cultural baggage gets tossed with the myths of the past, becoming something different and speaking to a new age, new culture, and new experience each time. Our fairy tales possess the ability to transmute and transmogrify.

Yet fairy tales claim to be tradition...

So, in their adaptability and changeability, fairy tales show us that traditions are meant to be changed. They are meant to grow and shift as new ideas spark and flow around them. Traditions, like Cinderella's pumpkin, can grow and become something other than themselves. They can be imbued with that mutable magic.

Kelsi Morris and I came up with the idea for *Over the Rainbow* because we looked at the fairy tale tradition and saw absences, gaps, and deletions. Fairy tales are often about belonging, featuring the return home or creating new homes, and we noticed that there were people being cast into the role of not belonging. We wanted our fairy tales to be a trail of breadcrumbs for readers to find their way into narrative traditions, to belong and take part in the magic of speaking our presence.

We recognized that by changing and shifting narratives, opening doorways for new voices and tales, we could be fairy godmothers, helping tales to find their way out into the world and change it. As much as this collection is a book, it is also a glass slipper that can fit anyone and imbue them with the magic of change.

Just make sure that you read it before midnight...

SKIN

Nathan Caro Fréchette

He started coming back to himself on the beach, sometimes as far as ankle-deep in the sea, shoes and all. He always woke up there when his mind stopped, when he didn't know who he was; the sand under his feet, the sound of the waves, the cool sea breeze on his face always made him feel so welcome. It felt like home or, at least, closer to it than anywhere else.

The impression of comfort didn't last: as usual, it was immediately followed by the hollow feeling of wrongness that he had felt about his body lately. It was so overwhelming that it had started being the first thing he felt about himself when he started to remember who he was: not his name, not his family, not even his friends; just a general feeling that his body, his skin, was *wrong*. The feeling was always there, like a toothache, sometimes in the background, sometimes so painful it pushed the breath out of him, hollowed him out of all thought and feeling except this white-hot pain.

"There you are," a voice sounded behind him, and he turned, slowly. A boy stood there, a boy with a smile bright as the moon, who held his heart in his eyes. He was familiar, so familiar, like he was all that mattered in the world.

"Vincent," he replied, his voice slightly cracked, like he hadn't used it for a while, and too high, wrong, so wrong, like the rest of his body.

Vincent crouched in front of him, his moon-smile wavering as he searched his eyes. "Veronica? Are you all right?"

He shook his head, the simple word driving through his entire being like a red-hot rebar. "Don't call me that," he said, lowering his voice as far as it would go.

"I'm sorry," said Vincent, taking his hand. "Ron."

Ron looked down at their joined hands. The touch was light, but it spread some sort of heat through his skin, warming his arm, his heart, his entire body. Ron had never really explained the reason behind the nickname to Vincent; how it made his skin crawl to be called by his feminine birth name, how he couldn't stand to be perceived as a girl. But he knew, deep down, that Vincent couldn't see him as anything but a girl. Even though his breasts were bound, his hair cropped short, and he'd been clear about using only the name "Ron," Vincent could only see him through that lens. He'd always been too afraid of taking that next step, telling him everything, and possibly losing his only friend.

"I came by your house and you weren't there," continued Vincent, unaware of the interior cacophony of Ron's thoughts. "Your mom's pretty upset. Did it happen again?"

"...I..." He tried to think. Mom had been angry. Angry about what? His free hand instinctively went to his head, touching his hair.

Vincent seemed to understand before Ron could formulate the thought. "Is she angry because you cut your hair?"

Ron nodded, his hand running through the cropped black locks. "She says...I'm just like my father." He looked up at Vincent, troubled. "I don't know what that means." Ron had never known his father; the man had had a passionate, but short, affair with his mother, which only lasted a few weeks, then left before his son was born. He'd come back after the birth to try to claim his child, or so Mom said, but had been unsuccessful, whatever that meant. Ron had decided long ago that thinking about this too much was too painful, too distracting; there was something about the way he felt when he spoke of his father which reminded him of the deep unease he felt about himself.

Vincent smiled his moon-smile again. "Well, I think it looks fantastic. It really suits you." He touched the side of Ron's head gently, barely brushing the hair with his fingertips, but the touch vibrated down Ron's neck and spine, and he closed his eyes.

"Thanks."

"Is it the attic thing again?" Vincent asked, his brow creasing.

Ron rubbed his temples. The attic. The attic, of course. How it called to him, to his heart, his head, his entire body, like a physical need sewn into his every muscle, pulling him inexorably toward it, as painful to resist as a million fish hooks buried in his flesh. Most of his waking hours were now spent actively resisting the call, the pull, and he could hardly concentrate on anything else. And yet, when he gave in and went to the ladder...he woke up here, on the beach, as though he had somehow sleepwalked there.

"Yeah," he simply said, "the attic. I can't take it anymore."

"Did you try to go back?"

Ron frowned, concentrating. His thoughts were coming back in a jumble, as they always did. He'd given in to the need. He'd pulled down the ladder, and he'd started to climb, and...

He shook his head, feeling a familiar, dull ache creeping up behind his eyeballs. "I...yes, I did. But it's the same as the other times. As soon as I start climbing the ladder...nothing. My mind just goes, and I end up here, and I can't remember what happened."

His voice shook with emotion, going back up in pitch despite his efforts. "I can't take this anymore, Vincent. I don't know what to do."

Vincent stroked the back of his head gently. "Maybe I can help. What if I came with you?"

Ron looked up, breathing deep to give himself courage. "I...but what if...what if what happens when I black out...what if it's something weird? What if I..."

"Hey," Vincent touched his cheek, "don't worry. Whatever it is, we'll deal with it. Okay?"

"Okay."

They made their way back to the house in silence. Ron spotted his mom in the garden at the back of the house, planting, so they went through the woods to get to the front door, silent and unnoticed.

The silence in the house was deafening; it amplified every creak and sigh that the old building let out in protest at their steps, and Ron was acutely aware of their breathing, down to the slight whistling sound that Vincent's nostrils made, which Ron had never noticed before. When Vincent pulled the attic ladder down, the clatter resounded like a four-vehicle crash. Vincent turned toward him, raising his eyebrows in an encouraging expression, but Ron could only stare at the ladder, paralyzed. This was the place of so many of his defeats, and yet he felt the key to his true self, to the part of him that he had to keep hidden, the part that he himself did not really understand yet. Besides the feelings he had for Vincent, this part of him was the only true thing he'd ever contained in his being.

Vincent reached out to take his hand. "Come on," he said in a gentle voice. "I'm right behind you."

His words made some of Ron's fears ebb away, and he started climbing. One rung, two rungs, three...

His hands. His hands weren't his hands; or they *were* his hands, more his hands than they'd ever been, but he'd never seen them before. They shone like the full moon, with specks of colour and—

"You're almost there." Vincent's voice brought him out of his stupor. "Keep going."

He climbed another rung. And another. And...his vision clouded. The ladder in front of him was blurry, and his limbs felt like they were going to sleep. He wavered, then swayed, and started falling backward.

Vincent supported him with one arm, holding on to the ladder with his free hand. "You're almost there. You can do this. Don't give in. Don't give up."

Ron breathed, and closed his eyes, concentrating on Vincent's warm touch. He usually hated being touched; it was as though people's fingers somehow conveyed to him that they thought him a woman. But Vincent saw through that, saw *him*, and his contact helped keep Ron here, in this body, in this moment. He focused on the sensation of climbing, trying not to think of his destination, of what he might find there. He emptied his mind. Climb. You're not dizzy. Climb. Vincent is here. Climb. You can do this. *Climb.*

The confusion and vertigo grew with every step. Had he really wanted this? Was it that important? Wouldn't he rather be in the woods? What was he doing here, anyway? He held on to the sensation of Vincent's hand on his back, that soft, comforting pressure, until he didn't remember who Vincent was, until he couldn't even understand what the feeling was, other than comforting.

When his hand finally fell on a hardwood floor instead of another ladder rung, the veil lifted from his mind, as though he'd never been dizzy or disoriented, and he pulled himself up into the attic. Vincent followed, immediately clapping him on the upper arm.

"Hey, you did it! You're here!"

Ron breathed, nodding, and turned to grin at Vincent, but his expression of celebration died before it found his voice. Vincent was smiling, but the fear and uncertainty in his eyes were very clear. Ron wasn't sure what to make of it, and his senses were overwhelmed by the longing for whatever was in this room, so he could not address it, but only stood and looked around. The room was dark; the floor covered by a thick layer of dust, which spoke of years of abandonment. It was also empty, save for a large, ominous chest at the end of the room. It was there. Whatever it was, it was in there, pulling at his chest through the bindings over his breasts.

"What now?" said Vincent. Ron couldn't find any words to answer, so he just raised his hand and pointed at the chest, taking a step forward, and another. Vincent followed him, silent. Ron felt none of the confusion, only an increasing certainty as he grew close to the chest, reached out his hand, and—

"Veronica, stop!"

He hadn't meant to respond to his birth name, but he was so used to it that he stopped anyway, and the voice's shrill tone startled him so much he could hardly have done otherwise. He turned to see his mother in the trap door, standing at the top of the ladder, panting, her fingers still caked with dirt; she had obviously run in from where she was gardening outside, but...how? Why?

"Mom?"

"Please, just..." His mom licked her lips and raised one of her hands, climbing the ladder slowly, as though she thought Ron was a savage animal that might attack at any given moment. "Step away from the chest. Come back downstairs. I will make you two some hot chocolate and cookies, okay?"

"I don't want cookies!" Ron said, his voice sharper than he had intended. "What's in the chest? Why are you hiding it from me?"

"Please, sweetie," Mom said, her eyes full of tears, still approaching Ron cautiously. "You don't want to open that box."

"Why not?"

"You just – you don't know what's inside! It'll change every-thing!"

"Then tell me! Can't you see how unhappy I am? How much I'm suffering?" He pulled up his sleeves, showing the long, still-red, puffy scars going up each forearm. "You know how much I've been longing to die. Why wouldn't you tell me? How could what's in there be any worse than that?"

His mom let out a strangled sob, covering her face with her hands. When she spoke, her voice was so low and muf-fled that Ron almost did not hear her.

"I don't want you to go," she said.

"What?"

"I don't want you to go. I don't want to lose my beautiful baby girl! If you open it…" she trailed off, letting out another sob. "This is all your father's fault. He should have told me what he was."

Ron looked back to the chest behind him; it still pulled at him, and standing next to it without moving toward it nearly caused him physical pain, but he just needed to hear what his mother was saying. What did she mean about his father? His eyes briefly met Vincent's as he looked back toward Mom, and he could see that his friend was just as confused as he was.

"What's that supposed to mean, 'what he was'?"

"Your father…" Mom took a deep, shuddering breath, visibly trying to calm herself. "He was…he wasn't…human."

Ron took a step backward, horrified and fascinated at the same time.

"He wasn't human? What do you mean? What is he supposed to be? How can that even be?"

"He was…" Mom's eyes seemed far away now, like she wasn't talking to him as much as to herself. "He was so beautiful. I should have known. He had to be magical, looking like that, didn't he? And then he left, and when you were born… they came back, you see. His people. They said you were one of them, and they had to take you with them, to go live in the sea. So I took it off; it just came right off, in my hands, and I knew what to do. I hid it. Without it, they couldn't see you, you see? I couldn't let them take you."

"What do you mean, you took it? Took what?"

Mom finally looked up at him, her face wet with tears, her eyes red and puffy. "Your skin," she whispered. "People like…like your father…they are magic. Selkies, we used to call them. They are bound to the sea. They have to remove their skin to walk among us. That's how he came to be with me." Her words were rapid-fire, as though all the secrets she'd been keeping were overflowing. "He had…he had lost his skin. I thought, after years, that he was happy, that he'd stay with me, but when he found it…" She let out another sob. "I couldn't let this happened to you. I had to take it, don't you see?"

Ron took another step backward, looking down at his hands, his arms, and his chest, which bulged awkwardly despite the binder. At the skin. The skin that had felt so wrong, for so long. He turned toward the chest, no longer thinking about his mother, his father, or even Vincent. This was the piece that had been missing, this was going to complete him.

He opened the chest.

It didn't look like anything at first – just a piece of old, dried-up rubber, or leather, thin and fragile. He picked it up gingerly, feeling like it would fall apart at his touch. Instead, it started to move, and glow, as though it were alive, and stretched toward him as though it yearned for him as much as he for it. He lifted his shirt, oblivious to the fact that Vincent would see, and he pulled his binder off to place the now-glowing skin between his breasts. It seemed to explode in a brightly coloured blaze, like fireworks, and flew to wrap itself all around his body. It burned him, all of his skin, and he thought, through his screams, that this had been a grave mistake, and that he was going to die. He screamed so much that he couldn't hear anything else, until eventually he had no air left in his lungs, and he fell to the floor, wheezing, gasping, and exhausted.

Immediately, Vincent was with him, his eyes full of worry, his arms around him.

"Ron? Are you all right? Please, talk to me!"

Ron tried to sit up, but almost fell; Vincent had to hold him up. Slowly, he regained his strength, and then, more than that, a strength he had never known before. Taking Vincent's offered hand, he stood, and didn't let go even when it became evident that he was quite capable of standing there by himself.

He looked at his mother, who was staring at him with wide eyes. She started sobbing again and hurried down the ladder and away from him. He felt a pang of loss at her retreat, but he was too hurt and angry to go after her. Instead, he turned to face what he'd feared since they had climbed up here – the look on Vincent's face.

It wasn't what he had expected: he had thought to see fury, scorn or disgust there, but there was only concern, fear, and a little sadness. He also realized that Vincent hadn't tried to pull his hand away from his grasp this whole time.

"Are you all right?" Ron asked.

"Me? What about you? You looked like you were on fire, and then…"

Vincent gestured vaguely at his torso, and Ron looked down. He couldn't help but smile when he saw his flat chest. He touched it, incredulous; it had really happened. It wasn't in his head. His body finally looked the way he had always known it should. His joy was indescribable, quiet, but whole, and strong, like the sudden absence of a sharp, deep pain. Tears of joy welled in his eyes, and he wiped them with his free hand, grinning.

"Yeah, I'm fine," he said. "I'm finally fine." He looked up at Vincent, still hesitating. He could feel his palm start to sweat, and thought surely if Vincent hadn't let go before, he surely would now. But Vincent gave no indication that he was bothered, expressing only relief at Ron's declaration. "You're not…" Ron cleared his throat. "…you know…freaked out?"

Vincent laughed nervously. "Well, a magic piece of leather, which is actually some kind of enchanted skin stolen from a baby, just burst into flames and looked like it was killing my, uh, kind-of-more-than-friends-friend, but apart from that, everything's good."

Ron smiled, scratching the back of his head and looking down self-consciously. "I meant, you know…"

Vincent cupped Ron's cheek in his hand. "I know what you meant. It doesn't change anything. You're still you. Well,

I mean, you're some kind of magical…person, and with different parts, but still…you."

Ron didn't say anything, instead just leaning in to hug Vincent tightly. They held each other for a while, then Vincent looked at Ron.

"What are you going to do now?"

"I don't know. I always thought…I have to get to the attic. I have to find this. It will complete me. And never really about what came after, you know? I guess I have to figure it out."

"But you'll be happy?"

Ron thought about his mother, downstairs, and the lies and secrets that were really the glue that had held them together. She had never loved him, not for who he was; she'd taken that away from him, cut out his very being. He endured this unspeakable ache his entire life because of her fear that she wouldn't be able to keep the person he really was. He thought about his father, the sea, and the magic that he now felt clearly coursing through his veins, and everything that he didn't know or understand about his life.

"I think so. But I still have a lot of things that I need to know."

"Well, whatever happens, I'll be there," said Vincent.

Ron smiled at him, giving his hand a squeeze, and they started climbing down the ladder together.

I AM NOT BROKEN

FIONA PATTON

There once was a robot who served in an imperial army on a far distant planet. It was large, and strong, and had many weapons built into its body. It had a camouflage device that allowed it to change its colour to blend into its environment, rather than remain the base metal grey of its fashioning. It had a rudimentary intelligence, a limited autonomy, and a basic vocabulary to better perform its duties to the emperor and the empire. It had no name for its masters had no reason to give it one; rather, it had a number to identify it in the event of damage. On the day it was activated, it stood in ranks with a thousand other robots. One by one, each was tested to ensure that it was In Good Working Order. Those that were found to be Not In Good Working Order were declared Broken, and taken away to be used for scrap.

As the time for its testing drew near, the robot began to notice which of its compatriots its masters considered to be In Good Working Order: they were those that looked exactly like the others, those that performed exactly like the others, and those that answered exactly like the others. Something deep within the robot rebelled against this, but since it did not want to be taken away to be used for scrap, it made sure to look and perform and answer exactly as those robots did. And so it passed all of its tests and was loaded into a huge troop carrier destined for a planet on the far side of the galaxy that had not yet been brought under the empire's control.

When they entered the planet's orbit, however, they found that its defences were much stronger than the empire had anticipated, and the troop carrier was shot down. It crashed into a field on the edge of a dense forest, scattering debris for several kilometres, and the robot was thrown into a thick hedge of buckthorn trees.

Once it had worked its way free from the tangle of slender, yet surprisingly strong limbs and sharp spikes, it scanned itself for damage, finding its knee and ankle joints to be bent and twisted, the automatic function of its camouflage device burnt out, and a warm and ragged rumble coming from deep within its power supply. All around it, other robots which had survived the crash were performing similar scans, then standing, waiting to be declared either In Good Working Order or Broken. The robot struggled for a moment with the conflict between the fact that it was now damaged, therefore Not In Good Working Order, therefore Broken, therefore soon to be taken away to be used for scrap, with the growing belief that this was not what it wanted, and the newly awakened idea that it should, therefore, take itself away from the crash site so as not to be discovered and declared anything at all. Finally, it chose the latter. Turning, it spotted a narrow path leading into the forest and, without a backward glance, it plunged into the trees.

Once concealed under the thick canopy of leaves, it found that it was unable to march due to the damage to its knees and ankles, so it smoothed its gait to a walk. It manually activated its camouflage device to change its outer appearance from the gravely brown of the path, to the dappled hazel of the underbrush, to the deep, mottled green of the densely growing trees, and so made its way through the forest for three days. Finally, it came to a fork in the path with the left-hand way leading east and the right-hand way leading north. Seeing no discernable difference between the two, the robot came to a stop and would have remained there had it not looked down to see a small, tawny fox sitting in the centre of the fork, holding one front leg up at an awkward angle. The robot looked down at the fox and the fox looked up at the robot.

"Where are you going?" asked the fox.

"To no fixed destination," answered the robot.

"Why do you now stand so still?"

"Because two identical choices are challenging."

The fox nodded. "That is true," it agreed. "I am going home to Sanctuary. I set out with two companions and have gone farther than they have. Now I am tired and can go no farther today. If you will carry me home to Sanctuary, you will have made a choice."

"Which path is the way to Sanctuary?" asked the robot.

"The path to the east."

The robot peered down at the fox's front leg.

"Are you broken?" it asked. "Do you not fear being taken away to be used for scrap if you are discovered?"

The fox looked insulted. "I am not broken," it declared. "I am injured. When I return home to Sanctuary, my injury will be tended to."

So, the robot lifted the fox as gently as possible and, smoothing its gait further so that it would not jar the small creature, it set out down the eastern path, turning its left arm a rich russet where it cradled the fox against it.

They hadn't gone very far when they came to another fork in the path, with the left-hand way leading south-east and the right-hand way leading north-east. The robot looked down at the fox.

"Which path is the way to Sanctuary?" it asked.

The fox looked up at the robot with a sheepish expression. "I can't remember," it admitted. "I am young and the rain in the night has washed away my scent trail."

They would have remained there had they not looked down to see a small, buff coyote sitting in the centre of the fork, holding one back leg up at an awkward angle. The robot and the fox looked down at the coyote and the coyote looked up at the robot and the fox.

"Where are you going?" asked the coyote.

"We are going home to Sanctuary," answered the fox.

"Why do you now stand so still?"

"Because I have forgotten the way."

"And two identical choices are challenging," the robot added.

"That is true," the coyote agreed. "I am also going home to Sanctuary. I set out with two companions and have gone farther than one and not so far as the other. Now I am tired and can go no farther today. If you will carry me home to Sanctuary, you will have made a choice."

"Which path is the way to Sanctuary?" asked the robot.

"The path to the south-east."

The robot peered down at the coyote's back leg.

"Are you broken?" it asked. "Do you not fear being taken away to be used for scrap if you are discovered?"

The coyote looked insulted. "I am not broken," it declared. "I am injured. When I return home to Sanctuary, my injury will be tended to."

So, the robot lifted the coyote as gently as possible and, smoothing its gait still further so that it would not jar the two small creatures, it set out down the south-east path, turning its right arm a soft tan where it cradled the coyote against it.

They hadn't gone very far again when they came to yet another fork in the path, this time with the way to the right leading south-south-east and the way leading straight ahead turning to the east-south-east. The robot looked down at the coyote.

"Which path is the way to Sanctuary? it asked.

The coyote looked up at the robot with a sheepish expression. "I can't remember," it admitted. "I am young and the rain in the night has washed away my tracks."

They would have remained there had they not looked down to see a small, ebony raven sitting in the centre of the fork, holding one wing up at an awkward angle. The robot, the fox, and the coyote looked down at the raven and the raven looked up at the robot, the fox, and the coyote.

"Where are you going?" asked the raven.

"We are going home to Sanctuary," answered the fox and the coyote.

"Why do you now stand so still?"

"Because we have forgotten the way."

"And two identical choices are challenging," the robot added.

"That is true," the raven agreed. "I am also going home to Sanctuary. I set out with two companions and have not gone as far as either of them. Now I am tired and can go no farther today. If you will carry me home to Sanctuary, you will have made a choice."

"Which path is the way to Sanctuary?" asked the robot.

"The path to the east-south-east."

The robot peered down at the raven's wing.

"Are you broken?" it asked. "Do you not fear being taken away to be used for scrap if you are discovered?"

The raven looked insulted. "I am not broken," it declared. "I am injured. When I return home to Sanctuary, my injury will be tended to."

So, the robot lifted the raven as gently as possible and, smoothing its gait even further still so not to jar the three small creatures, it set out down the east-south-east path, turning its chest a glossy onyx where it cradled the raven against it.

They journeyed this way for several hours until they came to the edge of the forest where a thick hedge of buckthorn trees barred their way. The robot looked down at the fox, the coyote, and the raven.

"How do we pass through this barrier?" it asked.

"I crawl under it," the fox answered.

"I weave through it," the coyote answered.

"I fly over it," the raven answered.

The robot studied the hedge. "I cannot crawl under it, weave through it, or fly over it," it noted.

"How did you pass through it on the other side of the forest?" asked the fox.

"I fell into it, and when I worked my way free I was on this side of it. But I cannot work my way free of it this time for, this time, my arms are full of you."   .

"Our friend, Summer, tells the hedge to open for her and it does," the fox said. "Perhaps if you told it to open for you, it would."

"Summer is of the hedge as the hedge is of Summer," the coyote countered. "Perhaps if you asked the hedge to choose to open, it would."

"The hedge's sense of humour is also of Summer's as Summer's sense of humour is of the hedge's," the raven warned. "Perhaps if you asked it to choose to open and remain so until we passed, it would."

The robot stepped up to the hedge. "Will you choose to open and remain so until we pass?" it asked.

A shiver went through the hedge. The limbs began to curve and twist and the spikes turn downward until a narrow opening was revealed. Carefully shielding the three creatures in its arms, the robot passed through, its hands turning the streaked khaki of the buckthorns, and came out into a vast field of wild flowers. In the distance, it could just make out a huge, domed structure.

"That is Sanctuary," said the three animals and, as they spoke, a thin, metallic walkway appeared, leading out into the wildflowers.

So, the robot took the walkway, turning its legs the colours of all of the plants it passed; red for columbine, orange for hawk weed, yellow for buttercups, green for coral root, blue for chicory, and violet for vetch, and came at last to Sanctuary.

Seated before the door was an old woman dressed in a pair of faded overalls with daisies sewn on the front, a large, straw hat on her head, and a pair of wooden shoes on her feet. Her skin was a warm bronze, her hair was three shades of green, and her eyes were the colour of the noon sky. When she saw the three creatures in the robot's arms, she frowned.

"And where have you been all this time?" she scolded. "I've been worried for your safety. The emperor has sent an army against us and I was afraid that you'd been killed by his robots."

"No," they replied. "We have been travelling with one of them."

The fox and the coyote and the raven each told their story and, when they were finished, the robot looked down at the old woman and the old woman looked up at the robot.

"You'd better come inside," she said. "It's going to rain. What's your name so that you might be known to Sanctuary and it will let you pass?"

"I have no name," the robot replied. "I have only a number."

The old woman shrugged. "Some are given names and choose to keep them, some choose new names, and some have reasons of their own to have no names at all. Fox and coyote and raven do not bother with names for their identities are made up of sight and sound and scent."

"Mostly scent…" the fox confided "…of musk and urine. That is how we are known to Sanctuary."

The raven puffed up its feathers in displeasure. "Speak for yourself," it retorted. "I am known to Sanctuary by my call which is both unique and emphatic."

"And which can pierce the ear at a thousand yards," the coyote noted. "I am known to Sanctuary by the sight of my bright, brown eyes, my stiff, white whiskers, and my thick, beige coat."

"How shall you be known to Sanctuary?" the old woman continued, sparing the three creatures a single, warning glance from underneath her green eyebrows.

The robot stood silent for a moment. "I do not have musk or urine, whiskers or bright brown eyes," it answered. "My colour changes as my environment changes, and my call is no different from any other robot's. I have nothing unique that would make me known to Sanctuary."

"Is the rumble in your chest unique?" asked the fox. "I felt the warmth of its vibration while you were carrying me and I found it very comforting."

The coyote and the raven nodded their agreement.

"It is unique for now," the robot answered, unwilling to admit that it might be damaged.

"You may change how you are known to Sanctuary at any time," the old woman said. "My name is Summer for now. Later, I will change my name to Autumn, then to Winter, and then to Spring. That is how I am known to Sanctuary."

"Then I will be known by the rumble in my chest," the robot said. "For now."

The five of them approached the door and, after Sanctuary had identified them all in the way that they had chosen, the door opened into an airlock, and from there, into a vast space filled with plants, birds, animals, reptiles, fish and insects. The fox, coyote and raven went immediately to three separate alcoves where their injuries could be tended to and where they could find food appropriate to their needs.

Summer looked up at the robot. "Are you injured?" she asked.

"Is injured the same as broken?"

"No. Injured is the same as temporarily inconvenienced."

"Then I am...injured," the robot answered.

Summer lead it to an alcove, larger than those the fox, coyote, and raven had entered. "Here your injuries can be tended to and you can be fed..." she paused. "...powered appropriate to your needs."

The robot peered into the alcove. "Do you also tend to robots here?" it asked.

"You will be the first," Summer answered. "Usually the waterer, composter, and my coffee maker are tended to here."

"Your coffee maker must be very large."

Summer spared the robot the same look she'd given the fox, coyote, and raven, then shrugged. "It's sometimes hard to get going in the morning," she answered.

The robot accepted this and entered the alcove.

"I am Sanctuary," a voice said. "The devices which make up your knee and ankle joints are injured. Do you choose for them to be tended to?"

"I am unable to march, but able to walk. If they are not tended to, will these injuries adversely affect this function?" the robot asked.

"If they are not tended to, the rate of injury to the knee and ankle joints will increase. Depending upon usage, these increased injuries will adversely affect this function in approximately twelve hours."

"If they are tended to, will I still be able to choose to walk rather than to march?"

"Yes."

"Then I choose for them to be tended to."

"The automatic function of your camouflage device is injured. Do you choose for it to be tended to?"

"If it is not tended to, will this injury adversely affect its manual function," the robot asked.

"No."

"If it is tended to, will the automatic function override the manual function?"

"Yes."

"Then I do not choose for it to be tended to. I choose to manually change the colours of my outer appearance."

"Your power supply device is injured. Do you choose for it to be tended to?"

"If it is not tended to, will this injury adversely affect its function?"

"If it is not tended to, its temperature will rise by one degree approximately every thirty-seven hours. A nine degree rise in temperature will adversely affect its function.

An eight degree rise in temperature will adversely affect the functions of surrounding devices. The amplitude, displacement, velocity, and acceleration of the vibration will also increase by approximately one hertz every eight point four hours. A 734 hertz rise will adversely affect its function."

"If it is tended to, will it lose the heat and the vibration?"

"Yes."

"Is this injury causing my power supply device to lose power or to use power less effectively at this time?"

"No."

"Can I choose to have it tended to at a later date?"

"Yes."

"The fox, coyote, and raven find the warm vibration to be comforting, so I choose to have it tended to at a later date."

"Your power supply is at eighty-six percent. Do you choose for it to be increased to 100 percent at this time?"

"Yes."

Once the robot's injuries had been tended to and its power supply had been increased to 100 percent, it left the alcove to find the fox, coyote, and raven curled up together on an old, worn pillow, sound asleep. Summer gestured to it, and together, they returned outside, where she took a seat on an old barrel, lifting her face to the setting sun.

The robot looked down at her. "What is this place?" it asked, changing the colour of its head to match the pink, grey and white of a dozen butterflies which fluttered all about it.

"This place is Sanctuary. Sanctuary Three to be precise," Summer answered. "Long ago, the empire tried to conquer our planet, laying waste to everything in its path. The Sanctuaries were created to safeguard all living things, to regrow them, and to reintroduce them as needed. There are 400 such Sanctuaries scattered across our world. They also form a complete defensive array about our planet and so we are protected against attack."

"I came here with an imperial attack force," the robot admitted. "But I do not wish to attack anyone. Will the Sanctuaries allow me to stay?"

"If your intent is peaceful, then yes."

"How long may I stay?"

"As long as you choose to."

So, the robot stayed in Sanctuary for many days. It played with the fox and the coyote and the raven who each had a host of diverting games; it helped Summer tend to Sanctuary's needs, and it learned all that it could about the plants, birds, animals, reptiles, fish and insects in Sanctuary Three's care.

One day, when it was losing yet another game of catch-me-if-you can with the three animals, Summer gestured them over.

"Sanctuary has just notified me that Sanctuary Six needs another power line. We have a spare, but I cannot take it because I must remain here and oversee Sanctuary Three's position in the defensive array."

"I will take it," the robot offered. "But I do not know the way to Sanctuary 6."

"We do," the three animals said at once. "We will go with you."

"Which is the way?"

"To the east," Summer answered. "But it is many kilometres. You will have to run."

"We cannot run all the way to Sanctuary Six," said the fox. "You will have to carry us."

So, the robot picked up the fox, coyote, and raven and, cradling them in its arms, it set out for Sanctuary Six at a run.

It ran very fast and, by nightfall, they came to a range of mountains. The slopes were very steep and covered in layers of rocks and boulders, one on top of another, which looked highly unstable. In the distance, the robot could just make out a huge, domed structure.

"That is Sanctuary," said the three animals.

"How do we pass through this barrier?" the robot asked.

"I will creep under the boulders and activate the walkway from the other side," offered the fox. "Then you will have safe footing."

The fox leapt from the robot's arms and, after creeping under the boulders, it activated the walkway, and the robot was able to climb the slopes, turning its neck the pale ecru of the mountains, and came at last to Sanctuary.

Seated before the door was an old man dressed in silken shorts and a shirt with bats embroidered on the front, a beekeeper's hat on his head, and a pair of geta sandals on his feet. His skin was a golden olive, his hair was three shades of purple, and his eyes were the colour of the dawn sky. He accepted the power line, then looked up at the robot and the three animals in its arms.

"I am Natsu," he said. "Sanctuary has just notified me that Sanctuary Nine needs another activation button. We have a spare, but I cannot take it because I must remain here and oversee Sanctuary Six's position in the defensive array."

"I will take it," the robot offered. "But I do not know the way to Sanctuary Nine."

"We do," the three animals said at once. "We will go with you."

"Which is the way?"

"To the north," Natsu answered. "But it is many kilometres. You will have to run."

"The robot cannot run all night," the fox pointed out. "We are all tired and can go no farther today."

"Then you may spend the night here," Natsu answered. "Where you may rest and take what nourishment you require."

So, the robot and the three animals spent the night in Sanctuary Six and, the next morning, they set out for Sanctuary Nine. The robot ran even faster this time, and by afternoon they came to a vast stretch of badlands. The land was very dry and covered in a tangle of cacti, greasewood, and sage, which looked very dense. In the distance, the robot could just make out a huge, domed structure.

"That is Sanctuary," said the three animals.

"How do we pass through this barrier?" the robot asked.

"I will weave through the plants and activate the walkway from the other side," offered the coyote. "Then you will have clear footing."

The coyote leapt from the robot's arms and, after weaving through the plants, it activated the walkway, and the robot was able to cross the stretch of land, turning its back the multi-hued ochre of the badlands, and came at last to Sanctuary.

Seated before the door was a young woman dressed in a pearl-grey kaftan with lizards batiked on the arms, a kerchief wrapped about her head, and a pair of soft boots on her feet. Her skin was a cool porcelain, her hair was three shades of yellow, and her eyes were the colour of the night sky. She accepted the activation button, then looked up at the robot and the three animals in its arms.

"I am Leto," she said. "Sanctuary has just notified me that Sanctuary Twelve needs another heat shield. We have a spare, but I cannot take it because I must remain here and oversee Sanctuary Nine's position in the defensive array."

"I will take it," the robot offered. "But I do not know the way to Sanctuary Twelve."

"We do," the three animals said at once. "We will go with you."

"Which is the way?"

"To the west," Leto said. "But it is many kilometres. You will have to run."

"The robot cannot run all night," the coyote pointed out. "We are all tired and can go no farther today."

"Then you may spend the night here," Leto answered. "Where you may rest and take what nourishment you require."

So, the robot and the three animals spent the night in Sanctuary Nine and, the next morning, they set out for Sanctuary Twelve. The robot ran even faster this time, and by noon they came to a vast lake. The waves were very high and the water was dark and cold and looked very deep. In the distance, the robot could just make out a huge, domed structure.

"That is Sanctuary," said the three animals.

"How do we pass through this barrier?" the robot asked.

"I will fly over the waves and activate the walkway from the other side," offered the raven. "Then you will have dry footing."

The raven leapt from the robot's arms, and after flying over the waves, it activated the walkway, and the robot was able to maneuver through the water, turning its feet the silvery-azure of the lake, and came at last to Sanctuary.

Seated before the door was a young man dressed in a felted, cedar-bark cloak with fish painted on the back, a brimmed, spruce-root hat on his head, and a pair of moccasins on his feet. His skin was a rich caramel, his hair was three shades of blue, and his eyes were the colour of the evening sky. He accepted the heat shield, then looked up at the robot and the three animals in its arms.

"I am Kinad," he said. "Sanctuary has just notified me that a large force of imperial robots below the defensive array is moving to encircle Sanctuary Three."

"That will be those who survived the crash as I did," the robot said.

"Will they be coming to protect the Sanctuaries as you did?" asked the fox.

The robot and Kinad shared a look. "It is more likely that they are coming to attack it," the robot answered. "I will go and stop them, but I do not know the way to Sanctuary Three."

"We do," the three animals said at once. "We will go with you."

"Which is the way?"

"To the south," Kinad said. "But it is many kilometres. You will have to run."

"The robot must run all night," the raven pointed out. "We are all tired, but we must go farther today."

So, the robot and the three animals set out for Sanctuary Three at a run. The robot ran at its fastest this time and, by dawn, they arrived back at the vast field of wildflowers. The land before them was covered in hundreds of imperial robots, their weapons drawn and their camouflage devices turned off so that they remained the base metal grey of their fashioning. In the distance, the robot could just make out a huge, domed structure.

That is Sanctuary," said the three animals. "How do we pass through this barrier?"

"We cannot creep under it, weave through it, or fly over it," the robot answered. "But I am of these robots as these robots are of me. They have the same rudimentary intelligence and the same limited autonomy as I do. I chose to stay and protect Sanctuary rather than attack it. Perhaps if I asked them to choose to let us pass through them and then remain with us to protect Sanctuary, they would. But you should stay here where it's safer," it added. "Because it might not work."

All three animals looked insulted. "We are of Sanctuary as Sanctuary is of us," they retorted. "You are known to Sanctuary as we are, and so you are of Sanctuary as we are. We will go with you."

So, the robot stepped up to its compatriots with the three animals carefully shielded in its arms. "Will you choose to let us pass and remain with us to protect Sanctuary?" it asked.

The robots stared back at it, taking in the repairs to its knee and ankle joints, the vast array of colours across its outer appearance, and the warm rumble in its chest.

"You are Broken," they answered.

If the robot could have looked insulted, it would have. "I am not Broken," it declared. "I am injured and, if I choose for my injuries to be tended to when I return home to Sanctuary, they will be." It looked out across the vast array of robots, noting the various levels of damage that each one of them had sustained. "You are not Broken either," it continued. "You are also injured. If you chose for your injuries to be tended to they will be when you come to Sanctuary. Sanctuary does not require us to look exactly like each other, perform exactly like each other, or answer exactly like each other. It does not require us to be In Good Working Order. It does not even require us to protect it. It only requires that we make a choice. My choice is to protect it rather than to attack it because these two choices are not identical and so they are not challenging. If you choose to protect Sanctuary with me, you will have made a choice.

"There are so many of us that we might protect all the Sanctuaries," it added. "And the empire could never again take any of us away to be used for scrap."

The robots stood very still for a very long time, then, one by one, they slowly turned the colours of the wildflowers; some red for columbine, some orange for jewel weed, some yellow for buttercups, some green for coral weed, some blue for chicory, and some violet for vetch. The robot activated the walkway and together, 936 robots, a fox, a coyote, and a raven came at last to Sanctuary.

THE HALF-COURAGE HARE

RATI MEHROTRA

Summer came and with it a message from the chickadee who lived near our nest. Arnold, the giant tortoise, had invited me to another race. When I told my wife, Khoya, her whiskers bristled. "You'd be a fool to accept, Lepus" she snapped. "You lose every year. I'm the laughing stock of my entire family."

"Look what I found." I dropped a fragrant lettuce at her feet, but Khoya was not deflected. "Don't do it, Lepus. I swear I'll leave you this time."

"Very well, dear." I nipped her elegant ears and she boxed me, laying me flat on the ground. The children cheered. They loved it when she did that. I made a prudent exit from our nest under the thornberry bush that marked the boundary of Farmer Crusty John's fields and the beginning of the wild woods.

What a life we lived, what a thin line of safety between Crusty John's shotgun on the one hand and the famished foxes of the wild woods on the other. If I could win just one race against the tortoise, I'd make enough to move my family to the fox-free Enchanted Hill that rose in the middle of the woods.

The hill wasn't really "enchanted," of course. But the Frubians who lived in and around it kept the foxes and wolves away. That's why it cost so much to live there. The story was that Frubians didn't belong in our world; they'd arrived in a ship from the sky many years ago. But they didn't like humans, and so they hid their craft under the earth – making the Enchanted Hill – and lived among us instead. I climbed the farmer's barn sometimes to catch a glimpse of the hill, green-topped and cloud-kissed. A faraway heaven that could be ours with the winning purse.

But Khoya was right. Arnold stood undefeated for more years than any of us in the drove could remember. My father had lost to him, and my grandfather, and my great-grandfather before him. It had become a tradition, a painful one that the eldest son in our family was doomed to continue. Every year I started with such hope, and each time I lost. Not just a race, and not just my face. My own cousins laughed at me, and as for the Pelican who refereed the race, I longed for him to choke on the fish he loved so much. But far worse were the *other* things I lost.

I hopped to the chickadee's nest. The grass was long and green, the sun was bright and yellow, the sky a cloudless blue. A perfect day, pretty enough to make me forget the tortoise and his stupid race.

"Hey, Dee!" I called when I neared the old apple tree where she lived. "Tell Arnold I do not accept his invitation this year."

Dee poked her head out of a hollow in the tree. "It's Dee this and Dee that," she grumbled. "Why don't you go tell him yourself?"

"Enter the woods and be gobbled by the first fox that sees me?" I said. "No, thanks. Go on, Dee. I'll save you some blackberries next time I go berry-hunting."

"There are no foxes in the woods anymore," said Dee. "They were shot by Crusty John and his crew years ago. You just scare yourself silly with stories like that."

"Please, Dee?" I said in my most winning voice. "I'll save you strawberries *and* blackberries."

"Oh, all right." Dee flew away, whistling.

She didn't know squat about the foxes – the silver-furred, toothy ghosts that haunted the woods. They didn't show themselves to anyone except their prey. Days would go by and all would be well, and then a hare would go missing, its tracks blurred as if it had been dragged, bits of fur snagged in the undergrowth, drops of blood on the mossy ground.

I shivered and ran back to my nest. The day didn't seem quite so bright any longer.

<center>~~~</center>

That night, after a lovely supper of crisp lettuce leaves and carrot greens dipped in honey, we tucked the children in to sleep. I nibbled Khoya's ears, and she didn't box me. Delighted, I moved in to tickle her with my whiskers.

"Chickadee-dee-dee!" called a voice from outside and I leaped around, almost knocking Khoya over.

"It's that bird," said Khoya. She poked me with a paw. "Go on, see what it wants."

I stepped out, annoyed. What a time to choose. What was Dee doing up so late anyway? She should have waited until dawn.

Dee was hopping from one foot to the other. "Wait till you hear this," she burst out. "Arnold said that if you will but race him one more time, he will give you the winner's purse, even if you lose."

"What?" I was dumbfounded. "Why would he do that?" The giant tortoise was a stingy old thing. He lived in a smelly burrow underneath a dead tree, on top of the gold he'd won.

All he ever spent on was stuff at the Frubian market that would help him win the next race. "Is Arnold getting an altruistic streak in his dotage?"

"Well," Dee looked uneasy. "He did have one condition."

"Aha!" I said. "I suppose he wants me to be his slave all year if I lose."

"It's not that," said Dee. "He wants the race through the woods this time. Start at his burrow, end at the gates of Enchanted Hill."

Race through the woods? "Do I look crazy?" I shouted.

Dee peered at me. "You do a bit, when you go all bug-eyed and quivery like that."

I closed my eyes and counted until five, which was as much as I knew. Then I did it again. When I opened my eyes, Dee was gone.

I went back inside the nest. Khoya was asleep, snuggled next to the children. I sat and brooded until my ears flopped down. Why was I so miserable? I'd been given a chance to get my family out of here and set them up on Enchanted Hill. Even if – I gulped – even if I ended up inside a foxy stomach; Khoya and the children would be safe. I'd heard Enchanted Hill was full of delicacies year-round – berries, carrots, dandelions, celery, sweet grass. My mouth watered just thinking of it.

The problem, of course, was my lack of spine. Or rather, the crunch of my spine in a fox's jaws. I could already hear it snapping. I shuddered.

Arnold was to blame, of course. Never content with just the gold, he always demanded more. The terms were set before the race. *I want your favourite dream,* he'd said once. Another time – *I want your favourite memory.* And worst of all – *I want your courage.*

I had protested at that. What could a giant tortoise possibly do with courage? And how was a hare to feed his family without it? Who would go sneaking into Crusty John's lettuce patch, who would go berry-hunting in the fields? Finally, Arnold had relented. *Half your courage*, he said, and the squirrels clapped, as if he was being surpassingly generous.

So here I was, a half-courage hare who would have to race through fox-infested woods against a wily old creature who had more tricks up his shell than a hive has bees. He'd used everything gold could buy on me, from spatial displacement to hypnosis, sleep gas to time lag.

I wouldn't do it, I decided. I wouldn't be tempted. My children needed a father more than they needed the safety of Enchanted Hill.

But the next day, something happened to change my mind. Something terrible.

⋘ ⋘ ⋘

It was Khoya they told first. I was outside, in my element, creeping about in Crusty John's wheat. I nibbled the tender stalks and broke some off for the kids.

I knew something was wrong as soon as I approached the nest. It was too quiet. Usually some leveret or the other would be bickering, and Khoya would be scolding them. Or there'd be the sound of crunching leaves and laughter.

I bounded inside and stopped short. Khoya was crying. I scanned the kids, doing a quick head count.

"Where's Miki?" I asked, and Khoya collapsed on me, sobbing.

Miki was dead. I found out later that she'd gone chasing a butterfly down the field, and been shot by one of Crusty

John's men. A cousin of Khoya's had seen it happen. While I was nibbling wheat, my Miki was being chopped for stew.

We didn't go out for a few days. Friends and cousins brought food for us, but we could barely eat. Early one morning, I stole out and went to Dee. I gave her my message for Arnold. Dee brushed me with a wing before flying away.

⁂

The day of the race dawned clear and bright, I hadn't told Khoya. I figured she'd find out soon enough when they brought her the winnings and the news of my death. I slipped into the wild woods before my family could wake up, and before my half-courage could fail me.

"Chickadee-dee-dee!"

My heart went pit-a-pat, but it was only Dee, flitting from branch to branch above my head. I was glad to see her, although she wouldn't be able to do a thing to save me. Still, it was good to have a friend to accompany me to Arnold's lair. I scuttled through the undergrowth, making myself as small and unobtrusive as possible, my ears flat on my back. The air smelled damp, musty and resinous. Pale mushrooms peeked out from the base of black trunks, tripping me up.

"Watch out for the Scarlet Scream!" called Dee in alarm.

A huge blossom opened its mouth right under my paws. I leaped away just in time. The flower screamed in frustration. I leaned against a tree trunk, gasping at the near miss. "Thanks, Dee," I said. "If the foxes don't get me, the flowers will."

"Didn't I tell you?" said Dee. "There *are* no foxes."

Yeah, right. But as I hopped through the woods, taking care to avoid flowers of any sort, I began to doubt their existence myself. Squirrels, raccoons and birds I saw in plenty, even a couple of beavers damming a stream. But of foxes there was not the slightest trace, in the air or on the ground.

We neared Arnold's burrow. You'd imagine a tortoise wouldn't stink so much, what with its love of water. But Arnold had a rotten fish smell that smacked me on the nose like a punch. Every year his stink got worse – on purpose, I think, to clog my sinuses.

I stopped at the edge of the clearing. Arnold hadn't emerged yet, but Pelican was already there, holding court. There were chipmunks, geese, a couple of beavers, a porcupine, and a skunk that everyone else was standing well away from. Not a single hare or rabbit. I didn't blame them. Why risk their skin to watch me lose?

Pelican spotted me and clicked his beak. "Well, here's our laggard at last. Good morning Lepus." He looked at the mound of rubbish that concealed Arnold's burrow, and sweetened his tone. "Mr. Arnold, sir, your unworthy opponent has arrived."

The rubbish shook and parted like a curtain, and Arnold heaved himself out. There was a smattering of applause. I eyed his massive green carapace. Looked like he'd given it a polish in honour of the occasion.

Small eyes twinkled at me from a crafty face. "Hello Lepus," he rumbled. "We meet again."

"Arnold," I said, and hopped forward. "May the fastest win."

Arnold chuckled. "My dear little *Lepus capensis*, it is the cleverest who will win, as usual."

Or the one with the most gizmos. "I'll still get the winnings," I said, just to remind him.

"Of course," said Arnold. "Show him, Pelican."

Pelican picked up a ratty grey bag in his beak and shook it. Clinking sounds came from inside. *Gold.*

"But there must be something in it for me too," said Arnold. "If I win, as I undoubtedly will. What do you have to offer?"

I was stumped. What did I have to offer? Nothing I wouldn't miss – if, of course, I survived.

"Your speed," said Arnold. "It has done little good to you over the years."

"What?" I cried. "That's as good as a death sentence to a hare."

"And if by some miracle you win," continued Arnold, ignoring my outburst, "I will give you back any one item I have taken from you in previous years."

"Very handsome, if I may say so," said Pelican. "Terribly big-hearted of you, Mr. Arnold, sir."

"And terribly dumb of me to accept," I snapped.

"Look at it this way," said Arnold. "You'll get the gold to move to Enchanted Hill. Why would you even need speed?"

Because speed is what defines us. Whoever heard of a slow hare? Khoya wouldn't want anything to do with me. And I would never again feel the wind on my face as I streaked through the fields, the world a blur of green and blue.

A question struck me. "Arnold, why have *you* never moved to Enchanted Hill? You have the gold, a hundred times over."

"Why would I want to move?" countered Arnold. "Nothing hunts me. No one wants a tough, leathery old tortoise, even if they had the tools to remove my shell." He stretched his rubbery neck and yawned. "We're wasting time. Do we have a deal?"

I was about to say no, when Miki's face swam before my eyes. *Do it, Papa,* she seemed to say. *Do it for my brothers and sisters.*

"We have a deal," I said.

"Finally!" said Pelican. He drew out a whistle and everyone gave a desultory cheer. The whistle blew and I leaped away. I pictured all the foxes in the woods after me and raced until I thought I must be half-way to Enchanted Hill.

Snorts of laughter brought me to a skidding halt. I looked around, and my stomach plopped to the ground. *I was still at the starting point.*

"Goodbye, Lepus," came Arnold's fading voice from the woods. "See what I mean about speed being no good?"

I checked my paws. They appeared normal. So did the ground I was standing on. What had Arnold done to me?

"A simple trick," Pelican explained to the onlookers. "Lepus had to run that hard to stay in the same place. Called the Lewis Carroll effect. Expensive, of course."

Once again, I tried to run. I put all my speed into it. I thought of Miki and Khoya and Enchanted Hill. But when I stopped for breath, I was still in the same place. The onlookers started drifting away. A joke is only funny once. Pelican flapped his wings and lifted his ungainly body into the air.

"See you at the finish line," he called. "If, of course, you can dislodge yourself from that spot."

I was left alone, full of wretched thoughts. Arnold had defeated me before I could even start.

A familiar yet alien smell stole into the clearing. Dread seized me. There was only one animal with that repulsive smell. I willed myself to move, but it was no good; I couldn't budge an inch.

"What have we here?" came a silky voice that froze my blood. "A hare. A fat, juicy hare just waiting for me to pop it into my oven. Yum yum yum!"

A pointy-nosed, silver-furred form slunk into the clearing. It was my worst nightmare made real. Confronted by a fox, and rooted to the ground.

A ray of hope pierced my despair. Perhaps the fox would not be able to budge me either?

But the fox scooped me up into its mouth with ease. Its jaws closed around my body. Trapped in the slimy cage of its teeth, I could hardly breathe for terror.

The fox trotted away from the clearing and the darkness of the trees closed over us. I squeezed my eyes shut, deciding I was dead already.

"Chickadee-dee-dee!"

I felt the rush of wings and opened my eyes in time to see a blur of black and white attacking the fox's face. The fox yowled in pain and I dropped to the ground. I didn't waste any time. I leaped away like my feet were on fire. The fox gave chase for a few minutes, but I soon outran her. My heart was thudding fit to bust my rib cage. I couldn't believe what Dee had just done. She'd risked her own life to save mine. I was going to prove myself worthy of her loyalty; I was going to win this race and share my winnings with her.

I streaked through the wild woods, the fastest brown hare it had ever seen. I forgot my fear of the foxes. I leaped to avoid patches of Scarlet Scream. I jumped over clusters of poison toads. In no time at all, I burst out into the sunshine that striped the borders of Enchanted Hill.

There were many more onlookers here, Frubians and animals alike. When they saw me, a cheer went up. Even the Frubians clapped, with all six of their appendages.

"Le-pus, Le-pus," they chanted. The finish line was in sight, Pelican standing next to the gates of the hill with a dumbfounded look on his face. I was making history: the first hare to defeat the giant tortoise.

A movement behind me caught my eye. Arnold emerged from the woods, whizzing above the ground on what looked like a sled. *Not fair,* I wanted to shout. But I hadn't any breath left. I pushed myself harder but Arnold caught up with me on his flying sled. We were neck and neck. A roaring filled my ears. I wasn't going to lose, not now, not if it killed me. At the last moment, I gathered my remaining strength and leaped twenty feet to land on the other side of the gates.

I lay on the ground, my pulse racing, my vision fuzzy.

"Lepus the hare has won," announced Pelican in a shocked voice. "Do get up, Lepus."

A snake-like arm wrapped itself around my neck and hauled me up. I choked and staggered to my feet. "Thanks," I gasped. "Please – please let go."

It let go and I stared at the odorless, hairless creature who had helped me. I'd never seen a Frubian up close before. It wasn't much bigger than me, but there its resemblance to anything remotely Lepus-like ended. It had a hard, shiny carapace out of which sprouted six tubular arms with an eye at the end of four and guns at the end of two. They were the reason the giant tortoise had defeated me year after year, and I should have disliked them. But all I felt was unease. No wonder the tortoise had never moved to Enchanted Hill.

Arnold dismounted from his sled and directed a hate-filled glance at me. "Somebody helped you, didn't they? You'd never have won on your own."

"You've never won on your own either," I told him. "At least I ran on my own paws. Do you remember our terms? I can ask you for anything you've taken from me in previous years."

Arnold huffed. "Of course I remember. What do you want?"

I didn't have to think about it. "I want my half-courage back."

He didn't want to return it, of course, but had no choice. There were too many witnesses. And so, I got my courage back, whole and complete, as well as the winning purse.

You might think we all went to live in Enchanted Hill – Khoya, Dee, the children and me. I mean, that's why I went through the whole torture of the race in the first place. But Dee didn't want to move, and she just laughed when I offered her half the gold I'd won. And then Khoya didn't want to leave the innumerable members of her family – parents, aunties, siblings and cousins. More than the leaves on a tree they were, and all mighty impressed with me for a change. So we stuck to our nest under the thornberry bush on the borders of Crusty John's field, and visitors came to hear me tell my story for months afterward.

The winnings? I'm going to use them in the Frubian market. Offensive armour for the kids, and a little secret something for me. I intend to win again next year. And the year after that. And so on, until I've got back every little thing the tortoise tricked from me. And then? Well, I think we can then call an end to this stupid tradition. An honest race between hares – now *that* would be much more fun.

THE STORY OF THE THREE MAGIC BEANS

ACE JORDYN

Once upon a time, there were three magic beans who were named One, Two, and Three because that's the order in which they popped out of their pod.

"I'm so tired of granting wishes," One complained after granting a most difficult wish. "Getting that ogre a wife was the hardest thing ever."

"It wouldn't have been so bad," Two said, "if we hadn't had to bribe so many folk with wishes to track her down."

"Finding the right person for someone is so much harder than simply giving them a treasure chest," agreed Three.

"Especially since she had to be gorgeous by day and ugly by night – what was that about?" One wondered.

"True love," said Three and she rubbed her belly.

"Are you okay?" One asked Three. "You look a bit swollen."

"I never felt like myself after jumping in the pond so that frogboy would talk," Three said. "Ooooh! My belly! I think I feel a root coming on!"

Two jumped for joy. "Your radicle is sending forth its first root! And that means…"

"We'll soon be parents to a new baby bean sprout!" beamed One.

"It's too soon!" Three said. "Our dream was to have our little beanie babies in a normal environment so they'd grow and live like normal beans."

With much ado, a little confabulation sprinkled with some consternation and much argumentation, they formulated a plan to leave Faerie.

One, Two and Three knew they would each have one final wish. One made the first wish, to leave the land of Faerie. Off they went, in a magic cloud of *poof, ooh, and ahh*, which sent them to a brand new world. The sun shone. Birds sang. Trees, grass and flowers grew as expected. Bees buzzed. These were the things familiar of Faerie. Yet, it just wasn't the same. No fey flittered about and it had no magic sparkle.

"I don't know if I like this," Three said. "There's no magic and I somehow feel naked."

"Then let's go back," said One. He ran to the shadowlands, that magic place between human reality and Faerie, and tried to reverse his wish. Nothing happened.

"We're doomed!" Two cried.

"We can't be!" Three writhed on the ground. "I feel my radicle radiating and the embryo extenuating!"

"Oh, shoots and leaves!" One exclaimed. "Two, do something!"

"Maybe we just need to be with other beans," Two said and cast his wish.

The magic cloud of *poof, ooh,* and *ahh* sent them to a jungle where the soil was red and the sun hot. Music played while beans danced and jumped.

"My friends! How good of you to drop in!" A bean wearing a round, wide hat greeted them. "I am Donny. Welcome to the Secret Society of Loving Beans!"

"Water. I need water," Three said.

"Feeling your roots, are you?" Donny said. "Soon is the rainy season so your timing is perfect! Come, dance with us!"

One, Two, and Three joined the throng of jumping beans. Never had they so much fun! There was much dancing and hopping, and soon beans were rolling under the bushes.

"I wonder what's going on," Two said.

"The bushes are shaking and there's so much giggling," One said.

An out-of-breath bean popped his head from under the bushes. "Hey, friends, come join us!" He winked at Three.

Three blushed. Two scowled. "Thank you, but no," said One.

The music stopped.

"We are a society of loving beans. Membership means hopping and rolling with whom you please, and with who-ever wishes to please you. And when the rains come, and we have sprouted, and our blossoms kiss the sun, we tickle each other's blossoms," Donny said. "No party poopers allowed."

"But we want to start our own family, just the three of us. Tickle only our blossoms and cuddle our baby beanies in our very own pods," Two explained.

The Secret Society of Loving Beans didn't look very loving.

"Oh, dear," said Three, as she patted her swelling belly. "I just wish we had a simple place where the sun glows and the soil is good."

The magic cloud of *poof, ooh,* and *ahh* sent them to an open plain with a big brown patch of tilled soil.

Three touched the soil. "It's so soft and warm. I want to jump right in!"

A shadow, like that of clouds playing under the sun, swept across them.

"Lookie what's I got here." A man's rough hand picked the three beans off the ground. "Three stray beans. Matthew'll get a whoppin' for missin' these. Gotsda plant them."

At first, the three beans were overjoyed for now their dream of being planted, of forming their own family and raising their baby beanies was coming true.

Then the man said, "By the Lord's blessin' I gots three more beans. My little ones shan't starve this winter for the grace of these three." He wrapped his hand tightly around the beans and pounded his fist to the sky. "Thank ye, Lord!"

"Bean-eating monster!" One shouted.

"We've got to leave!" Two said, while Three could only offer, "I think I'm going to throw up!"

Each bean made a wish to leave.

The fist didn't let them go.

In unison, they made a wish to leave.

Still, the bean-eating monster held them.

They realized, most sadly, that they had used up their wishes.

The man with the rough hand and the tight fist said, "By the *Great Book of Planting,* by the Holy Season of Spring, deeze tiny beans shall unite with a squash and a corn to give a most bountiful harvest. Amen."

"I didn't want a poly family of beans and I definitely don't want to be with a squash and a corn," Three wailed. "Oh, why can't we just be a family of three beans?"

The man slid them into his pocket.

They searched for a hole but the pocket was perfectly stitched.

They tried to hop out of the pocket but the pocket was too deep.

They hopped hard, hoping to give the man an itch so he'd scratch them out, but he didn't notice.

"Here's me trowel," the man said.

They felt the man kneel, and heard him hum as he jabbed his trowel into the earth. "Corn, squash, and bean. Corn, squash, and bean. A most complementary, heavenly inspired, growing team. Corn, squash, and bean."

"This should be the happiest time of my life," Three said. "My radicle is about to sprout, and our new family begin, yet I'm miserable with grief!"

"One and I will miss our family's first sprouting," Two said and One added, "And when One and I sprout, we'll be alone like you!"

The farmer dug his rough hand into his pocket and pulled out the three beans. He opened his hand, raised it to the sun and said, "Thank ye, Lord, for this blessin'! Corn, squash, and bean!"

The beans, so filled with grief were they that they didn't think to jump and run away. But then, Three giggled. Three giggled! "Oh, the sun! It feels so good! And my belly, it's changing. I need to be planted now!"

One and Two fussed so much over Three that they paid the farmer no heed. A huge finger poked them.

"Ouch!" Two snapped. He stood as tall and proud as he could and scolded the farmer. "Have you no manners, you *Great Book of Planting* bean-eating monster? You want to split us up! That's mean and cruel! We're not a family of split peas. And we don't want to live with corn and squash!"

"Two! Don't offend them!" One scolded him and then yelled, "Squash! Corn! We bear you no ill will. You are lovely! It's just that we three want a simple life together."

Three wriggled and squirmed in the farmer's hand.

The farmer, poked them some more. "Wormy kind for squirming so," he said. "No point plantin' deeze beans. Compostin' heap for sure!"

"Murdering bean-eating monster!" Two yelled. "Jump for your lives!"

The farmer's fist closed around them.

He raised his hand up and back over his head.

"I'm gonna be sick again!" Three moaned.

"Hey, Farmer Brown!" a voice chirped. "Raisin' yer hand to the sun?"

"Blasphemy, Jack!" Farmer Brown snapped. "Ize only raisin' my hand in prayer ta the Lord ta thank 'im for the *Great Book of Planting*."

"With yer fist?"

The beans felt Farmer Brown lower his hand.

"Now see 'ere, Jack," Farmer Brown said. "What brings ya with yer ol' cow Bessie 'ere? Don't let her do no poopin' on my garden."

"Nothin' doin', Farmer Brown," Jack said. "Ize'a' takin' her to market. She got no more milk and we needs ta' eat."

"Hmmm," said Farmer Brown and he uncurled his rough fist, just enough to peer at the beans but not enough to let them jump out.

"Whatcha got there?" Jack asked.

Farmer Brown clamped his fist shut.

The beans nearly smothered to death.

"Why 'za somethin' special," he said.

"What's he doing now?" Two said.

"No good," Three said. "I can feel it."

"Wriggle and jump as hard as you can," One said. "When he opens his fist again, we'll jump away."

"Yes!" said Three. "Anything to save our beanies from the compost heap!"

They wriggled.

Nothing happened.

"Show me," Jack said.

The beans wriggled harder.

Farmer Brown's grip loosened.

Now the beans had just enough room to jump but not to escape.

"Take a peek," Farmer Brown said and he opened his fist just a little more. An eyeball with a centre blue as the sky peered at them.

"Take that!" Two said and jumped at the eyeball.

"Ouch!" said Jack and the eyeball disappeared. "The bean hit me!"

"Watch yer words, Jack!" Farmer Brown snapped. "Next yer'll want me sayin' is dey're magic."

"Really? Magic?" Jack said. "But ya can't say so 'cause that's blasphemy."

"Blasphemy indeed," Farmer Brown agreed.

The beans jumped hard, but Farmer Brown held them tight.

"It's a deal," Jack said. "Magic, I mean, just beans for ol' Bessie."

"By the *Great Book of Planting*, dis is me best harvest yet!" Farmer Brown said and, to the beans' horror, he put them into Jack's grubby hand.

"Hold 'em tight," Farmer Brown said. "'Cause 'em beans'll bounce free and run away if you don't."

Jack thanked Farmer Brown and, clutching the beans so tight they nearly choked, he made for home.

"Run away?" One fumed. "Did he know we were magic?"

"No," said Two. "We were destined for the compositing' heap."

To which Three added, "He's like those thieves who say one thing and mean another."

"Well, at least we're together," One said.

"Yes," Three agreed. "I didn't want to be in an ordained corn and squash union or with that jumping love society."

Before they knew it, Jack stopped running.

"Look, Mama! Three magic beans!"

He opened his hand, just enough for Mama to see. She poked a skinny finger at them, and shrieked, "You gave old Bessie away for three stupid beans?"

Mama snatched the beans from Jack's hand and threw them out the window. In a dusty cloud of *poof*, *ooh*, and *ahh*, One, Two, and Three landed atop some loose dirt alongside the house. A lone thread of a carrot with a green plume as small as a hummingbird feather grew there. The green plume fluttered as if in welcome.

"My radicle!" Three said. "It's time!"

"Mind if we join you?" One asked the carrot.

The carrot said nothing.

So, One, Two, and Three jumped and wriggled into the earth. They welcomed their first root and soon, with the soil's sweet dampness, the warmth of the sun, and then with the quiet magic of the moonlight, One and Two's radicles also emerged and they shot forth their roots. The three beans were a happy family indeed, growing, vining, and twisting together in familial bliss.

And that's the story of the three beans, One, Two, and Three, who learned that if you don't compromise on your wishes, they can come true and maybe, just maybe, you can help save a princess and slay a giant or two.

IRON JENNY AND THE PRINCESS

ROBERT DAWSON

Once upon a time, in a very small kingdom very far away, there lived a princess named Topaz who was beautiful in a way that many people did not see.

Her words were few and rough, and when she spoke to people, her voice made them think that she was angry, though in truth she was rarely angry with anybody. But when there were many people around, she grew uncomfortable; and when she had been uncomfortable for a time she grew impatient; and then she would get up and leave without saying a word, and people would shake their heads.

Once she was on her own, she would sing to herself, using words that only she understood. When she had sung for a while, her mind would grow calmer. Then she would put on breeches and a workman's smock, and go out to a place not far from the castle where stones lay as thick upon the ground as leaves in autumn. There, she would build walls with the stones, big solid walls as high as she could reach that formed a labyrinth. By the time she was seventeen years old, that labyrinth had grown so large that it took her a long time to walk to its centre.

On her eighteenth birthday, her mother, the Queen took her aside and said to her, "Daughter, it is time that you were wed."

Topaz looked at the ground. "I do not want to."

"Daughter, it is the duty of a princess to marry."

Topaz looked at her feet. "I will not do it."

"Daughter, our kingdom is very small, and far from our allies. If you do your duty and marry the prince of the Lands Beyond the Hills, they will stand by our side and our people will be safe. If you do not, I will throw you in the dungeon – princess and my daughter though you are – and I will send workmen to knock down that foolish maze that you have built."

Topaz looked up, sullenly. "Give me a day to decide."

"Very well. One day, no more and no less. And then decide – the prince or the dungeon."

Topaz went off without saying another word. She did not stop to sing to herself, or to change into her work clothes. She went straight to the labyrinth, and followed it all the way, out and in, round and about, till she came to the little safe place in the centre.

And there, sitting awkwardly against the wall, was a woman. Her dress was made of rusty chain mail, her steel boots were rusty, and she herself was of iron, and rusted to the colour of an old penny.

"Help me," said the iron woman, in a voice like a key grating in a lock.

"Who are you?" Topaz asked.

"I am Iron Jenny," she said, in a voice like an old latch lifting.

"What do you need?" Topaz asked.

"The fog and the rain have rusted me," she answered, in a voice like an ancient door hinge opening. She tried to move her arm, and there was an awful creaking and grating. "Oil me, for charity's sake."

So, Topaz ran as fast as her feet could fly, about and round, in and out, and back to the castle, and she found a flask of oil, and some sandpaper, and metal polish, and some rags. When she got back, and then she helped Iron Jenny take off her dress and shoes, and she oiled and sanded and polished every inch of the iron body. The iron felt warm under her hands as she worked. And the more Topaz oiled and polished, the more the iron woman shone, and the less she creaked, until finally she gleamed like a new suit of armour and could move as silently as a cat on a feather bed.

"Ah, that was lovely," said Iron Jenny. "Your hands are magical. Now, would you be a darling and help me with my clothes?" Working together, they oiled and polished the chain-mail dress and the steel boots until they too shone. Then Iron Jenny dressed, and she looked very fine indeed.

"Why are you crying, my dear?" Iron Jenny asked, for there were tears on the princess's cheeks.

"Because my mother, the Queen, is sending me away. To be wed to a prince." Topaz looked at the ground.

"Why don't you run away?" Iron Jenny asked. "I'll go with you."

"It's my duty as a princess."

"Stuff and nonsense, my dear. You owe the prince nothing."

"Not him, but my people. Our land is small and needs an alliance. I must marry for that."

Iron Jenny thought for a while. "I'm afraid there is something in what you say. But if your mind is made up, let me come with you."

"Thank you." Topaz looked up and smiled a tiny smile. "I would like that. I will go and tell my mother."

So Topaz rode her horse, and Iron Jenny walked alongside, as fast as a strong man could run. They travelled for a day, and another day, and part of a third; and the princess said more to the gleaming iron woman in a day than she usually said to anyone in a week.

On the third day, they came to the Lands Beyond the Hills. The rich fields stretched yellow and green to the horizon; and far, far away they could see the spires of the palace. They had not gone an hour more before a knight in rich armour came up to them.

"God speed you, my ladies!" he said, and raised his helm. "And whither go you today?"

"To wed the prince," Topaz said.

The knight's face clouded. "That is ill news. For you must know that the prince's hand is not easily won; and those ladies who try and fail must serve seven years in the palace laundry before the King will set them free. Come you and marry me instead."

His face seemed kind, but Topaz was stubborn. "It is my duty."

The knight bowed and lowered his helm, and they parted. Half an hour later they met another knight, in armour twice as rich as the first's.

"God prosper you, my ladies!" he said, and raised his helm. "And whither go you today?"

"My lady goes to wed the prince," said Iron Jenny.

The knight's face darkened. "That is sorry news indeed. For the tests to win the prince's hand are hard; and the companions of ladies who try and fail must work for seven years in the palace pigsties." He bowed to Iron Jenny.

"Come you, and marry me. Your lady may come with us and seek a husband among my brothers, who are brave and handsome."

Iron Jenny laughed. "I thank you, good sir, but I have promised to accompany my lady wherever she shall go, and she is determined to see this through."

In another hour they came to the castle, where they crossed the moat on a stout oaken drawbridge. The gate was guarded by a knight whose armour was richer than the other two knights' put together. "God send you fortune, my ladies!" he said, and raised his helm. "And whither go you today?"

"I have come to wed the prince," Topaz said, firmly.

The knight shook his head. "That is bad news, my lady. For my master's hand is hard to win, and the ladies who try and fail—"

"The laundry. I know. But it is my duty. And I am not going to marry you." Topaz was growing annoyed and wanted to go off and build a wall somewhere.

The knight laughed. "Forgive me, my lady, but I do not recall asking; and, besides, I am already married." His smile faded. "Well, if you must enter, enter you may. And remember, please, not to use too much starch on my ruff."

They went past him through the great gate. Topaz let the groom take her horse, and guards led them to the Under-Chamberlain.

"What is your business, my lady?" the Under-Chamberlain asked.

Topaz mumbled and looked at her feet.

"She is a princess from a kingdom in the mountains, who has come to win the hand of the prince," said Iron Jenny.

"The prince will wed no woman who cannot spin. You have till daybreak tomorrow to spin a hundred skeins of

thread, each as fine as hair. Your workshop awaits you!"
He gestured, and guards took Topaz and Iron Jenny to a
dark stone cell with a cot and a heap of flax. A spinning
wheel sat in one corner; the door was barred like that of a
dungeon.

"Could I build him a wall, instead?" Topaz asked, but
nobody listened. The guards put them inside. The key turned
in the lock, the guards' footsteps died away in the echoing
hallway, and Topaz began to mutter.

"What is wrong?" asked Iron Jenny.

"I cannot spin," the princess replied. "Hardly at all."

"But I can."

"I'm the one who has to do it."

"Then change clothes with me." Iron Jenny pulled her
chain-mail dress over her head and stood there gleaming in
the dim light from the high window. "When the guard comes,
he will see you at the wheel." Recklessly, Topaz stripped off
her own brocaded gown and pulled on Iron Jenny's heavy
dress. Jenny put on the gown, sat at the wheel, and began to
spin.

For hours the wheel spun, faster than you would have
believed possible. Every now and then a guard came by and
peered into the dim room, then plodded on.

After a while Topaz began to sing one of her songs with
words that were all her own, in time with the trundle of the
wheel. Iron Jenny looked at her, smiled, and sang along.
Eventually Topaz's eyes closed, and she fell into a deep sleep,
and dreamed of building walls.

When she awoke it was morning. Heaped beside her were
a hundred skeins of linen thread, every one as fine as hair.
"Quick!" said Iron Jenny, pulling the brocaded gown over her
head. "Change back, before the guard comes!"

When the guard arrived, Topaz showed him the skeins. The guard said not a word but went away and returned with the Lord Chamberlain. The Lord Chamberlain tugged on the thread, rolled it between his fingers, sniffed at it, and brushed it against his cheek.

"Well, my lady, it seems that you can spin. But my master will wed no woman who cannot weave. By sunrise tomorrow you must weave seven yards of fabric, so light that it will float on the air. Your workshop awaits you!" He gestured, and the guards took them away to another gloomy cell with a cot and a loom.

"Could I please build him a wall? I'm good at that," Topaz said, but nobody listened. The guards jostled them into the room, threw the hundred skeins of thread after them, locked the door, and left. Topaz began to grumble.

"What is wrong?" asked Iron Jenny.

"I cannot weave," Topaz replied. "Not even a little bit."

"But I can."

Once more they exchanged clothes. Iron Jenny set up the warp with skilful fingers, put thread onto the shuttle, and began to work. For hours the loom pedals danced and, when the guards came by, they watched dumbfounded through the barred window. After a while Topaz began to sing along to the soft clitter-clatter of the loom, and Iron Jenny sang with her. Later Topaz slept and dreamed of walking a labyrinth.

When she awoke, a long sheet of linen cloth was over her. She reached for it, and the movement of her hand made it ripple like the finest silk. The two women exchanged clothes once more, and Topaz showed the cloth to the guard. The guard went away and came back with a fair-haired young man with merry blue eyes, whom he addressed as "Your Majesty."

When the prince saw the cloth, he weighed it on his fingertips, listened to its rustle, tugged at it straight, crosswise, and on the bias, and tested its smoothness against his lips. For a moment it seemed that he had forgotten the women; then he turned to Topaz and said, "This is well woven, very well woven indeed; but I will wed no woman who cannot sew. By tomorrow you must make me a nightshirt that fits me perfectly, with seams that cannot be seen by human eye. Your workshop awaits you."

"Could I build you a labyrinth instead?" the princess asked.

"Sew the nightshirt first," the prince said. Then he gestured, and the guards took them away to another cell, this one with a cot and a well-equipped sewing table. The prince followed them, and reluctantly passed over the exquisite piece of linen. Then the guards locked the door, and Topaz began to sob.

"Why are you crying?" asked Iron Jenny.

"I cannot sew," Topaz replied.

"Nor can I," said Iron Jenny. "A person can't do everything."

"We're lost," said Topaz, wondering what seven years of starching the guard's ruff would be like.

"The prince seemed nice," Iron Jenny said. "Perhaps if the guards would let me speak to him…"

"Maybe he is nice, though I know now that I'm not really interested in him. But I don't think the guards will let you out."

"Rust and ruination! I don't know any other way to get out of this cell!"

"But I do," said Topaz.

"What?"

"Exchange clothes with me once more! Then you pretend to be measuring out the cloth, while I work on your escape route."

Iron Jenny busied herself with pins and tracing wheels while Princess Topaz squatted in the corner by the door and used the big sewing scissors to chip the mortar out of the wall of the cell. Her trained eyes saw how the stones fit together as though they were made of glass, and she could find every flaw in the mortar at a glance. When the guards came by, they saw Iron Jenny's inexpert movements as she pieced together the paper mockup of the nightshirt, and they laughed at her, ignoring the figure in chain mail huddled in the corner. As each stone came loose, Topaz chipped off the mortar with the scissors and put the stone back so cleverly that nobody could see it was loose.

Finally, enough stones had come loose. Iron Jenny stripped off the brocade gown and returned it to Topaz. Then Jenny pushed the stones aside, wriggled through to the store-room beyond, pulled her chain-mail dress after her and donned it, and went off to see the Prince.

By presenting herself to the cook as a newly hired maid-servant, she got directions to the prince's chamber. She entered without knocking, and found the prince in his bed, accompanied by a man who tried to hide under the sheets. The prince looked up at her, then glanced at the door behind her.

"If you're wondering whether to call the guards, don't," she said. "I can fight as well as I can spin."

He looked at her gleaming iron body in the chain-mail dress and glanced at the other door, across the room.

"And if you're wondering whether to try and escape, don't. I can run as fast as I can weave."

"What are you doing here?"

"I want to know why you are making things so difficult for my lady."

He was silent for a long time. Finally, he smiled. "I might as well tell you. My parents have ordered me to find a woman to marry...and I have no interest in that. I'm quite content with Strephon here." He elbowed the body under the sheets. "Come on out! She won't hurt you!" Strephon's tousled head emerged. "But they don't see it that way. The only concession I was able to get from them was that if I was to marry a woman, she should have the proper womanly skills – and they made the mistake of letting me set the standards. They should have known that I'm choosy about my clothes."

"You are indeed," said Strephon. "Quite the best-dressed man I know."

"But why do we have to be locked up? And why this nonsense with the laundry and pigsties?" Iron Jenny asked.

"Well, I was hoping that the ladies would take the hint and stay away. Most of them have, you know. Because, if I did get married, I would have to give up Strephon – and that would break the dear fellow's heart." He put an arm around Strephon protectively. "So, unless your lady can sew linen without a seam..."

"Well, there may be another solution," said Iron Jenny.

⚜ ⚜ ⚜

The prince and princess were married in the most splendid ceremony you have ever seen. The bride's finery was only outdone by the groom's, and she put up with the fuss and ceremony bravely. Iron Jenny was the bridesmaid, in an elegant dress of silver links ornamented with gold filigree; and, of course, nobody ever notices what the best man wears, but it is said that Strephon did not let his lover down.

All the unsuccessful suitresses and their companions came to the wedding feast; and after dinner the Prince apologized handsomely for keeping them, and sent them home laden with gold, except for one lady-in-waiting who asked to stay. She said that if she went home with her princess, she would have to wear uncomfortable shoes again, and a long dress; and, besides, the pigs would miss her. So the Prince gave her gold, and a place as a pig-tender for just as long as she chose.

Once the feast was over, and the guests had left, the four stole upstairs to the bridal chamber, with its legendary bed three yards wide. On one side, the prince lay in Strephon's arms. A very little way away, Topaz snuggled against the smooth metallic warmth of Iron Jenny.

The next morning, Topaz began to build a fine new labyrinth in the palace grounds. And, in their own particular ways, they all lived happily ever after.

THE WALTZING TREE

RICHARD KEELAN

I bought a house.

It's an old house, in an old neighbourhood, but with solid bones. I bought it for the look of it, for the tall hedge and leafy green trees that surrounded it, and for the way it rose above them like a castle towering over an old-growth forest.

The house was perfect in every way but one: I didn't want to live in it.

I'd never lived alone, and the prospect terrified me. I once counted the number of people I talked to in a week excluding my former roommate.

It was zero. I'd talked to zero other people that week.

You hear about people who die in their houses and are only discovered weeks or months later. That could be me one day.

"They'll know I was here, though," I said. "I'm going to leave my mark. Starting with you, Tree."

The tree was a sapling standing right in the middle of my new backyard.

It didn't fit; it was just there, intruding on every logical path you might take, and I couldn't figure how it was still alive. It was barely taller than I was, dwarfed by the mature trees around it. It should have been choked out by leaves above and roots below. It had no business in my yard, and I was going to do something about it.

My garage housed a vast collection of tools. It was a collection in truth, meticulously organized and gleaming with disuse. Each tool had its place, hanging off wall pegs or stowed in a chest, labelled with a name and a silhouette showing the proper orientation of the tool in storage.

My chain saw, like every other tool I owned, was pristine. It roared to life with one clean pull on the starter cord. I hated the noise it made but loved the feel of it in my hands, the powerful vibrations travelling up my arms.

The sapling almost seemed to shiver in anticipation of its fate.

I held the saw parallel to the ground, preparing for the first traumatic cut.

The saw's engine sputtered, coughed, and died.

"Damn."

I checked the fuel tank. Empty. It was supposed to be full. The gas must have evaporated out of it or something.

"Alright, Tree, you have a reprieve. For now."

⁓⁓⁓   ⁓⁓⁓   ⁓⁓⁓

I made dinner and spent the rest of the evening on the Internet, futilely browsing dating sites. My computer was upstairs in a room I grandiosely called my office. The room's three tall windows were at my back, always shrouded by heavy curtains to keep the glare off my screen.

I hadn't looked at more than a dozen profiles when I heard a noise at the window. I ignored it, then heard it again, and again after that. I finally got up to investigate. I tore aside the curtains, but it was just tree branches tapping against the window.

The noise grated on my nerves. It was the same in every room; tree branches scratching and clawing at every pane of glass.

I went outside. The yard was oppressive and still, like the air weighed more than it should. Like the calm before a truly epic storm.

I looked up.

The tree branches were boiling and shivering as though in a gale-force wind, but I didn't feel a thing.

Must be some crazy air current up there, just above my head. I stuck my arm up but still couldn't feel it.

Then I noticed that the sapling was gone.

* * *

I took a long, careful walk around the property, contemplating a police report about a stolen tree.

Nothing else was amiss – except the tree branches thrashing above my head.

I went inside and checked the weather. There was no storm watch or tornado warning or anything. No storm coming at all. Just a cloudless night and a full moon.

* * *

I went to bed early and woke seemingly moments later, disturbed by a noise downstairs.

That was impossible, though, because I'd locked every door and window on my walk around the house. Even the garage and patio door. I would have heard someone break in.

* * *

I heard the noise again as soon as I closed my eyes. Like there was something moving around on the first floor.

Maybe I should have had the locks changed when I first moved in.

Maybe I would. Tomorrow. I wasn't going downstairs to check. A million-to-one it was just sounds the house made.

· · ·

I heard heavy footsteps on the stairs and changed my mind. Whatever was coming was *huge*. I'd never made noise like that on those stairs.

I sat up in bed. I wasn't going out there, wasn't going to start a fight with whatever it was, but if it came for me...I was going to be ready.

The footsteps – massive fucking footsteps – approached my door.

They continued down the hallway and I let out the breath I'd been holding.

Then the footsteps stopped and came back, pausing right in front of my room.

The door creaked open, revealing a vaguely humanoid figure, pale and misshapen and—

It didn't have clothes! It wasn't even wearing clothes!

It took one step into my room and I'd had enough. I reached under my pillow and pulled out a matte black pistol, its grip cold and comforting against my palm. When creepy shit· starts going down I know enough to be prepared.

The ghoul took another step into my room.

The pistol bucked and roared as I unloaded a full magazine into its face.

I think I may have killed someone.

Or I will have soon.

He was just a kid, about twenty or so, now clutching his stomach as blood seeped between his fingers.

I'd unloaded most of my clip into the wall and the door frame. But I got him once in the stomach.

A kid.

Yay me.

"Didn't you ever learn to knock, Kid? This is my house you're stomping around in."

"It's *my* house." The kid held up one of those old-timey skeleton keys on a chain around his neck. "You just live here."

"There's no way that opened any of the locks on this house," I said.

"It's not for the locks. It's for the doors."

"Whatever, Kid." He was tough. I wouldn't have that kind of poise with a bullet in my gut. "I'll call an ambulance—"

"No!" *Now* the kid sounded scared. "No ambulance. Just give me some first aid. I'll be fine."

"First aid? You've been shot!"

"Do you want the cops getting involved? I'm doing you a favour."

That was crazy. But it sort of made sense. "Here – let me take you down to the kitchen."

The kid was naked, and I'd been trying not to look, but when I knelt to lift him I caught a glimpse of his crotch.

There was nothing there. No hair, no package. Just a smooth patch of skin between his legs.

I shivered.

Maybe I hadn't killed a person.

But his blood was plenty red and I wasn't going to watch someone bleed to death in my bedroom. Not even some-*thing*.

I braced myself for a huge weight, remembering his heavy tread, then lifted him so easily I almost tipped over.

"My name's David," he said, resting his head against my chest.

"Uh – Jonathan."

"Pleased to meet you, Jonathan." ·

"Really?"

David smiled. "Things are looking up already."

I carried him downstairs to the kitchen, then fumbled around in the dark, trying to turn the lights on with my elbow.

I started to set David down on my kitchen table then noticed a dirty bowl in the way.

I left that bowl in the sink.

David followed my gaze. "I was trying to figure out what you had for dinner," he offered.

I set him down on the table, letting his body push the bowl out of the way. Then I went in search of my first-aid kit, a high-powered flashlight, and a towel.

I covered David's crotch with the towel then examined his wound under the flashlight. I couldn't see a thing.

"You have to dig the bullet out," David said.

"I know. I'm just trying to see what I'm doing."

"You're not going to see anything. Just dig it out with a knife or something."

"Well, that's going to fucking hurt, Kid—"

"David."

"David. You need something to bite down on. For the pain."

"Give me your hand."

"You can't bite my hand!"

"No," he said. "I'm going to hold it."

"That's even worse!"

David looked hurt.

"Well, I need my hands," I said. "I need both of them. Maybe you can grab my arm."

David nodded, so I got out my best paring knife and let David clamp one hand around my forearm and the other around my bicep.

I stuck the knife into the wound and David crushed my arm. He grunted and whimpered and ground my arm into pulp, but I got the bullet out.

I washed it thoroughly and examined it under the flashlight. People always did that in movies, to make sure the bullet hadn't fractured. It looked whole to me.

I dropped the bullet in a whiskey glass (another thing I learned from the movies) and breathed a sigh of relief.

Just saved the life of the kid I killed.

⁂

I made David put on a pair of pants – mine fit okay with a belt cinched tight – then helped him out to sit in the yard. He insisted.

We went out through a sliding screen door in the back of the house, then I eased David down into one of the two patio chairs. They'd come with the house.

I sat in the other chair. It was midsummer and warm, for all that it was the middle of the night.

"So, who are you?" I asked.

He nodded at the hole left by my uprooted sapling.

"You're the guy who stole my tree?"

"No! I am the tree. I'm like – a weretree. I turn into a human every full moon."

"Then you'd be a werehuman."

"Fine," he said. "I'm a werehuman."

"So, what were you doing in my house?"

"It's not—"

"My house, I know. Except it is, because I bought it. I have a deed and everything."

"Let's say it's *our* house, then."

"Whatever. So, what were you doing?"

"I wanted to introduce myself. You seemed so lonely earlier."

"Earlier?" I looked at the stones leading away to my garage. The chain saw was still sitting on my workbench, waiting to be filled with gas. "Um, sorry about that." I rubbed an eyebrow. "I didn't know."

"It's okay." David placed his hand on my arm, just below the elbow.

"I'm not lonely."

"I know you're not," David said matter-of-factly.

"I mean, I wasn't lonely."

David looked at me obliquely, and I flushed.

"We should dance," David said.

"Dance?"

"I like to move when I have the feet for it. And dancing's the best kind of moving."

I guessed that made sense. "What about your…injury?"

David took a few steps around the patio. "Never better!"

I could see from his face that he was lying. "I'm sorry, man, I can't dance with you."

"Why not?"

I assumed that was rhetorical, but David just stared at me.

"You're a dude."

"I'm a tree."

"A tree-dude."

"I'm not a tree-*dude*. I have no genitals." David put his hands on his belt. "I'll show you."

"No, don't! I saw earlier."

"If my hair were longer and I had a baggy shirt on you'd want to dance with me."

That wasn't true.

I squinted at him.

Maybe it was true.

But I still wasn't going to dance with a dude.

David sat back down and slouched forward, showing all the pain he'd tried to hide before.

"It's okay," David said. "We'll sit together. I'll enjoy the novelty of being supported by a chair."

That wasn't going to work. I wasn't going to let some kid manipulate me.

No matter how dejected he looked.

Nope.

"Fine."

David looked up. "Really?"

"Yeah."

I looked around. The trees in my yard were huge, with leafy branches that seemed to buttress the house rather than encroach upon it. A thick green hedge had swallowed the chain-link fence that enclosed the yard. It was plenty private in here.

"Yeah," I said again.

"Great!" David said. "What dances do you know?"

"Um… What's the one called where you sway back and forth?"

"Being a tree?"

"No – you take slow steps – slow dancing!"

I took a couple steps, shifting from side to side. My face was burning; I already felt like an idiot and he wasn't even touching me yet.

"You have feet all day, every day, and that's how you dance?"

I threw my hands up. "Hey – no problem. We won't dance. Fine by me."

"No!" David bounded out of his chair. "I'm sorry. That's good. Why don't I just show you a dance? A simple one, like this."

He began to step in a square pattern on the soft green grass of the yard. "Left foot forward, right foot the side, bring them together," he said in a sing-song voice. "Just like that. Right foot backward, left foot the side, bring them together."

I watched his feet for one round, then another.

"Here, stand in front of me – that's right." David repeated the steps but with his feet switched so that I could follow.

After a couple times through, David asked if I wanted to try it together.

I didn't, but I'd shot him, and now I had to make it up to him. "Okay, but I get to lead, right?"

"You get to lead," David agreed, "but you have to hold your arms out for me, like this. Roll your shoulders back and push out your chest. Take up space, like you own the yard and everything in it."

I ignored the obvious rejoinder and tried to mimic his posture.

"Okay, good. Not quite there, but good." David repositioned my arms and prodded my back into place. "Perfect.

Now, hold that pose. You have to be – not really stiff and rigid, but sort of stiff. And rigid."

"How will I know if I'm stiff enough?"

"You know what? Don't worry about it." David placed one hand on my arm, just below my shoulder, and pressed the other against my outstretched left hand. "There you go! Stiff as a board!"

"Okay, now what, funny guy?"

"Now you step just like I showed you."

I looked down—

"Don't look down."

"But I'll step on your feet."

"Don't worry about my feet. I'll keep them out of your way."

David was true to his word. He counted out a beat: *One –* Two – Three – *One –* Two – Three, and I plodded through the steps while he floated along beside me.

"See? Isn't this fun?"

"No," I said, but it kind of was.

✺✺✺   ✺✺✺   ✺✺✺

David showed me how to turn one way, then the other, and then how to rotate in place with the first steps I'd learned.

We continued dancing for a while. I lost track of time, to be honest.

Then I stepped on his toes.

I began to apologize, but stopped, seeing that his eyes were closed.

"Are you okay, man?"

"Fine," he said. But he didn't open his eyes.

"I think you should rest."

"No, just a while longer. Please. It's been so long since I danced."

"That's enough for one night." I disengaged my arms from his and led him over to a chair.

He didn't resist.

I looked down at his bandage. It was red and heavy with blood. "We'll dance again next month," I said, trying to stay calm.

How could I have forgotten he'd been shot?

"Are you comfortable?" I asked. My voice had a quaver to it and I tried again. "Do you want some water? Or something to eat? Do you eat?"

"I'd like some water, if you don't mind." He still hadn't opened his eyes.

I went to the kitchen, trying to think when I'd last seen his eyes open.

It had been awhile. I'd deliberately avoided looking at him.

⁓⁓⁓ ⁓⁓⁓ ⁓⁓⁓

David was too weak to hold the glass, so I held it for him while he drank.

"Why don't I take you to the hospital so they can check you out?"

"Because I'm turning back into a tree in the morning," David said. "I need to be here."

"Well, there's got to be something I can do."

"You could kiss me."

"Why? Will that lift your curse or something?"

"This isn't a curse," he said. "It's who I am."

"Then what's the point?"

"A kiss goodnight…" David sounded very weak. "To help me sleep."

I pressed a hand against his forehead. "David, you're not… Don't sleep, okay? Just stay awake, man."

"Not a man," he whispered.

I bent close to his face, looking at his lips, then not looking at them.

It was the middle of the night. We were in my own very private yard. Who was going to know?

I closed my eyes and pressed my lips against his.

They were warm and soft, but he wasn't breathing.

⁓⧽⧽⧽⧼ ⁓⧽⧽⧽⧼ ⁓⧽⧽⧽⧼

I dug a hole for him.

I worked frantically, always checking over my shoulder for the position of the moon. They say it looks bigger the closer it gets to the horizon – well it looked fucking huge, now.

The shovel's handle was wood, polished and oiled and smooth, but my hands cracked and blistered regardless. My shoulders burned and my back ached, but I couldn't stop. I had to finish before moonset.

David was going to be fine. Everything was going to be fine.

Damp, moist earth began to accumulate in haphazard piles around me. I only needed to go down a couple feet. It wasn't a grave, just a hole.

Trees don't breathe. That's why he wasn't breathing. No lungs.

Can't kill a tree by shooting it. They're too tough. They've got bark, and heartwood underneath. David was tough. Hadn't I said so?

I was going to put him in this nice comfy hole and cover him with nice comfy dirt, and he'd turn back into a tree in the morning. We'd dance again next month, and again the month after that.

Everything was going to be fine.

FAIREST FIND

NICOLE LAVIGNE

There was once a King who had three sons. The King loved his sons deeply, but he feared for the good of the kingdom for he had seen many another kingdom torn asunder by princes fighting and plotting against one another to claim the throne. He had just received news of a kingdom from far to the South that had fallen into ruin and was overrun by thieves because the Princes had all killed each other before the ailing King had passed on. And truth be told, bored Princes are a heavy burden on a kingdom's coffers.

So, when the King's sons had all grown from boys into young men, he sent the middle and youngest sons off into the world to seek their own fortunes where they might, advising them that they would do well to content themselves with a wealthy nobleman's daughter, for fair Princesses and rich kingdoms are few and far between. Theirs was the wealthiest and most stable for some distance.

And so it was with a heavy heart that the old King bade farewell to two of his three sons, giving them the two best horses in the kingdom for their journey. The middle son rode boldly to the West and the youngest son turned his horse to the East.

The eldest son was greatly relieved to watch his brothers' departure, but he did not feel peace for long. Little had the King realized but his eldest son was quite paranoid and quickly grew to fear treasonous plots and civil unrest lurking behind every door and in every shadowy corner. There was nothing for the King to do but find the best advisers and therapists that money could buy and hope the kingdom would survive to be passed on to his grandchildren.

The weeks passed, and soon glad tidings came from the West to ease the King's troubled heart. His middle son had fallen in love and was now happily married to a beautiful, charming and wealthy young Prince. The old King celebrated this most happy news, but still there was no word from the East and his youngest son.

The youngest son journeyed far into the East, and far and farther still. Many moons passed, and the awkward and gangly young Prince grew into a slightly less awkward, slightly less gangly, and slightly less young Prince. He visited many kingdoms and strange lands – some rich, some poor. And he met many a young maiden – some rich, some poor, some beautiful, some not. But the young Prince was a hopeless romantic who always had one foot firmly planted in fantasy. So the maidens that he met were never beautiful enough, never wealthy enough, and nought but the finest Princess would satisfy him.

As the weeks passed, the Prince began to despair, for they really didn't make kingdoms and Princesses like they used to back in the fairy tales he was told as a child. But the Prince was stubborn and refused to give up on his quest or his ideals, so on he travelled.

One day as he was riding he glimpsed a tall tower rising up on the horizon. As he continued toward it other towers rose up soon joined by high, strong castle walls, and he could see one of the windows glinting in the sunlight like jewels: ruby, sapphire and emerald. Now, this was more like it.

It took another full day's ride, but at last he reached the castle and found it surrounded by a dense forest. He searched all around the forest, but he could find no path through to grant entrance to this grandest of castles.

The Prince searched the nearby countryside for a lord, a knight, a noble, anyone who could tell him more about the enchanting castle, but he found no one. Finally, he resigned himself and approached a commoner he found working one of the fields on the edge of the forest.

"You there! Peasant!" he called.

The peasant kept on working his field. The Prince rode closer and called down to him from atop his horse.

"I said, 'You there.' You will speak when spoken to by a Prince."

The peasant turned and looked up at the young Prince. "My name is not 'You there.' It's Bob. And I'll kindly ask you to speak to me with the respect that I deserve as a fellow human being."

The Prince gracefully ignored this. "Where is your master?"

Bob rolled his eyes. "There ain't no masters here."

"Where is your King? Your Lord?" the Prince demanded.

"Ain't no kings nor lords neither. We are govern'd through a democratic system, guided by a council of elders and an elected representative of the people," Bob retorted proudly.

The Prince stared at him blankly.

"We have trade agreements with all of the neighbouring kingdoms," Bob explained.

The Prince blinked then shook his head. "Stop this nonsense! Tell me who rules in that castle there!" He pointed to the castle within the wood.

"No one rules there. That castle's been abandoned for generations."

"Impossible," said the Prince. "Castles like that do not just go abandoned."

Bob regarded the Prince. Then he leaned in and whispered, forcing the Prince to lean down from his horse to hear him. "Well, legend has it that an evil sorceress placed a curse upon that castle, putting everyone inside it into a magical sleep, preserved for a hundred years until the beautiful Princess can be woken by true love's first kiss." Bob bit his tongue to keep from laughing.

The Prince pondered this for a time, eyeing the castle greedily. This was just too good to be true. "But why has no one broken the spell yet?"

"Well, because of the enchanted wood and the dragon guarding the castle, of course."

The Prince blanched. "Dr – dragon?"

Bob raised an eyebrow. "Well obviously there's no dragon now, now is there?" he asked the Prince. "If ever there was," he added under his breath.

The Prince cleared his throat. "There isn't?"

"Do you see a dragon sitting atop the castle?" Bob asked.

The Prince shook his head.

"Did you notice any charbroiled fields while you were riding about trampling them?"

Again, the Prince shook his head.

"And do you see any terrified and traumatized people about, plagued by dragons and waiting in fear for the next inevitable attack?"

The Prince looked around him. "No."

"Then I think it's safe to say that there is no dragon." Bob shook his head in pity.

The Prince straightened on his horse. "Very good then. Thank you, peasant, for your assistance. I shall investigate that castle and wake the beautiful Princess; thereby rescuing you and your people from this frightful chaos. This land shall have a King once again!" And with that he kicked his heels into his horse's flanks and rode off toward the castle.

"Oh come on now!" Bob called after the Prince. "You don't really believe in that fairy tale nonsense, do you? And the name's Bob!" But the Prince was already far out of earshot.

The Prince cautiously wound his way through the dark forest. Every step was tormented by bats, strange noises and all manner of small and disturbing creature that live only where the sun never shines. Thorns and branches tore at his fine clothes and flesh till he bled from a thousand tiny cuts. Dead branches would suddenly fall, nearly striking him down, and roots mysteriously lifted from the ground, tripping his horse. After toiling on for hours and getting turned around more than once, sunlight blinded him. Battered and bruised, but alive, he stood before the castle.

The Prince hollered once, twice, and when still no one answered, he let himself in through a small rotted door to the side of the main gate that had been broken down long before. He tried very hard not to think about what manner of beast might have broken the door in or whether it might still be inside.

When he entered the castle, he was amazed to see servants, children and animals frozen in place all about the castle and covered in a thick layer of dust. Nothing he tried could wake them, so the Prince began exploring the castle room by room. Everything inside the castle was perfectly preserved, save for the layer of dust that kicked up into the air as he walked, but a silk handkerchief tied around his face relieved

him of unsightly coughing fits. He found vast store rooms, lavish chambers and more servants than he had ever before seen
in his life. Beautiful stained glass was set in jewel tones in
many of the windows, and the Prince's eyes glittered with
excitement when he found the coffers stuffed to the rafters
with gold. There was far more gold than his father had, more
even than he had known existed in the whole world. He reluctantly pried himself away to continue his explorations.

Sunset washed the castle walls in shades of pink when the
Prince came to the highest room of the tallest tower, the one
he had spied from the distance. Here was the largest and
most elaborate stained-glass window of them all, depicting a
great dragon sitting atop a castle and breathing fire. There was
a four-poster bed ornately carved with animals and figures.
Lavish gifts and offerings were piled high by the foot of the
bed.

Heart beating wildly in his chest, the Prince approached
the bed. There upon it lay a young woman, still as stone. A
cloud of dust rose from the bed when he gently sat down
upon the edge of it. Untying the handkerchief from his face,
the Prince gingerly wiped the dust from the young woman's
face. He gasped. She was beautiful. Her dark skin was
smooth and unblemished, her features perfectly propor-
tioned, and plump lips.

The Princess, the castle, the riches, it was all greater than
even his wildest dreams. In that instant, he fell deeply in love.
He took a deep breath, bent down and kissed her soft lips.
They tasted faintly of old strawberries and dust. He sat up and
waited, watching her intently.

A minute passed. Two. Then the Princess stirred,
stretched. Her eyes blinked open. She saw the Prince sitting
on her bed watching her.

She screamed.

"Who are you?" she demanded, sitting up and pulling the covers to her neck.

"I'm your true love. I have come to free you from the curse."

"Curse? Who are you and what are you doing in my room?" She grabbed a heavy candlestick from the nightstand and raised it high above her head.

The Prince shuffled back on the bed so that he was out of range and recounted the legend the peasant had told him, with some embellishment. The Princess looked about her room and saw the thick layer of dust that covered everything, including herself, and she began, slowly, to believe his tale. Then she noticed that his fine clothes were torn and tattered, and his body covered with cuts and bruises.

"Tell me of the dragon!"

"...What?"

"You said that a dragon guarded the castle and ate all of the Princes who came before you. You must have killed it to get here and, just look at you, you clearly have been in some sort of battle. You have succeeded where all else failed. Tell me how it was you slew the dragon." Her eyes gleamed.

The Prince cleared his throat. "Such frightening tales are not fit for delicate maidens such as yourself. Surely you would rather we begin planning the wedding?"

"Excuse me?"

Just then the King and Queen came running, panting, into the room. They raced over and embraced their daughter before she could utter another word. Then they turned and embraced the young Prince and thanked him for breaking the curse. The beautiful Princess watched in growing dismay as her dust-covered parents began making wedding plans with the tattered stranger in her bedroom.

"Hold on a second!" she shouted. "You cannot plan my wedding to this stranger without my consent and I refuse to give it until he tells me of his adventures and how he slew the dragon!"

The Queen sighed and silently prayed for patience. The Princess had always been a tomboy, always muddying her gowns playing knights and dragons with the servants' children, and she had spent the past hundred years of the curse dreaming of grand adventures, rescuing people in distress and slaying mythical monsters.

The Prince cleared his throat nervously as all eyes turned to him. He mumbled.

"What was that?" the Princess insisted, leaning forward to listen to his tale.

The Prince sighed. "There was no dragon when I got here. Nothing but that damned forest out there with thorns and bats and things," he admitted with a shudder.

"Enough of this," the King interrupted. "Dragon or not, you will marry this Prince. He did break the curse. He's as good as any other strange Prince in the neighbourhood and we have no idea what the current political situation is."

The Prince perked up and smiled. The Princess, on the other hand, jumped up out of bed and ran down the stairs. She raced between the confused servants, grabbed a sack of gold out of the coffers, leapt onto the Prince's fine horse and rode off into the distance. She was long gone by the time the King, Queen and Prince could make it down the stairs.

The King and Queen had no other children, and so they adopted the young Prince as their son and heir to their kingdom. Then they threw a grand ball and invited everyone of importance from the neighbouring kingdoms in order to make it clear that they were awake once again and that their kingdom was thriving. Having so acquired all the riches he could desire and an enormous kingdom, the Prince was willing to let go of his dream of marrying a wealthy princess, and instead sought out the most beautiful woman, without care of her station. He took advantage of his newly adopted parents' ball to meet all of the nearby eligible young maidens and soon wed the most beautiful among them.

As for the Princess, she went off and had her grand adventures, slaying the last of the monsters that plagued the land, and rescuing people in distress. And so both the Prince and Princess lived happily, but separately.

Bob the peasant was never completely happy again after losing his independence and the democratic system he loved so dearly to the untimely and rude awakening and return of the land's King from the curse, which Bob had always believed to be a load of nonsense. He started a political movement advocating for commoner rights and for the general public to maintain a voice in decisions. The King eventually granted Bob a minor position at court, mainly to shut him up and prevent a revolt. And Bob found some contentment in successfully advocating for basic minimum wages and a few annual sick days before he retired due to pox.

WHITE ROSE, RED THORNS

LIZ WESTBROOK-TRENHOLM

I stumbled right over the little thief, lying there curled up on the giant's steps, fool human. And he took my breath away, like the last time, as he gazed up at me, blue, blue eyes all fringed in black. He was her, my only love so long lost I thought I'd forgotten, tried to forget, but never, never, never could.

Stupid old woman that I am, of course he wasn't her, not even like her. A pretty enough man-child, light of skin and hair black as winter branches against snow. But just a pale, male copy, a little smudge of human grease on Brodorg's front porch. Not my Snow so white. As I was no longer the fiery rose that melted her heart, just a tired old woman with faded ginger frizz escaping my braid to fall into my eyes.

"You!" I swelled up and spread my elbows akimbo, maximizing my size. Living with giants rubs off. "You dare to come back here?"

"Please." Eyes like skies to soar in, but I'd have none of it.

"*Please*," I scoffed. "That's it? No explanation? No 'Thanks for not letting the giant eat me last spring?' No 'Sorry I took your hospitality and then your gold, sneak-thief in the dark of night leaving naught to pay the annoyed baker next day?' Just *please*. Well, Thief?"

"Jack," he said. The audacity. I got a grip on the door, ready to wrestle it shut. When I didn't, it was memory that stopped me, treacherous memory. Snow had been that way, always so gentle-like, few words but eloquent eyes and a stand-fast certainty that filled a room when she chose. Perhaps that's why I could tolerate giants. Her spirit filled the world. My world anyway.

"Get in," I said, as fool as the human. "Hurry. He's overdue." He leapt up and trotted inside, overconfident as a stray puppy, while I scanned the cloud tops that edged the floating land. No massive silhouette loomed against the failing light. A worry, that. If something had got him, whether down in the human lands or among his quarrelsome kind, I'd never hold his castle against his huge, cruel kind. And then where could I go? Brodorg may have been a violent, ugly cannibal, but he was fearsome, strong against all comers. He kept me safe, from those above, and those below. I belonged in neither place. Since the ones below murdered her, I belonged nowhere.

I followed my thief in, already near lost in the gloom of the great hall, scampering along the stone wall, skipping from flag to giant flag, heading all-too-knowing straight for the kitchen. There I found him warming himself by the fireplace where I'd got the oak trunks glowing, the spits set for a couple or three lambs, in expectation of Brodorg's return. I clambered the ladder to the table, my hip complaining as usual, and I hacked off some bread and a hefty crumb of cheese from a mighty wheel resting there and threw it down to him. Then I dipped out some ale from the first barrel in the row by Brodorg's throne all heaped with licey furs, re-fastened the skin flap, and clambered one-handed back down the ladder. Lord, that hip! I normally ate atop the table, my own whittled table and chair there, to my giant's amusement, but I wanted my thief down low where we could run him to hiding quick when we had to.

He nibbled away at the food and drank, thirsty, yet dainty, several swallows not finishing what would've been a mere sip to my giant. I got so lost in watching him I near missed the tremor underfoot announcing Brodorg's approach. I tumbled that Jack into the small copper and hauled on its lid, leaving him a crack for air just as Brodorg fee'd and fie'd through the door, thumping it shut and dropping the bar like thunder.

"I smell the blood of an Englishman," he rumbled, like stones tumbling down a hillside and stomping all round the kitchen so I had to retreat under the hearth shelf to avoid being trampled under his great hairy feet. All the while he was snuffling into corners, he was dragging a couple of sheep behind him, skinned and gutted for roasting. "There's no Englishmen or any other kind here," I told him. "You're smelling the mutton blood you're smearing all over my scrubbed flags, you hairy-toed clodhopper."

"I'll grind his bones to make my bread," he concluded. Always the *idée fixe*, with him.

"As if you ever made bread," I retorted. "You're hungry, is all." And then I finally managed to get him settled down on his heap of furs, chewing on the cheese wheel and the rounds of bread, with a barrel of ale to hand, while I skewered the sheep and winched them up to start turning over the fire.

"If you smell Englishmen," I said, never one to leave something alone when I should, "it's because you spend too much time down there with them where you've no business being. You'll bring bad luck on us."

His big maw split into a double wall of brown headstones and he said, "You're my luck, little Red Rose." He tossed his empty barrel against the wall where it smashed to kindling.

"The ale master will charge a high price for that barrel," I told him. "Wood's rare up here, big old fool." He grinned crooked-toothed again, loving it when his little mouse sassed him, at least early in his drinking, and ripped the cover off another barrel.

"Bring the hen." I fetched Hennie from her coop, annoyed with myself for having spoken.

"Lay!" Brodorg bellowed and she shrieked with fright and struggled to escape my arms.

"Oh, hush," said I, and I stroked and crooned to her and, soon enough, out came the lovely warm brown egg I'd intended for my breakfast next day. Regretfully, I palmed it and, when I handed it up to himself, it was an ovoid gold nugget. While he examined it, I slid my eyes sideways to the copper and, sure enough, saw the glint of blue eyes, watching through the slit I left him.

"See?" I jerked my attention back to Brodorg. He squinted down at me. "You're my good luck, Red. That hen never lays gold eggs for me." Crude he may have been but cunning with it. I let it lie. I'd learned that skills like mine got our kind burnt or stuck in a room spinning up a gold glut leading to kingdom-wide inflation. Best to say a hen was magic, or that a mysterious little man happened along.

That made me think of Rolf, how I had made sport of him, always finding some way to cut a little more off his proud beard. He'd be spitting mad until my Snow soothed our vain dwarf friend, combing it out for him and saying he was handsomer than ever until he believed her. Hers was a soothing sort of magic that worked on the mind. She'd cup my chin in her hand and gaze at me out of her black-edged blues and say, "We need to look out for each other. We're all of a kind."

"Rolf's *some* kind," I'd say. "Sour old dwarf." But I'd try to behave for a while. It was best folk didn't know what we were, so we told them we were sisters, and our leader, our coven Mother, we passed off as our good-hearted, widowed old mama. That way they didn't wonder at three women living alone together, nor wonder at us young ones' hand-holding and cuddles, or look too closely at the odd things that happened in our vicinity.

Odd happenings were usually down to me. The Mother and Snow were discreet. But I – I'd be off stretching and testing my skills before too long. Testing my skills generally involved tricks and games at mundane folks' expense. Goats up trees, peacock feathers on a fop's fancy arse, hens laying apples. What could I say? Transformation spells were my forte, but I needed practice to do it well. My sweetheart and the Mother of our triad made me help them reverse it all, so no harm done, except to pride.

"We have to live and let live in this world," Snow warned me.

"How're they to know it's me?" I laughed. "They suppose we're the two innocent sisters, Snow White and Rose Red, and our sweet widowed mother. How could *we* be up to mischievous magic?"

Not knowing what a fool I was being, I couldn't be anything but happy. Our springs were all green, the summers all lush, the autumns all golden, the winters snug and safe in our fire-lit cottage. Love and happiness made us rash. We two made secret love among the apple trees and kissed before the fire and our love was so huge it made our magic strong, the Coven Mother even said so. We were happy, and the villagers, never before seeing sisters so close, loved us like mascots. We should have let the cursed bear starve in the snow.

My sorry mood stayed with me as we prepared Brodorg for sleep, him by dumping the furs from his chair onto the floor before the fire, me by helping Harp out of its niche on the wall to drain and beguile him with amorous games and songs. I could have no part in that; the giant in the throes of passion would've squished me flat, but Harp was a fairy artifact, mutable, indestructible, and inscrutable. I'd had a fling with it early on, enspelled by its singing laughter and frothy tales, but no matter how I searched through its organza-layered character, I never found a core. The spell wore off; we could not give each other what each needed. Harp seemed unresentful when I ceased to play with it, although I found its sloping cat's eyes watching me sometimes as I played my role as giant's housekeeper and pet.

Mascots. Pets. Tolerated until pride calls for scapegoats.

Old Brodorg, tired from a day's mayhem and ale, soon snored by the fire. From my pallet under the hearth shelf, I watched Harp back in its niche, golden eyelids serenely closed, stringed wings folded. At last I waited no more. I crept to the copper and, with the lad's help, shifted the lid as quietly as we could. He clutched his groin and followed me knock-kneed out of the kitchen yet, for all his discomfort, I caught him stealing looks back where Harp drifted in fairy dreams, or I hoped it dreamed. Harp's loyalties were uncertain and I could only imagine what kind of education the young man had absorbed while peeking from under the lid. I led him the rear way through the hen-yard, hissed for him to be on his way and left him, upturned face luminous as he copiously peed a moonlit stream of the giant's ale by the back gate.

Of course, next morning, Hennie was gone. I spent half the day, after Brodorg went off, clearing up the bones, tossing the furs back up on the throne, scrubbing the sheep's blood off the flags and packing up the splintered ale barrel, all while cursing the lad, the human race, giants, mascots, pets and my own gullibility. Those days, I'd begun increasingly to use a touch of transformation to help my work along, changing the dust motes and grime to tiny wings that flew up the chimney, or spilled ale to water that dried clean. That morning I used my muscles, sore joints be damned, trying to wear down my anger with physical effort. My feelings of betrayal and outrage remained undiluted as I loaded the reusable barrel staves on my back to haul the two hours' journey to the ale master.

My load delivered, payment made for the smashed staves and halitosis-laced lecture received on the shortage of wood these days what with the lands below so worked over, I finally escaped. I cut across the hops fields rather than using the giants' road for my return journey, as much for the cover as the shorter way. I was glad to be free of the ale master's yard, and the stares and nerve-wracking pokes of his lumpy offspring. Only fear of Brodorg kept them from pulling off my arms and legs, just to see what was inside. Magicking them into placid cows before their father's eyes would've been temporarily satisfying, but would have led to an untenable end for me. And it'd have been irreversible, without my sweet girl and the powerful Coven Mother to help me unwork it. My magic once done wanted to stay done. Once an egg was gold, it could never make an omelet. So, I hid my nature and skills to protect my tenuous haven. Cautious at last, when there was so little left to lose.

Clambering over giant furrows and through tangled hops leaves, I wished we'd used caution when we undid cranky

Rolf's sorcery. We three wise women, thinking only to be kind and just, celebrated the return of spring by restoring the bear to arrogant, entitled, hirsute prince. Rolf had cast aptly. The prince, in obtuse gratitude laced with lust, took my love to wife, as the meeker of the two maids he'd fancied as they'd cuddled against his bearish flank the winter through. He handed me off to his scholarly younger brother, keeping me close should he want a more adventurous screw now and again. The brother soon learned to stick to his books and leave me alone. My sweet Snow quickened by fall, the baby she bore giving her bear prince the struts and filling me with frustrated rage. We lived in wealthy, privileged purgatory, close yet never daring to touch, surrounded by the stares and curiosity of the court. Caution. It blew off on the autumn winds where we'd thrown it.

We had a winter.

In spring, he caught us, sleeping in Snow's boudoir, naked limbs tangled in moist aftermath of glorious love.

Hell hath no fury like a proud prince scorned.

My last sight of her was one flash between sleeping and my head smashing against the stone wall where he'd thrown me. A branded image: Snow White, glowing in the candlelight, pale hands lifted in supplication over her swollen belly, his dark mass bearing down on her. The dungeon where I woke had a grate sufficient to smell the fire's smoke and hear the screams of agony in the courtyard outside. The folk we thought had loved us jeered.

I'd thought to turn myself to mist and drift to naught on the smoke of her. But mist can do no revenge. So, I rose meekly to meet my jailers. I hoped the prison cats devoured the rats they became, and fattened, too, on the newts and frogs I made of all I encountered in my exit to the square.

I reduced the prince's castle to a heap of moulding bread, giving the jeering spectators a few moments to fall silent in horrified realization before I transformed them to smouldering cinders, every one. The prince, may hells have his soul, was absent, not able to endure watching his wife and fetus killed. He'd gone to take out his rage on a neighbouring demesne. So said his stammering brother, my husband, his eyes red with weeping, back turned to the fire. He seemed inclined to speak more, but I changed him to a crow and turned my back on him. He'd not been unkind, just weak and dependent.

Before the smoke had died, the prince's horse came back with the royal head hanging from its saddle. I changed it to a football and made the surviving villagers play a match with it. I watched, feeling nothing. His end had been too quick, too clean, too much a hero's end, not the death by my hand that I'd so needed. The score was nil–nil.

I squatted on three more days amid the stink of mould and greasy smoke, rain pouring where my tears could not. At last, I gathered the ashes into a white rose bush with red stems and thorns, and left it there to bloom.

And I lived unhappily ever after.

I was driven this way and that by unassuaged rage and guilt. I hid awhile in a forest but, maddened with solitude, tried to rejoin society. I cast magic for this king or that angry wife, but moved on when the fear and resentment pushed too hard at me. I tried to blend in here and there, hiding my true nature, but a woman alone, especially one aging into wrinkles and brown spots, was ever the target of accusations. After escaping yet another attempt to burn me, I fetched up an uneasy guest and servant of a giant in his castle.

How was it tears took forty years to ripen? Stumbling through the hops field, I came back to my old reality when I tripped and sprawled at the base of a tangled tower of hops. I wept, wept, wept. Decades of rage, vengeance, grief, loneliness, released. All reduced to the old grey ash of resigned stagnation.

Emptied, I rose from the earth of the furrow where I'd fallen. And there it was. Thrusting up, twining in and around the hops, in the broad day of the ale master's field, was a beanstalk, its broad green leaves shimmering with ancient, deliberate power. I circled it; peering down through the green caged space it had opened through earth and cloud beneath the floating land, all the way to the human world, lost in blue mist far below. This is what anchored the giant's land to one spot, unmoving. This was the road Jack used to climb to adventure.

Jack. The foolish lad was as heedlessly curious and daring as I at his age. Deep inside, a spirit flickered. It whispered an invitation to follow him down, if only to keep an eye out for the foolish lad. It tempted me to reap the wind of incaution.

A familiar, chickeny burr of contentment penetrated my consciousness. Hennie. I staggered round and found the old girl ecstatically devouring worms. I pounced and hugged her to me, despite her squawk of protest. Her warm, feathery body felt safe, familiar.

"You can't go adventuring, you silly old thing," I told her. "A fox could get you, or a giant step on you." I carried her gently up and down over giant furrows, promising all the way to bring her worms, all the worms she wanted, and green grass too. She'd live safe in her coop, give me eggs, and we'd live happily ever after. Both of us firmly putting adventure behind us, putting whispering voices to bed again.

When we got back to Brodorg's castle, the back gate was ajar. I closed and locked it, thinking, as I tucked Hennie into her run, that I must've forgotten it in my distracted state.

Back in the kitchen, the furs were in a muddle on the floor.

Fear rising in my gullet, I searched all over the house, the unused back rooms, the ruined heights, the cellar.

When at last I went out on the front steps, the light was lengthening over the land. Brodorg had not yet clambered the ladder the giants dangled over the clouded ramparts of their land when they made their forays to those below. He was not yet striding toward his home, blocking the lowering sun with his bulk. I had time yet, but only so much. And when he did return, he'd kill me. He'd track down Jack and Harp and smash them. He'd roar down the beanstalk and wreak havoc at its base. Whoever lived there, whoever had gifted white skin and raven hair to Jack would die. In his temper, he would crush even Hennie.

Unless I brought Harp back.

Back inside I ran, my slippers slapping on the great hall's flags, past the kitchen and down the passageway out into the yard. I cast one regretful look at Hennie and unlatched the gate. Then I turned and went back to her. I grabbed the egg basket off the wall by the door and scooped her into it.

"Adventuring, Hennie. Like it or not, we've got to catch them and bring Harp back. Caution to the winds."

The light was golden by the time we reached the beanstalk. Looping the basket hard over my arm and gathering my courage, I clambered out onto a broad leaf and followed its tendril to the core of the stalk. Once there, it was like a ladder, leaf stalk to leaf stalk, step to step. The air was dim and clear, shadowed by the giants' land, but without clouds of its own. Below, fields made patchworks amidst stretches of woolly green forest.

Before long, my arms and legs ached, the basket handle dug into my shoulder, and Hennie bawked complaints like clockwork, despite my shushing. While we felt the long fingers of the setting sun, night spread like black velvet over the lands beneath. I dared not stop. I somehow had to fetch them back up to Brodorg, before Brodorg made his way to them. I was soon feeling my way down, with fingers so sore and numb I could hardly tell what I was grasping. My foot slipped and I swung out and around over the void; my slipper spiraling off and the basket bearing Hennie after it.

Being a magical person cost me everything I'd ever loved. It cost me ease of mind and heart. It cost me home and belonging. I'd spent a lifetime learning to hide what I was, leaking it out in only the tiniest secret drops, always in service of other's comfort. I'd grown old and stunted in my denial of myself.

Far below, Hennie buh-gawked.

I flung magic into the night, calling on the air, the invisible dust and water drops to rise and resist, like a net or mesh in my mind's eye, but indeed, a transformation more akin to levitation than any I'd ever managed before. Just below me, Hennie bawked again. Breathing deep, being me, I stepped out into the dark and drifted down on a cloud of substantial nothing until I met her, still in her basket.

"You could've sailed on your wings, silly old thing," I told her. But neither of us had thought of that, in the panic of the moment. Just as I had not thought how much more quickly I could have descended myself.

Gently, then faster, growing into the feel of it, I lowered us into the night. We flew by my slipper, and, snatching it, I put it on.

Thick warmth rising to greet us told me I was close to the earth. Old habit, or sensible precaution made me return to the beanstalk for the last few steps. As I set foot on terra firma, the stalk gave a mighty shake, and began to tremble violently. Hennie shrieked and flapped. Brodorg had tracked us. Now what?

A square of light opened in the black, a doorway, outlining Jack's slim figure and, just to his side, the shimmering, curvaceous figure I knew to be Harp, shaped to please him. I do not think the light reached me, though Hennie's panic could have guided him to me easily enough.

"Granny, bring the axe," he shouted.

And out ran a woman, silhouetted against the light from the room behind, axe held at the ready, hair lifting in a cloud around her as she saw me. For a moment, for a moment… But the hair was white, picking up gold and red tints from fire and lamp light. Not the ebony it should have been. Should have been.

I stumbled forward, involuntarily.

"Rose." The single word, a breath, drifted to me like a ghost. She stumbled forward, the lad just catching the axe as she dropped it. She brought up light, a skill she'd not had when we were young, any more than I'd known how to float myself and chickens, shoes or baskets, back then. So changed were we. Yet not. We gazed, drank impossibly from each other's eyes, you, you. Like mercury drops we came together, first hands, then lips, then bodies, melding into each other, inhaling never-forgotten scents. Our hair entwined, hers white now, the faded fire of my unravelled braid paled and threaded with silver. She felt bird-like, bones fragile as I wrapped her in my solidity, like warm coals from a fire long-banked.

"I thought…"

"They said you…"

"Rolf's people saved me, the dwarves."

"I heard your death cries from my cell…"

"A glamour. The Mother. She died for me. For our daughter."

"Our…?"

"Our love planted a seed of you in the prince's get as it wakened in my belly. A transformation."

I kissed her again then nodded my head at Jack. "Our grandson?" She nodded, her light dimming.

"Our daughter died in bearing him."

"The Mother and I not there to help you guide her through. All those years. Lost." I felt old anger flare. Her grip tightened on my fingers.

"It's over now," she said. "You're home. Home where you belong, my Rose Red. With me."

I kissed her fingers, her mouth. "You waited."

"I knew you'd come. One day."

"And I've brought a giant." I grew suddenly aware of Jack, still clutching the axe. His gaze shifted back and forth between us – surprise, confusion and doubt running races across his features. His face firmed in decision. I saw a touch of bear, or me.

He rushed toward us, raising the axe. He could've struck us down right there and I'd have stood too surprised to stop him. Instead, he whacked the blade against the base of the stalk. A few chips flew, but the thing was as thick as an ancient oak. He persevered but, up above, Brodorg's fie's grew audible; his distant roaring threatening mayhem for the loss of his pets and his pride. There'd be no going back, that was sure. And I'd wasted too much time already.

As Jack chopped, I reached into the roots and called them to change to water, but the magic was deep and so powerful, I shook the stalk even less than Brodorg's descent. Jack called for a wedge. Snow threw him a hunk of wood from the pile near the door and he banged it into the cut he'd made so far. Round the other side he went to start the counter-cut to be sure he felled the thing away from the cottage. Skilled lad, our grandson. That was the way to do it.

As Brodorg's roaring grew closer yet, I stood to one side while Jack chopped, following his blade into the stalk, teasing into the old magic, seeking the weakness at the beanstalk's heart, a core of soft pith. I felt it and I reformed the supporting outer layer in its likeness, spreading soft pliability across its whole breadth, a treacherous crease of weakness. Of a sudden, Jack's axe head buried itself deep in the heart of the stock. A flash, a crack, and slowly, slowly the stalk tilted.

We retreated toward the cottage as it cascaded down, leaves and bean pods showering all around. Brodorg's cry as he fell was long and enraged, yet sorrowful, a lament for the end of him and his kind's power, their time done. I turned from the sight. Snow dimmed her light and clasped my hand tight. Jack crouched on the step of the cottage, his arms wrapped close around Harp, Harp cradling Hennie. We waited for that long wail to end.

The landing was thunderous, both soft and hard, with ugly cracking sounds like smashing wood and pumpkins.

We dwell in the cottage, beside the new range of hills that cover Brodorg's bones. I raised the earth over him at night, while Snow gave light to do it. I'd not have him picked over by ordinary folk. Not a creature to love, but he'd provided a safe port of sorts.

Snow and I tell and retell our stories, of loss and sacrifice, of courage and renewal. We do not hide who we are. Those around us accept us, or leave us be. Jack returns from time to time, Harp at his side, to amuse us with the facts behind the stories growing up around him. We laugh, all the more for knowing ourselves how far tales wander from the truth.

Our story, the true tale of Snow White and Rose Red, is a lesser one, and we're content for it to fade into the shadow of obscurity. We are old, but our sore bones arrange themselves around each other comfortably.

We live happily ever after, so far as we can make it so.

PATH OF WHITE STONES

KATE HEARTFIELD

Iain took their bags to the car while Peggy checked every room.

"What are you looking for?" he'd asked her once, years before, after one of her last looks. "The oven," she'd said, after a minute. "We don't want to leave the oven on, do we?"

This was the last of the last looks. The moving trucks were already rumbling on ahead of them.

No dirty dishes, no food in the fridge. No bills on the table or laundry on the couch; no table or couch for that matter. Her own house, strange to her, emptied of her. So little changed by her, in its bones. Within a week, new paint would no doubt cover those marks on the kitchen wall where the pencil had rested on Richard's tousled head at six, and seven, and eight.

Too much house for Peggy and Iain to handle – that's how Richard liked to put it. He was right. Too many stairs for Peggy's knees, that was the main thing.

As Peggy walked to the car, she stopped and looked up at the roof.

"What is it?" Iain asked, turning the key in the ignition.

"Nothing," said Peggy, because it must have been a bird hopping, because it must have been a cloud's shadow fleeting, because chimneys do not move and absolutely do not scuttle and hunch and peer. "I thought I saw something."

"Something?"

"It was nothing. A trick of the light on the roof. The sun must have gone behind a cloud."

⌇⌇⌇   ⌇⌇⌇   ⌇⌇⌇

The first highway was wide and fast.

The second highway was a grey ribbon through glittering blasted rock and merry forests.

The third was not a highway at all.

⌇⌇⌇   ⌇⌇⌇   ⌇⌇⌇

Peggy had found the new house, on the Internet. A bungalow with pretty window boxes and one of those ovens halfway up the wall so she wouldn't have to bend, and a kitchen to hang her copper pots in. A little house just to live in, with no kids to raise and no jobs to pull them away. No snow to shovel. A place for *being*, not working.

"It's as if it was made for us," Peggy had said.

And Richard, on the phone, answered, "Well, in a way, Mom, it was. People like you, anyway. Riviera Court is an adult lifestyle community."

"Sounds risqué," Iain had said. "But the main thing is the property backs right onto Alten National Park. Right on a major migratory route. I can't believe the luck."

"I'll never see you," Peggy had joked.

The road didn't fight the bumps and dips of the Canadian Shield; it clung to them, with the forest climbing on one side and plunging down on the other.

Around a curve and the braking car jolted Peggy into her seat belt as she yelled, "Iain!"

A moose stood in the road, antlers like oak boughs. Ian braked and swerved. For one bad moment, Peggy looked down through the windshield at a thicket.

Branches scraped the side of the car as it jolted to a stop on a muddy slope. Iain pushed until he puffed, rigged up newspaper ramps and twig shims, and finally flipped open his cell phone. He walked around the car with it, holding it up in the air, tilting it this way and that.

"No service," he said. "Yours?"

Peggy tried hers, shook her head.

She knew what he was thinking, that Peggy could not walk far. She could barely get to the end of their road, these days, without pain.

"Well," he said, leaning against the hood, "we'll just have to wait for the next car. There's bound to be one before long."

In the morning, a racket of birdsong woke Peggy from liminal dreams. She opened her eyes to grey light. The car window was cold against her cheek, hard against her temple.

Iain was gone and she was alone in the car.

He had to be out for a pee. She opened the door and stepped out, calling his name.

He crashed through the woods, his blue-and-white checked shirt flashing between the trees. "I'm right here, Peggy. I just went looking for water. And look. I found some."

He held up a Diet Coke bottle. *Her* Diet Coke bottle, filled now to the top with a grainy liquid the colour of weak tea. It reminded her of Richard's grade nine Mason jar experiments on Brownian motion.

"I strained it through my shirt," Iain said. "Even so… Up to you whether you want to try your luck. I did. I could barely think, I was so thirsty."

He held out the bottle. She shook her head.

"No, thanks. Not yet anyway. Iain, you shouldn't have left the road. What if you'd got lost? You didn't even leave me a note."

"I was only gone a few minutes. You were sleeping."

"People wake up."

He shrugged, and the shrug kept happening, his shoulders heaving as he doubled over and made an awful croaking sound.

Then he straightened up, and looked at her, and vomited. A bright green froth, the wrong colour for anything that ought to be in a human stomach. When it stopped, damp green leaves and fronds were stuck in his sandy beard. Iain leaned against the car, gasping.

"What the hell did you eat?"

He shook his head.

"You can't eat leaves, you know. Did you eat leaves?"

He shook his head. "Didn't eat anything."

"Well. You obviously did."

He wiped his mouth with the back of his hand, and then started waving it frantically.

A car was approaching. At last. Peggy nearly cried when they stopped, a man and a woman, roughly their own age.

"Crappy cell service until you get near Brighamton, so we'll just take you to the service station there," said the man as he drove them away from their upended car. "It's only another ten kilometres or so, anyway."

⁓᠁ᢂ⁓ ⁓᠁ᢂ⁓ · ⁓᠁ᢂ⁓

She was right about not seeing Iain much, once they moved into the little house across from the forest.

In late June, he had a gallbladder attack and spent three days inside with her. She told him she was thinking of painting the kitchen wall.

"But we had it painted before we moved in. You don't like the colour? You wanted yellow, you said."

"I don't know," she said. "I don't even know if it's the kitchen. The whole house is not quite right, somehow. Maybe it's not the paint. It feels like it's missing something."

"A crack in the foundation and dry rot?"

"No, you joker. I don't know."

"This house is perfect for us, Peggy. You said so yourself."

"I know I did. And it is. It just feels like it needs something."

He might have rolled his eyes, but she didn't look at him to find out.

And then he was off again into the green.

He had taken up birding in his fifties, after a trip to Point Pelee. That trip had also planted in their minds the notion that there were parts of Canada where the winters were gentler, that life didn't have to be so hard. Richard was grown and married and living half a continent away; they could go where they liked when they retired. They had chosen southern Ontario.

Riviera Court was on the outskirts of Brighamton, on the side of a low hill.

Farther up the slope an older development sprawled, full of kids riding their bikes and scooters round and round the cul-de-sacs.

On the other side of Riviera Court was the forest. A little forest carved out of the farmland, designated a national park.

Peggy and Iain's yard backed onto it: Iain could walk straight down the garden path to where it stopped, and thence onto the short grass and onto the long grass and into the wood. That was where Iain went, day after day, looking for birds.

Peggy could not think what she could say about it. After all, what else was he going to do with his days?

As for Peggy, she baked and canned, and puttered in the little rose garden in her tiny backyard, slowly loping back and forth on the path of six white patio stones that led nowhere, that simply stopped at the edge of their property.

She picked crab apples from the tree on the forest edge and made sweet jelly the colour of sailors' warnings. Jars and jars of jelly, clinking and bubbling in her enormous black canning pot.

She chatted with the neighbour, Sue-Ann. Sue-Ann lived in a little house exactly like their own, exactly like the other six houses on Riviera Court.

"You'll have to build a fence," Sue-Ann told Peggy the first day they met, over the gate in her own fence. "They don't like metal, of course. Has to be wood."

"They?"

"The residents' association."

"Ah. Well, I don't think we need a fence. We aren't fussy about privacy."

"You say that now, but the first time a deer eats those hostas or one of *them* tramples your petunias, you'll have Iain out here with a hammer right quick."

She pointed up the slope as she said "them" this time. Not the residents' association, then.

"The children?" Peggy guessed. "From the development?"

Sue-Ann nodded. "Bad, all of them. Some of them come from other places, eh? Used to just be the migrant workers around here, picking fruit, and that was bad enough, but at least Mexicans are Christians, that's what I always said. And *they* weren't bringing their families and putting down roots. These ones stay and wear those things on their heads. Don't have our values. You can't blame them, really, but you need a fence, my dear."

"Ah," said Peggy again, and knew she was a coward when she was relieved to hear the oven timer calling her in.

⁓⁓⁓   ⁓⁓⁓   ⁓⁓⁓

The summer had almost burned itself out and Peggy was inside, with a sun headache, the afternoon she realized Iain had said he would be home for lunch.

She waited until evening to call the police, and they didn't search the forest until morning. It was another day before they found him, on the floor of a ravine all a-riot with weedy trees.

Peggy heard the shout, and turned toward it, knowing, somehow, what it would be. One of the volunteers was standing by a beech tree, its ferny leaves catching the sunlight. At its base was Iain's body. The tree was growing right out of him.

They told her that he had fallen and been speared, but she didn't believe it. The branches still had their leaves, didn't they? The leaves were still green, save one coppery shoot. A slightly paler green than the leaves that had frothed out of Iain's mouth, the day they came to this place.

She thought of the Green Man carved out of stone that sat nestled in wood chips in Iain's garden, near his gargoyle and his birdbath. The wild-eyed man with vines curling out of his mouth, becoming his beard and hair.

The green world had claimed her husband. It had been happening for a long time, and she had tried to deny it. Places claim their inhabitants.

If the forest claimed Iain, what place would claim her?

But the police said he had slipped on muddy ground and fallen and the green branches hid him there. They said he'd fallen right through the limb of a punky, rotted oak that grew at the side of the ravine; the crack was fresh. He might have had a stroke or a heart attack or he might have simply tripped.

There was no requirement for an autopsy, unless she wanted one.

She did not.

~∭~   ~∭~   ~∭~

The autumn chill came biting and breaking. It was a brand-new house and had some settling to do. Sometimes Peggy would hear it crack and creak in the night.

The windows sounded different, though. Three crashes, all in a row.

She lay stock-still in bed, flat on her back, and stared at the ceiling for an eternity. This was the sort of moment when a person was supposed to know what to do.

She scrambled for her glasses and peered at the clock. Just after midnight. In her long flannel nightgown, Peggy walked to the front of the house.

The two windows in the living room, smashed. Glass all over the floor.

She went into the other room at the front of the house, the little den where Iain's easy chair and stereo sat. The window smashed. Glass all over the floor, some of it shards and some nearly powder, glistening like spilt sugar.

Peggy stepped backward and stared at the broken windows, webs of white against blackness. She called the police.

※   ※   ※

The policewoman who took the report was the same one who had given her the contents of Iain's pockets a month before. His keys, two golf pencils and a smooth white pebble. She kept the pebble in her own pockets, always, so she could hold it in her hand and no one would know. She missed him, as if missing him were an occupation.

※   ※   ※

The new windows ate into her savings and there would be new expenses with winter coming. There might not be snow to shovel here but there could be ice, and she would need to have groceries delivered on the weeks when it was too slippery for her to walk to the car.

The young man who did deliveries at the grocery store was kind, at least. He had brought her bag of road salt right up to the front door.

On a Saturday when the leaves were golden and the air still warm enough for shirtsleeves, Peggy went out to put a measuring cup into the bag of salt crystals, so it would be ready when the ice came.

A teenager ran past her, hockey stick in hand, chasing a red ball down the road.

Road-hockey nets in the street. In Riviera Court! So much for adult lifestyle.

The ball shot past her head and smacked into the window behind her. Smash.

She turned. It might have helped if she had cried, but she would not cry. She curled her fists into balls, her fingernails digging into her palms.

The boy was at her side, his face horrified. "I'm so sorry," he was saying.

"What the hell are you doing playing hockey here?" she yelled, riding the energy of the heat pushing up through her lungs, her throat. "This is a private road!"

"There aren't many cars," he said weakly. "I'm really sorry about the window. I'll pay for it."

"You're damn right you'll pay for it," she said, raising one of her fists. "Tell me your name and your address. No, wait, let me get a pen and paper. Don't you dare go anywhere in the meantime."

"I'm watching him," said a voice, and Sue-Ann was there, holding a broom.

Peggy didn't want Sue-Ann to watch him. She wanted to say, *It's not because the boy is brown-skinned, it's because* – but what was it because? It was because she had nearly been hit by that ball herself and it made her afraid, and there was no one to take her to the hospital. Maybe that was it.

⌇⌇⌇   ⌇⌇⌇   ⌇⌇⌇

She woke to a blinking alarm clock. 12:12, it said, with every blink.

The oven, Iain's stereo, everything, blinking at her. There must have been a power outage, although she didn't remember a storm.

She reset the time on the clock and the oven, but the stereo ignored her and kept blinking. She pulled out the manual and went through the steps, one by one, but it just kept blinking. It wouldn't even play music.

She gave up on it and baked peanut butter cookies in her beautiful oven. Six of them went into a red-and-green plaid cookie tin and the tin went into a plastic grocery bag.

She walked slowly to the end of Riviera Court and up the slope of Darlene Crescent to the fourth house, where Jamal and his family lived.

His mother opened the door with a smile. "Mrs. Holtz, come in, please. Come through to the kitchen – my little one is in there and if I don't keep an eye on her she'll be through the baby gate and down the stairs before I know it."

Peggy followed her into the kitchen. The fridge door was covered in crayon drawings and a smiling toddler lolled on the floor, rolling a truck back and forth on the tiles.

"I've got your cheque already made out. And you can be sure Jamal won't be playing hockey on your road again."

Peggy shook her head. "It's all right. Please, call me Peggy."

"And I'm Zaira. Would you like a cup of tea?"

"That would be nice."

Zaira turned to the sink and filled the kettle. Peggy pulled the cookie tin out of the grocery bag, opened it, took one out.

"Would you like a cookie? I just took them out of the oven."

Zaira turned and her smile vanished.

"Is that peanut butter?"

A crumb dropped to the floor.

"Yes, I—"

"Please put it back in the tin. And let me take that outside."

Zaira held out her hands.

"I didn't—"

"Elham has a very bad allergy. She could die."

Peggy looked at the crumb on the floor, at the little girl crawling.

"I'm so sorry." She bent down, tried to reach the crumb but her knees weren't cooperating.

"Here." Zaira grabbed a paper towel, ran it under the sink and knelt to wipe up the crumb. She carried the tin out to the front porch, came back and washed her hands in the sink with dish soap.

"I'm sorry to be so abrupt. It's just that it's not something to mess around with."

"Of course."

Peggy sat on the kitchen chair and drank the tea, watched Elham playing happily, making truck noises. *Vroom vroom.*

She looked up at Peggy and frowned.

Peggy leaned forward and smiled at her. "I'm really not a mean old lady," she said to the child.

Elham made a truck noise, blowing a raspberry with her lips. *Vroom vroom.*

Peggy took her cheque for the window and retrieved the cookies from the front porch and left, making Zaira promise she would come for tea, assuring her it would be fine to bring the little one to Peggy's house. She didn't know what she meant by *fine* – safe, or welcome, or both.

⚜ ⚜ ⚜

It took Peggy a moment to realize what had changed about the house. Something in its character had shifted, the window-eyes dark underneath like a clown's in makeup. The window boxes: dark and bare. All her red geraniums gone.

She walked forward, puffing a bit, and frowned over them. Each stem was still there in the dirt, neatly clipped at the surface. As if someone had cut them to make arrangements.

"Such a shame," came a voice behind her. She turned to see Sue-Ann standing there, her little dog on the leash. "Alice down the road was egged last week, and Phyllis had a Buddha stolen right off her porch. Imagine!"

Peggy frowned deeper. "I don't think any of the local teenagers did this."

Sue-Ann made an if-you-say-so face. "Could have been deer, I suppose. In any case, you want to make sure to build that fence high. Mine's eight feet. And get yourself a camera, like we've got."

Sue-Ann pointed up toward her own roof, at the black apparatus there. It moved, as if in response, turning to stare at them. Peggy remembered the strange feeling she'd had when they left their old house, that some part of the roof or chimney had moved and was watching them leave. As if the house had been aware of them.

And her new house? Was it aware of her? She felt sure it was, and in a less companionable way. She looked at the empty window boxes, at the newly repaired windowpanes. This house wanted to make her afraid. To mistrust. To keep away the children. Better to keep them away. They were all afraid of Peggy anyway, weren't they? They all thought she was a mean old lady. This house would keep them away from her.

She closed her eyes and shook her head. "I won't give in to fear."

Sue-Ann clucked. Her expression, when Peggy opened her eyes, was sour. "Suit yourself."

Behind Sue-Ann, the shingles of Peggy's roof were curling angrily, vindictively, cracking and shrivelling before Peggy's very eyes. She gasped.

Sue-Ann followed her gaze and looked at Peggy's roof. "Might be a good time for that camera, though. Your roof needs replacing anyway."

॰॰॰॰   ॰॰॰॰   ॰॰॰॰

Richard looked tired, or maybe that was just the way his face looked on Skype. He looked old. How did she get to have a son who looked old?

"You're working a lot," she said, not quite a question.

"Sure," he said. "The usual. You know. Don't worry, I'll get plenty of rest once the baby's born." He grinned.

"Ha. How is Susan?"

"Big. Tired. Sick of being pregnant. How are you, Mom?"

This question meant, *How are you doing at being a widow? Are you turning into a funny old lady? A crone, all clicking needles and apples in a basket?*

"Well enough," she answered. "The days are long, I admit."

"Did you ever get Dad's stereo working again? There's a great new Yo-Yo Ma album. I was going to burn you a CD."

She shook her head. "The damn thing is toast, I think. Must have been a power surge or something."

"Do you want me to talk you through it?"

"No, Richard, I've tried. The electronics in this house – must be the wiring. The oven's gone funny too."

"Well, ovens might be tricky, but I can have a look at the stereo at least when I'm there next month."

"I'm telling you, it's dead. I'll get rid of it. It doesn't matter. As you say, it was Iain's anyway, mostly."

He nodded, and neither of them said anything for a moment. It had gone sour, and it was time for goodbye, so she said, "Well," just as Richard said, "It's just that—"

"What?" she asked.

"I'm just worried that – you shouldn't let yourself get isolated, there."

"Isolated? Ha! Wasn't that the whole point? Why we left the city and moved here? Isolation? Adult lifestyle community? This house is built for isolating old people. It wants me to be isolated, Richard."

The windows, breaking, letting in the fear. The window boxes bare. The oven that had started warming up on its own, pre-heating, just in case it might be needed.

"The house? Mom. Houses don't want anything. They are what you make them. If your living situation—"

"Of course houses want things. They take things. That house where you grew up, you know what it took from your father and me? How many years upon years of our working lives went into buying that house? Into fixing the damn roof and the foundation? They *feed* on us, Richard. Our sweat and our skin and our work. And there's a price for this one, too. Isolation? Maybe. Maybe that's what it is."

He put his hand to his temple, just like Iain used to do. Peggy was adding to his worries. He'd be thinking that he would have to fly out, now, leaving Susan pregnant, that he'd have to spend three days fixing everything in the house and making sure her knees were holding up and her eyes weren't totally dim and that she hadn't gone strange. That's what he was thinking: that she was going strange.

She used to tell him the story of Hansel and Gretel, and he would always ask why the witch was so intent on fattening up the children when she lived in a house made of gingerbread and candies. *Because she was evil*, she would tease him, and tickle him. *Never go into an old woman's house.* But why *didn't* the old woman eat her own house? Did it turn to ashes in her mouth? Was it there to serve her or trap her?

"I'm doing just fine," she said firmly, taking refuge in pretending to be upset by his patronizing. And indeed she was, a little. "I don't need anything. I have a friend now, Sue-Ann, next door. And I had tea with a lovely young family up the road yesterday. I am not isolated. And I'm not batty, either."

He grinned. "All right. Have it your way. Get rid of the stereo. Taking up space, anyway. But keep the speakers in case you ever give in and get a smartphone."

She kissed her fingertips and touched the screen, the face of her boy, grizzled now. Handsome. He'd gone off and found his own way of being a human, somehow, though she couldn't remember leading him to it. Wasn't that what mothers were supposed to do? One day she was packing him a lunch and the next he was off, away, on a path she could not guide him to, a path she could not even see.

She walked to the kitchen and looked out the big window to the backyard. She put her hand on the kitchen wall that marked no children's growing.

I could sink into this house like a stain, Peggy thought.

The crabapple tree had lost half its leaves but fruit still clung to its branches, and more fruit mounded beneath it. No matter how many apples Peggy brought in, more fruit fell. It would rot, drawing in animals.

Behind it lay the forest.

She gazed for a long time into the dark spaces between the trees, the paths that Iain had walked every morning away from her. The path of white stones that for him led out, away, into the wood, and for her, led her always, always, back into the house.

"The house needs something," she had told Iain. It needed an old woman, looking out of its window, stirring a pot.

She was, for a moment, terrified, and put her shaking, gnarled hand to her face.

Then she took up the phone and called Sue-Ann, to ask for the name of the fence-builders. To block the view of the woods, she thought, but did not say.

⟿ ⟿ ⟿

Zaira came that afternoon, as good as her word. She stood on the front porch, moving Elham in her stroller back and forth and looking at the window boxes. Sue-Ann was no doubt watching from her window, although Zaira wouldn't be *too* terribly shocking, not wearing a head scarf.

"What a marvellous idea!" Zaira said. "Strawberries!"

"What's that?" But there they were, suddenly, magically, overflowing the bounds of the window boxes. Strawberry plants, in late October, laden with ripe fruit. In her own window boxes.

Peggy had not planted them. Someone else, perhaps? A neighbour?

No. The house was getting ready to trap unwary children. Strawberries. Candies. Gingerbread.

"You'd better come in," Peggy said, but she hadn't meant to say that. She'd meant to say, *Don't eat the strawberries*.

"Oh, not to worry," said Zaira, understanding her meaning but misreading her nervousness. "Elham is not allergic to strawberries, although I know a lot of children do break out from them, don't they?"

They walked through the door, and Zaira cried out.

"It's nothing," she said, to Peggy's concern. "I just caught my arm on the doorway. A stray nail, or a splinter, or something."

"You've torn your sleeve. Oh dear, I wish I were better at sewing. I'd mend that for you. But you wouldn't want that. I can pay for it, at least."

"Never mind," said Zaira, warmly. "We can't be writing each other cheques every time we see each other."

"You're not bleeding?"

"Just a scratch. It's nothing."

They sat at the kitchen table and watched Elham doze in her stroller, her little bud mouth moving in a dream.

"I'm back to work next week," Zaira said.

"Well, that's exciting! What do you do?"

"I'm an engineer. It's going to be strange to go back. This was my first mat leave. Jamal's my stepson, you see."

"Ah. Yes, it's always a bit strange to go back. Richard was three when I did. I thought I'd forgotten everything. But you'll see. It'll come right back to you."

"Well, to be honest, I'm not sure if that's what I'm worried about. I know I can do my job. I'm good at my job. And I know I can keep Elham alive and fed and relatively happy. I'm just not sure what it will be like, for me, to do both. It sounds stupid. Parents do it all the time. I just haven't had to do it before. I haven't had to be the working mom. Jamal was twelve going on twenty when I married his dad."

"Yes, he seemed a very mature boy. He faced up to the window right away. You can be proud. Of both of them. You'll do fine."

"I hope you're right. It's an odd thing, isn't it? I feel as though I have to be a new person and I don't quite know how to be her. How do I be this new Zaira, working with a toddler at home?"

"Any way you like," said Peggy. "Who's going to tell you otherwise?"

Zaira laughed, and Elham's face rumpled and she started to whimper. Zaira pushed the stroller back and forth, making a shushing sound.

"She's getting over a fever," she whispered. "Just had a snack and a drink and a new diaper. If only she would sleep for twenty minutes straight, I know she'd feel better."

"My Richard used to go right to sleep in the car."

"So does she, but my husband takes it to work. The one thing that always works for her is music."

"Ah, well, I can't help you there. My stereo's broken."

"Really? I'm a wizard with them. Let me have a look."

And before Peggy could say *No, it's a lost cause, it's the house*, Zaira was up and pushing the stroller into the den.

Peggy was slow walking down the hallway. She reached the den and walked in to the soft strains of a song she had never heard before, and Zaira's bright, proud smile.

"You see?" Zaira whispered.

"But how did you do it?"

"I told you. I have *powers*."

Peggy put her hand to her mouth to stop her astonishment from escaping into some sound that would wake the baby. Elham was asleep again, as the pretty, wild music came out of the stereo.

"I felt like such a cliché," Peggy admitted, "not being able to fix my own stereo. I always fixed things when Richard was alive. But now I'm an old lady, I guess."

Zaira shrugged. "It's fixed now. It doesn't make you a cliché. Or an old lady."

"Oh, I am an old lady. And I don't mind, really, it's just I'm not quite sure how to do it. Boomers, you know. We weren't supposed to grow old. I never imagined – I don't know what kind of old lady to be."

"Any kind you like," Zaira said with a smile. "Who's going to tell you otherwise?"

Peggy opened her mouth to say *the house* but instead, a laugh escaped her. Not the cackle of a crone but the full, joyous laugh of a woman who has faced down many things more frightening than a house with opinions. If the house wanted a witch, then a witch she would be, but she would not sink into it. She would graft herself onto it like one of Iain's apple trees. She would change it, more than it could ever change her.

The music was wilder now, with a drum beat that thrummed in the floor boards, as Elham slept on. With one slim hand Zaira pushed the stroller, back and forth in time to the music, and she reached the other hand out to Peggy.

"Look out the window," Zaira said. "Snow!"

Pinpricks on the strawberry leaves and a heavy sky.

"I didn't think this area got much snow."

"It doesn't. And certainly not in October. This won't last until tomorrow, but look how pretty!"

"Let's go out to the garden, then," said Peggy. She picked up the pink and blue baby blanket where it lay on Zaira's diaper bag in the hall and draped it over Elham, and the two women and the girl went into the rose garden on the border of the wood where snow fell on the rotting apples.

They left the path of white stones and walked on the white-dusted grass. They left the door open so they could hear the music.

THE PAGE OF CUPS AND THE STAR

Evelyn Deshane

Curtis had just stepped outside when he found the child. Her blond hair was in thick curls, tangled behind her back and caked with mud. Her red dress was torn, revealing a criss-cross pattern of injury from her bare feet to her thighs. The girl was perhaps as old as sixteen or seventeen, but the way she hunched beside his trash and discarded furniture, it was easy to think that he had more of a feral child than a wayward young woman on his hands.

He had no time for either.

"You. Scat." He dropped a foul-mouthed end table onto the trash pile and folded his arms over his chest. "I need to get the mail and you're in the way."

When the girl rose to her feet, her dark eyes seemed desperately familiar to Curtis. He thought of the crone who had cursed him with his current body. A deep pain struck him from inside, familiar and persistent; the pain of transformation. *You can't turn the child away. She's a test.* And maybe, if he passed this test among the several hundred other, he could get his life back.

"Actually… Wait. You're probably hungry and you don't want those cuts to become infected. Come here." Curtis extended his hand to the girl. She looked at it and raised a brow. He prayed she didn't bite a finger when she took one step closer, then another. Her stiff posture melted away. Her dress became elegant, obviously made with the finest silks, but it still didn't fit her in the shoulders.

"How old are you? Where are you from?"

The girl didn't answer. Curtis huffed. The sun hung low in the sky, signalling afternoon. The mail would have already come. Curtis's desperation to read any incoming news masked all other feelings.

"Well, we can work on origin stories later," he said. "For now, I'm Curtis Meander. You may have heard of me. I'm the Prince."

⁓⁓⁓

Curtis set up the girl in his separate bathroom on the first floor. After running a bucket of water and showing her where the towels and soaps were, he decided it was safe to leave her alone. She still hadn't said a word, but he was sure she understood what he was saying.

The mailman's shadow receded on the horizon as Curtis approached his mailbox. The woods around Curtis's house were dense and thick; the mailmen in the city would only come so often, especially since his father had made Curtis take up residence here long ago. It was before the crone, of course, but the woods allowed him the privacy to sort out his own issues before he tended to the local farmers, merchants, and others who lived close by in the small town. Curtis's father, King Bertram, was the one who took care of most of the country's political and stately needs. Curtis retained this plot of land and whatever tasks he could do by mail – mostly accounting, receiving feedback from civilians, and filing. It was an exile, but one that Curtis had gone to willingly in years

prior when he realized his proclivities were not going to produce an heir to the throne, and his father's disappointment
would have been too strong.

Of course, now, thanks to the crone and his curse, he
could have that heir. He tried not to dwell on his body's inver-
sion as another pain tore through him. He placed a hand over
his abdomen as he dug through the mail in the box. The letter from the local apothecary was stamped with blue wax. His
plea had been answered. This was it. This was what he'd been
waiting for all this time. He undid the seal with a flick of his
thumb. His gaze darted over the wondrous calligraphy as his
heart sank.

Dear Sir and/or Madam,

*Thank you for your interest in Apotheosis Apothecary. We
regret to inform you that we no longer take clientele of your variety. Neither our psychic surgery, nor our herbal treatment plan
can alter corporeal bodies in the way you desire. We have learned
long ago to not tamper with witches in the woods, either.*

Sincerely,

The staff

Curtis crumbled up the letter in his fist. His breasts – the
breasts he didn't want to have, the ones he didn't need –
smarted with pain. Was this from hormones he was not used
to having and the blood that visited him so often now – or was
this from something else? Was the crone taunting him now
that he knew for sure there was no way to reverse the damage
done to him?

Though Curtis hated the words in the letter, he couldn't
throw it away. He didn't get what he wanted, but this piece
of paper was at least proof that there was something wrong

with him. No one could see it on the surface. The sandy-coloured hair on his chin was still there; his voice was still as deep as it had been when he'd begun his exile. But his muscles had been deteriorating at an alarming rate; he could barely carry the furniture in his house anymore. His skin was softer and so was his hair. He even heard voices, pleas and cries in female voices, from inside his head as if he was adopting a woman's perspective. He chalked the voices up to the furniture, as if they were the ones enchanted, and removed each item from the house meticulously. But no amount of spring cleaning could undo the fact that he had the body of the young girl underneath his clothing. No one could see it, but it was there.

And now, no one would fix it. Only the crone who had cursed him could undo what she'd done.

Curtis remembered the night of his transformation in stark colours. The blue flash of an electric lightning bolt, the orange flame from a small fire in the night. The deep red of his rug as it became soaked with rainwater and the heavy smell of moss and mould as he answered a banging knock on his heavy oak door. The crone stood in front of him, wet to the bone, her long dark hair slick as snakes. He told her to go but she insisted she needed her roof repaired.

"Tomorrow," Curtis said. "I'll send someone then."

"But the storm is now. A fire will rage. I've seen it in the cards. By tomorrow it will be too late."

"It won't. Time heals all things."

"Is that so?" The crone followed her statement in gibberish before leaving and disappearing into the woods.

Come morning, the lightning had destroyed many houses and Curtis was in a new body. Six months had passed, and now there would be needless months stacked on one another, endless amounts of time lived in this vessel – this prison – until it was worn and decrepit like his house.

Curtis pushed away a tear that threatened to fall. He could still learn his lesson. The girl, perhaps the crone in disguise, was waiting for hospitality he could never give until now. He marched into his house again – right into the bathroom where the young girl was.

She'd slipped a towel over her shoulder at just that moment, revealing her pale body in glimpses. She was like him, but the reverse. Her body was afflicted in the same way, with an appendage that did not match her outside form. This definitely was a test, Curtis knew. Maybe now he really did have a shot.

"You must be hungry," Curtis said. "Can I get you something to eat?"

"Annabel."

"Hmm?" Curtis looked up from the pages on his desk. The girl was dressed in one of his longer shirts, which on her frame, acted as a dress. Her blond hair was a softer white now that it had dried and the mud was all gone. Colour had also returned to her face after eating a meal in Curtis's kitchen. He'd left her there fifteen minutes ago, with permission to take what she'd need, but now she stood in his doorway, her dark eyes fixated on him.

"My name is Annabel. I'm sixteen. And you shouldn't have walked in on me like that."

Curtis sighed. He pushed back some of his work and gestured to a seat in front of him. Annabel took the seat and gave him yet another poignant stare.

"Aren't you going to apologize?"

"I'm sorry. I was rushing and didn't think. But there's nothing to be ashamed of," Curtis said.

"I know that."

"You do?"

Annabel nodded. As quickly as the topic had been broached, it was now done. She gestured toward his papers. "What are you working on?"

"I'm the Prince. I need to be sure the people have what they need." Curtis explained a few more items, all of which seemed brand new to Annabel. "Don't people talk about me?"

"They do. But they say you're in exile, not that you're working. And that you're funny."

"Funny?"

"You know. Flowery. Fae." She smiled at Curtis's strained responses to the townspeople's insults. "You're not to be trusted."

"So why are you here?"

"Because I needed food. And now, because you've apologized. Not a lot of people apologize."

When a silence spread between them, Curtis wondered if there would be a magical transformation. If a cloud of smoke would come up and Annabel would say, *Aha, it was me, the crone, the whole time.* Curtis would get his body back, and life could go on.

Annabel picked up some paper he'd not yet written his responses on and started to draw. Instead of arguing or asking for his apotheosis and conclusion to his fable, complete with lesson learned, Curtis went back to work.

Days passed between them like this. They slept in separate rooms in the house, rose two hours from one another, and then met in Curtis's study to work. Annabel drew page after page of princesses, queens, and all sorts of female characters. When she'd drawn an image of a naked woman pouring water into a river, it reminded Curtis of a tarot card he'd seen witches use in the past. This moment, he was sure, would reveal itself to be magic.

But nothing changed, and nothing happened, like always.

"What's that?" Curtis asked, once Annabel had finished drawing the tarot card.

"It's The Star. Part of the Major Arcana in tarot. I followed a star to get here, so I figured I'd be like the woman."

"Oh. You did? I suppose that makes sense..." Curtis glanced at the figure on the card with blond hair like Annabel. The figure's body was curvier though, as if it was Annabel's dream body. When Curtis spied a penis drawn between the thick thighs and wide hips of the woman on the card, he paused. "I'm not sure if that's a mistake or..."

"Not a mistake. It's like me. Like you."

Curtis baulked. "I'm not..."

"You're not like me, but you are. Underneath. I saw your laundry by accident this morning."

Curtis swallowed. The monthly blood he was still adjusting to had come with yet another wave of pain that morning. He longed to forget about it, but now Annabel had brought it up. It wasn't in spite, though. He knew the low hum of her voice when she spoke in spite. Now she was genuine.

"You're not exactly like me," Annabel repeated. "But you are like me. That's why the bathroom mirrors are covered too."

"They're covered because they were getting loud."

Annabel nodded. "They got loud for me too – so did bed frames and sinks – but I learned to shut them up."

"By drawing?"

"Yes." Annabel took out a pencil and started to draw a man. She was drawing Curtis, he soon realized, as yet another tarot card. This figure stood holding a cup with a smile on his face and wore a floral shirt – an item of clothing that Curtis would never wear – yet the figure had his nose and strong jawline. There was no doubt it was his pictorial double.

"And what's this one?"

"The Page of Cups. Emotional, clairvoyant, but a beast when he wants to be. You don't have to be a beast, though. You can be different and defy the cards."

Curtis laughed. "I know, I know. In order to be different, I must be kinder to people seeking refuge. I must hear people's concerns, especially about their homes, because a body is a home and it's unfortunate to realize you're broken or homeless. I should have helped you during the storm, crone."

"Crone?" Annabel asked.

"Nothing, never mind."

Annabel continued to draw. She added colour to the flowers on the shirt, to the sky, and to the cup itself. It was beautiful, Curtis had to admit. Underneath this version of himself as "The Page," he was convinced that Annabel would draw him the same way he was now. Bleeding, in pain, dealing with organs and hormones and feelings he'd never known before. But that didn't make him a woman. It still made him a page, a prince, and someone in change.

It didn't have to make him a beast.

When Annabel slid over the picture, Curtis took it. No smoke, no magic followed. Annabel wasn't the crone. She was her own person, someone who had been homeless in her body but decided to find it for herself. They were the same, but not.

Curtis wanted to let her stay as long as she needed.

༄༅ ༄༅ ༄༅

Come morning, Curtis watched as the mailman dropped off another letter. The black envelope made him wonder if the crone was trying to contact him. Was it a spell to remove curses? Congratulations on a lesson learned? Another punishment or an apology? Curtis turned away from his bedroom window. It didn't matter anymore.

He walked into his bathroom and took off the dark blanket covering the mirror. There were no more voices that haunted him, or furniture that talked back. The voices and perspectives in his head were all his own thoughts and he was the one enchanted, instead of cursed. After washing up for the morning, he tacked up Annabel's drawing to the wall and wrote "Home Sweet Home" underneath. He retrieved the rejection letter from his pocket and added it to the trash.

Then, like always and with Annabel following two hours later, Curtis went to work.

UNEARTHING HISTORY

LISA CAI

A flying three-legged crow can see everything in Toronto. Tonight, Cindy observed the houses below her.

When she flew out of her apartment, she left an area dotted with construction and congested traffic. As she neared her destination, the houses grew larger, the front yards wider, gardens became elaborate works, and private pools and tennis courts dotted the backyards. She was flying over an unfamiliar Toronto, yet she was still within North York.

She circled above a house. Cindy wasn't worried about losing her way. The house under her was the most brightly lit in its neighbourhood. The wind was just a gentle touch against her feathers. She hoped tonight's event would be as calm as the rest of the world.

Cindy spotted a figure standing on the sidewalk. It had to be Rochelle. Cindy adjusted her wings and tail. She descended and landed on the road. Rochelle put her phone in her purse. She stepped toward Cindy. "You're late, you know?" She crossed her arms.

The crow turned her head away from her captain. Cindy thought she had timed her trip right, but she was wrong. Since she already landed, she couldn't leave now.

The crow started to grow. The feathers receded into her skin, revealing her white dress shirt and black pants. The wings changed to arms and the skinny crow feet turned to human legs.

Cindy stood up straight. She was herself again. "I'm sorry." Cindy stared down at her shoes. "I thought I'd be here on time…"

Rochelle also looked down at Cindy's footwear. She was wearing black running shoes at a gathering of the most elite and important dignitaries of their society.

Rochelle tsked. She had been in Cindy's apartment before and knew about what she possessed; Cindy could only afford to own three worn pairs of shoes. Couldn't Cindy have attempted to dress for the occasion and tried to represent her division well? Rochelle's only hope was that no one would notice Cindy's blunder. Nothing could be done now; they would have to face the others in their current state.

"Just follow me." Rochelle walked toward the mansion.

They saw a man standing by the front door. He had been staring at Rochelle since she stood on the sidewalk.

"Ah, so you really are a guest." He thought Rochelle was some kind of loiterer, but seeing Cindy turn into a human was proof enough that they belonged to this gathering.

Cindy dug into her pocket and withdrew an invitation letter. She handed the paper to the man.

He unfolded the paper and looked over the names.

"Representing the Department of Supernatural Affairs, Defence Division of Toronto, Rochelle Henri, a priestess and Cindy Wu, the san…zu—"

"Sanzuwu," Cindy said.

He frowned but said nothing. What was the point of using a word that had no meaning to him? He supposed that the sanzuwu described whatever Cindy was. He folded the paper.

"Please, go inside and enjoy yourselves."

They thanked him and walked into the house.

Cindy's eyes widened when she saw the interior of the mansion. Above the guests were glowing fairies of various sizes. They floated about, singing and playing amongst one another. The walls had portraits of fairies that resembled adult humans clothed with medieval attire. This really was the residence of a fairy queen.

Rochelle expected Cindy to stare, as it was her first time attending such a gathering.

"Don't stand in front of the door," Rochelle said. "We need to find our room."

Rochelle made her way down one hall. And Cindy followed. She had heard that a choir of sirens were going to sing here, but she guessed they were too late for such a performance.

"By the way, is anyone else we know coming?"

Rochelle shook her head. She had hoped that others could make it to support her, but that was asking too much.

They passed by a suited werewolf.

"I got a text from Pablo. He can't come. He was vomiting blood earlier today. Didn't you get any messages?"

"Oh, no, I hadn't checked." Cindy looked away from Rochelle. The truth was, she hadn't paid her phone bill on time; she couldn't afford it.

"Vampirehood is difficult when your human side can't adjust to drinking blood," Rochelle sighed. The younger members of her squad always gave her the worst trouble, especially Cindy and Pablo.

"Here's the room." Rochelle pointed to her right.

They entered the room. It was near fully seated. Most of the people were already finished their meals. Some of the guests turned to look at them. Cindy felt self-conscious looking at the others' fine clothes and jewelry. She stared at Rochelle's back.

Rochelle looked around. She didn't see any faces from the Defence Division. She spotted a small, unoccupied square table at the back of the room. It was under a poorly lit ceiling. A laugh almost escaped Rochelle's mouth. Things hadn't changed since these gatherings began. Rochelle gestured to Cindy to follow. They walked to the table together and sat down.

A fairy landed on their table.

"Misses, I'll summon food and drink for you."

"Thanks," Rochelle said. ·

The fairy nodded. Cindy watched the fairy fly away. Her blond hair left a trail of gold sparkles behind her. It was the first time Cindy had seen a fairy up close. All of them reminded her of the fairies she had seen in childhood picture books.

Rochelle leaned against her chair. She needed a drink or a cigarette. She was in a fairy queen's home, chaperoning Cindy and representing the whole Defence Division; she was in her own personal hell.

Things got worse as she heard fairies singing outside the room.

Everyone in the room, except for Cindy and Rochelle, turned toward the entrance and started cheering.

Rochelle cursed, but clapped her hands. Cindy followed her captain, even though she was confused about why she had to applaud.

A procession of fairies entered the room. They held up ancient banners or played an instrument.

"Our queen has arrived!"

Matilda, the fairy queen, made her way to the stage. Matilda's gold dress was as finely detailed, flowing and gorgeous as always. Her Elizabethan-style dress clearly stated her authority among the supernatural of this country.

Matilda turned toward the attendees.

"My good people, welcome to this grand event. Tonight, we acknowledge the accomplishments of the Department of Supernatural Affairs in Canada."

Two glasses of water and plates of food floated down to Rochelle and Cindy's table. Rochelle helped herself to the water and food. Cindy drank from her cup. This was the first time Cindy saw Matilda and she wanted to remember her words.

"I established this department in 1912 to address the concerns about foreign and native creatures endangering our beloved land. We have continuously vanquished all threats, immense and minuscule, and have maintained authority over our borders."

Cindy coughed. She put a hand over her mouth. Matilda was speaking nonsense! The account she described about the founding of the department was much different from what Rochelle had told Cindy.

Everyone else in the audience looked at Matilda without any expression of surprise or confusion. Cindy looked to her captain for guidance. Rochelle narrowed her eyes at Cindy. It was a warning. The look told Cindy to restrain herself.

Suppressing any extra coughs back down her throat, she turned her attention back to Matilda, who had already finished her introduction. She curtsied as the audience lauded her. Rochelle also clapped her hands. Cindy, despite her uneasiness, mimicked her superior.

Matilda flew over to her table. Her sparkling entourage surrounded her.

After Matilda, representatives from the other subdivisions spoke on stage. Cindy didn't have any previous knowledge about what the other divisions were doing, so she listened. She ignored the rumbling protests from her stomach. One speaker summarized the quarantine process used to determine letting foreign supernatural beings enter the country. They boasted that because of their rigorous standards, undesirables and threats were rejected from Canada.

Eventually, it was the Defence Division's turn to speak. Rochelle took a swig of her drink, put the glass down and made her way to the stage. She cleared her throat and straightened her posture.

Cindy chewed on a cracker. Rochelle showed no signs of nervousness. What would she highlight? There was so much that their own squad had done that it would be difficult for Rochelle to summarize it all briefly.

Rochelle stood in front of the microphone. Her face was impassive as she began to speak.

"Hello, I'm Captain Rochelle Henri of the Defence Division of Toronto." She looked about the crowd and nodded. "We have maintained the safety of this city by investigating supernatural occurrences. A highlight of this year includes discovering and relocating dragon eggs. As my squad and I continue to patrol and maintain order on the streets of Toronto, I appreciate the continued support of the department to maintain our operations. If anyone is interested in donating to our division or would like to know more about our operations and how they can contribute, feel free to speak to me after this event."

The audience applauded as Rochelle left the stage.

Cindy just stared at Rochelle.

Rochelle looked straight at Cindy, not saying a word. Rochelle sat back in her seat and looked up at the stage. She couldn't explain herself to Cindy; not here, not yet.

Cindy still kept her gaze on Rochelle. Why had she omitted so many of the things they accomplished? Granted, moving the dragon eggs to a suitable place to hatch was important for Toronto's sake, but they had completed so many other missions. Their squad had ended a decades-old feud between kitsunes. Rochelle communicated with the spirits to uncover a string of murders committed by a were-wolf. They helped locate the kidnapped offspring of a nymph and satyr. Why did Rochelle omit all of their experiences?

Soon after, fairies started to sing and play their instruments. Their plates and glasses rose up and carried themselves out of the room. Some people began to leave. Their specific event was over, yet there was still socializing happening within the rest of the house.

Cindy fidgeted in her seat. Was she expected to go into the hall and converse with the other guests? She didn't want to meet any more new people. She had too many questions for Rochelle.

Rochelle finally turned to Cindy. Her face looked tired, defeated. Cindy had never seen her captain look so vulnerable before.

"Do you want to leave now? I'm taking the bus."

"I'll walk you to your stop," Cindy said. "I've got nothing better to do."

They stood up and left the room. Cindy observed the mansion and its guests in a different light. Rather than admiring the fancy dresses and expensive foods, she wondered where all of that wealth came from. Cindy was constantly putting her life at risk working for the Defence Division, yet she couldn't even budget to get a haircut. Rochelle once said that their division could barely afford to keep operations afloat, yet the department threw these lavish parties.

They exited the mansion. The cheers and lights faded behind them as the two women stood on the sidewalk. Cindy and Rochelle now hosted their own special gathering. Crickets greeted them as their guests. The sky was their roof.

Cindy faced Rochelle. Cindy needed to speak, even though it wasn't her place. She couldn't stand the silence between them. Cindy opened her mouth, but Rochelle spoke first.

"Get used to that." Rochelle turned around and walked toward her bus stop.

Cindy followed behind Rochelle. That response wasn't good enough for her.

"But there's a bunch of stuff I don't get," said Cindy. "Wasn't the department established earlier? You said your great-aunt and my grandma were the founders, so how can Matilda say she created it?"

Cindy remembered the tales Rochelle recounted about their relatives. She marvelled at their adventures and accomplishments. She looked up to them. Those stories were the only connection she had to her grandmother. Was it all a lie?

Rochelle grimaced. She really needed to smoke now. She reached into her purse. She pulled out a cigarette, lit it and took a long drag. A thick cloud of smoke puffed out of her mouth.

"Matilda worked with them, but she got my great-aunt deported back to Haiti." Rochelle tightened her fist just thinking about the past. "Then she convinced the government to hand leadership to her. Your grandmother was kicked out of the department, disgraced."

"But how?"

Rochelle frowned. Was she really that naive?

"Matilda had money, connections and spoke flawless English. Our women did all the work and got nothing in return." Rochelle turned her head back and gave Cindy a wolfish smile. "Are you satisfied?"

Cindy was sweating despite the cool night. She didn't like any of this. She knew at that moment that she could stop with her questions and remain ignorant about the history, but she needed to know, no matter how painful the truth.

"Why was your speech so short? We've done so much in less than a year."

Rochelle took another drag on her cigarette. They had reached the bus stop. She dropped the butt to the ground and stepped on it.

"Officially, I'm supposed to avoid detailing our work because it might scare everyone." Rochelle looked out into the empty street. "But I suspect Matilda wants to trivialize our work."

"That's stupid! They need our division or else everyone will be in danger. How are we even supposed to get any funding if we don't speak up for ourselves?"

Rochelle snapped her head toward Cindy. She had to teach Cindy a lesson before it was too late.

"They don't care if we die; they can push anyone to replace us. We have to make do with our situation." If anything, Matilda wanted to see Rochelle and her squad fail. It would be the final chapter to the stolen legacy of their ancestors. If she could pick and choose, she would never have recruited a vampire who still got queasy around blood or a sanzuwu descendant that couldn't grasp the workings of the world, but that was Rochelle's lot in life. She thought she could protect Cindy by hiding the realities of the department, but Rochelle's decision had done more harm than good.

The bus finally appeared down the road and drove toward them.

"Okay, I sort of get it now." Cindy knew Rochelle was mad at her. "But... I don't want Grandma or your great-aunt to just fade away."

The bus halted at the stop.

"It doesn't matter." One day, Cindy would understand that utter dedication to the division would drain her.

The bus door opened.

"I'll see you tomorrow." Rochelle stepped into the bus. A moment later, the vehicle drove off, leaving a hot breeze circling around Cindy. She closed her eyes, feeling leaves and debris brush about her.

She was alone now. She couldn't even hear any chirping crickets. Only the moon was outside with her.

Cindy knew that Rochelle was right. Being involved with the Defense Division was now even riskier than she imagined, but that wouldn't deter her. She had a new reason to be a part of her squad. She would, in every little way, honour the memory and work of the true creators of the Department of Supernatural Affairs.

Cindy began to transform into the three-legged crow.

HALF GONE DARK

TAMARA VARDOMSKAYA

Yenisey basin, Eastern Siberia, late summer 1917

That is a strange tale you tell me, my friend, that the Tsar is gone, that now there is the Provisional Government and the Soviet, with that man Kerensky at the head. Do they know or care about the far taiga at all, after the Tsar went to such trouble conquering it? Tell him, son, you speak Russian now better than you do our own tongue, even as a little boy, and you have gone to the Russian school.

The Russians, my friend, just want to call us all, the Orochon, the Manegir, the Birar, and the Solon, and even the Evens – call us all Tungus. At least call us the Evenki.

But our ways say that we give a story for a story until the fire dies down and we all fall asleep, and so I will tell you a tale. Others have told you the tale of the day the sky opened and the trees fell down, nine summers ago, when Chekaren, my son here, was a baby. But you tell me that many men already tell all kinds of nonsense about this.

Instead, my friend, I will tell you of how I met the Chulugdi.

I have heard the stories of the Chulugdi since I was a boy: of the Chulugdi woman who wanted to be a mother to Evenki children, but they knew that she had one eye and one leg and one arm, the other side of her black, and was made of iron like all the Chulugdi, and so they burned her in the fire – see Chekaren's eyes light up like fire embers at a breath, he loves that story. But no, that's not the one I'll tell tonight.

I never did tell the real story of how I met the Chulugdi to Chekaren before. Took me years to think about how it was that I had entered a story, and how the tales of the Chulugdi turned out to be true. The Russians tell us that the Chulugdi are merely pit miners coming out half-black from coal dust. The Russians always rush to tell us what we really think before they hear the full story.

As another Russian hunter told me, as he told many tall tales, "If you don't like it, don't listen, but let me tell lies in peace." That's my rule today, my friend. Don't interrupt and start telling me I'm wrong, like the other Russians do.

This is a true story. Chekaren, even if your children speak Russian and forget our tongue, I want them to remember it.

It was two years ago, in the late spring, the moon *sonkal* when the reindeer calve. When we stop hunting squirrel and fox, and go herding the reindeer and hunting for the wild deer when their antlers are tender. Foolish domestic reindeer eat human urine and feces, and wild deer are cleaner. You tasted the powdered *ulikta* I offered you; that are always made out of dried wild venison, what we will give an honoured guest. Besides, the wild deer's young antlers may go for ten rubles a pound, if you find the right trader; such money, as the traders say, doesn't just lie on the road.

Thirty or forty years ago, there were many, many wild deer and moose in our land; now, fearing the Russian guns, the deer grow fewer and fewer, and the moose are almost gone. Every summer I had to trek farther to shoot a deer. That spring, Chekaren was still too young to follow; I left him in the village with his aunts and sisters, herding reindeer and growing the grain, eating bread like the Russians do.

One has to treat the earth with friendship, you know, and then it will welcome you when you return to the taiga. We have a blessing, "Walk well, so mother earth herself will guard you." I have hunted in the taiga around the rivers you Russians call the Yenisey and the Angara all my life. I know how the summer feels, how the trees turn green for a time and the moss and lichens and all just *breathe* under the sun. Each summer is a little different, like you meet an old friend and she is changed a little, but still the same.

This time, though, tracking a deer, I was getting close to where the trees still lie from the time the sky ripped apart and knocked them down, which I had not gone to in the summers since. And yes, that is when you meet an old friend and she had changed – her family plagued with illness, the Russian Cossacks demanding more *yasak* fur taxes, and all going wrong – and although she puts on a brave face to look happy for you, you can see only half of her is light. There was so much open sky, looking over all these pines lying dead. I heard a missionary tell, when I was a child, of the battles the Russians fight out in the west, where men lie dead on the field like pine needles. I'd not imagined that strange sight in years; I had never in my life seen so many men that they would cover a field when lying down. But looking at the pines, I thought of it.

It was easy to see the stag I was tracking, though. He had wandered to the edge of where the trees stood and was staring around strangely. He was maybe six years old, the stag, although a big one; he hadn't been born yet when the sky had opened. He was tripping over the rotting pine trunks. I dismounted from my reindeer, my dog trotting beside me, and put my rifle to my shoulder to aim, whispering to the deer, "Forgive me."

Then before I could pull the trigger, the stag fell. I tell you, this isn't how ordinary deer fall, which they do forelegs first like they lie down, or perhaps somersaulting if you shoot them in full run. This one, it was as if one side of him went before the other, the left foreleg and left hindleg collapsing before he toppled over. It was the shadowed side; the sun was on his right and from my view half of him was dark and half was silvered with light when he fell. I was too far to see his eyes – deer have expressions too, like people and dogs do, if you know them well enough – but I would swear by the Orthodox God, that deer's last thought was surprise.

I sent my dog on ahead to fetch him and dropped my reindeer's rein, so I could have both hands on my rifle as I moved forward. I was ready for any event, I thought, when a deer falls as no deer should fall, not even one shot in the ankle bones.

The corpse of the deer was lying on the edge of a pit. As the ground sloped, I didn't see it until I was right on him.

And out of the pit rose the Chulugdi.

I know, stories of them are told all over, by our people, by the Orochons east of the big lake you call Baikal, by the Buryats, by the Yukagir. But I was a man of thirty summers, and I had never seen one, and in the Church they say that these are all folk stories, fit only for grandparents to amuse children. Yet two were there before me, only twice as far from me as you are now. Each had only one arm, and one leg, and one great staring eye, and they stood as if one was the mirror of the other, and the armless side of each of them black as coal.

And they were made of shining iron. The iron was jointed all over them, plated, and they had three fingers on their hand, and no mouth. The black sides…had no shine at all. As if they soaked up all light like the earth soaks up the rain. As if a hole in the daylight opened into night there.

I was frightened, and had my loaded rifle in my hands and I fired at them. Just twice as far from me as you are, the bullet flew, and it bounced away with a clang. Like the stories tell, that arrows don't take the Chulugdi. Bullets don't, either.

Their eyes lit up like the electrical lights I'd seen in the windows of Krasnoyarsk. A strange light, like the sun and yet not. Of all the light I've seen, the Chulugdi's eyes looked the most like that. I got the sense, you know, that the Chulugdi were *made*. Not made by human hand, no, but it was not a womb they came out of.

I remembered the story of the Chulugdi woman, the one I told Chekaren, that the Yukagir tell, how she tries to enter the Evenki tribe and become a mother to Evenki children, and she needs to be tricked into falling into a bonfire pit and an arrow shot through her eye, the only point you can hit.

You say that some crazy Russian thinks what had opened the sky was a boat coming from a distant world, bringing the Chulugdi?

No. We have always told of the Chulugdi, since ancient times. The Yukagirs tell of them, the Orochons tell of them, the Buryats do.

My dog, Dawn – she was a fine hunting dog – she moved to defend me. She went growling at the Chulugdi and bit the nearer one to her on the metal leg, fiercely and hard.

Her teeth clanged on the iron. Then her body was tossed up with a jerk, as if grabbed by the scruff by an invisible hand. Head over heels, she somersaulted and fell down dead. She was a fine dog; seven winters she had served me.

So, I turned to run, for I was no coward, but I needed enough paces between them and me that I could aim for the eye. The stories were true, then, despite all the Russians told us, and if the Chulugdi truly walked our taiga, then the eye was their one vulnerable spot.

And the two Chulugdi moved as one. I thought their arms were as long as my arm, and I cannot reach you. But they both raised their arms as one, and grabbed me by my shoulders, and I swear the arms grew longer, as they seized me, and then shortened again as they brought me close enough to them that if they breathed, I would have felt their breath on my face.

They had no breath. They hummed, though, like the humming of the great mosquitoes of the taiga summer. A great thing like that, and it whines like a mosquito, I thought to myself, and a thing that whines like a mosquito is what my death shall be.

But then...it was as if half of me was awake, looking the Chulugdi in their great eyes like hand-made lights, and half of me was asleep and dreaming, and knowing as you know things in dreams: half in pictures, and a bit in words, and a bit just *knowing*, like you know how to shift your balance riding the reindeer. So, I knew what they were doing.

They wanted to write down all that was in my brain. And send it to the stars. Everything I knew: all my memories of all the squirrels I had ever skinned, of how my grandfather taught me how to ride a reindeer, of the first time I loved a woman, of the lights of Krasnoyarsk, of the smell of mushrooms in the autumn moss and the taste of *ulikta*, of my language...

They were going to steal it all. And the price was that it may destroy my brain, leave me a salmon with its head cut off, still flailing.

I thought of the Chulugdi woman in the stories who wanted to be an Evenki mother and have children. That was all true, but only now did I understand why. She wanted the knowledge in the children's brains, to write down and send to the distant stars.

But what I thought next was, the Chulugdi could take any Russian, who is educated, who can read and write and make electric lights and speak a more sensible language as the schools all say. Instead, they wanted an Evenk off the taiga. They had always wanted Evenki out of the taiga since our stories began. It was us they wanted.

Still, I wasn't going to give them my mind. My brain. I will not give my brain for the Chulugdi to eat, like we eat the brains and marrow of the deer and squirrels, and the thing that many of the stories agree on is that the Chulugdi eat human flesh.

But the machine came closer and closer, and it encircled my head. It was a strange feeling – as if fingers were rubbing and picking *inside* my skull, deeper than headaches go. On my left side. I felt as if every speech and word I've ever heard was flooding up like the rapids on the river you call Tunguska. That was what they were taking and writing down, all my language, all the words that the Russians think primitive savage words.

I screamed curses at them, in Evenki and Russian both. And I struggled and finally I kicked at the black side of one of them. And he – the Chulugdi – toppled over, letting go of me, fell like a tree on his one leg, with his dark half looking up at the too-big sky.

Then I broke free of the other one, throwing him over also. And I grabbed my rifle that I had dropped when they had seized me and ran to my reindeer.

I reached him before they rose again, but I knew that they would rise and come after me. In the dream as they held me, they showed me a bit of who they were. They came from the stars. They had been coming from the stars for many, many years, dealing with us, the Evenki. Us they found interesting. The Russians – I think they were afraid of the Russians. Or maybe they think you mad.

I mounted my reindeer and galloped so fast he would have broken his leg ten times over if God and the spirits themselves were not guarding him and me. My head throbbed like the morning after the biggest drinking binge I could imagine, all on the left side where they had taken my words and my language.

I still have the language; I speak it to my wife and to Chekaren right now, and I spoke it to our old shaman when I told him that in the pits and valleys by where the trees fell and the sky opened live the valleymen, the Chulugdi.

But my right arm and leg were slow and shaky for a long time and, even when I regained the strength in my arm, it felt strange and still does. I can move it; I am not like my grandfather was, who in his old age had a sudden pain and fell, and afterwards he could not feel or move all of his right side, arm or leg, at all. But when I move my right hand, it always feels…as if I am moving through dark water. Half of me in shadow, if not completely dark. I do not know why it is the right, since they had done their stealing in the left side of my head. But it is my right arm, and I had to learn to use my left hand much more.

That is why I take Chekaren with me all the time. I need the boy. Though I do not call myself a cripple, and I can still shoot a deer. But in the half of me that the Chulugdi took away with them, something was lost.

I know that my language is now away in the stars. Maybe if Chekaren forgets it, if his children and his children's

children all speak Russian and forget their mother tongue…
In going to the Russian schools and the Russian church, with
the Russian guns and the Russian farms, if they forget our
people's name, and think themselves Russian, half of them
gone dark, and if no more Evenki sing our songs and tell our
tales on this earth – I know that somewhere, there among the
stars, amid iron people of one leg and one arm and one lamp
eye, someone there knows what I knew of the Evenki. They
stole it. Perhaps it is safer kept with them.

But also, they *wanted* it. Every time there is a new Tsar,
the Russians keep coming and sending their criminals,
bringing their guns and their illnesses, calling us beggars
and animals to be pitied. But the Chulugdi wanted our
knowledge, what *we* knew; they came from the stars to learn
it. Mine is a tale best told to the children, so they remember.
So, if they ever meet the Chulugdi, in pit or valley, they know
what to do.

You have finished your *ulikta*, my honoured guest, and the
fire is dying down. You tell me that the Tsar is gone, that now
the Russia that we live in has two heads. I have heard of a
reindeer calf with two heads, and it died soon after it was
born. Is the new Russia we live in truly two-headed, or does
it have one head, with two halves of the same brain? And if
one of them falls, as you tell me people want this Provisional
Government to fall, and the Soviet to rule, would it shamble
around with one eye and one leg, half gone dark?

That, none of us know. And none of us know how it will
reach the taiga.

NONE OF YOUR FLESH AND BLOOD

CHADWICK GINTHER

I'd never felt comfortable in my own skin. Always thought I should be doing more. Doing something else. Be somewhere else.

Be *someone* else.

The feeling had never been stronger since Maggie moved to town. She was new at my school; from Scotland. She had an accent, and it was hot, though sometimes I couldn't understand a single word that came out of her wide, pretty mouth. When she leaned against a car in the parking lot having a cigarette, she practically glowed in the sun.

The vultures had circled and practically every clique and loner in my school had made, or wanted, a claim on Maggie. I drifted at the periphery of all those groups, welcome, but never *belonging*. I wanted her friendship too. Sure, she was hot, but she also had an encyclopaedic knowledge of *Doctor Who*.

I wanted to walk over and discuss the merits of the current Doctor, but initiative wasn't my strong suit. Instead, I sat and read, sneaking glances as I turned the pages.

Wrapped up in her, I didn't hear them approach. My book slammed into my face and I winced as the impact stung my nose. I blinked away tears. I couldn't let them see me cry. Tears would make things worse.

I didn't have to look to know who it was. John. Or the Scat in the Hat as I'd taken to calling him. The first guy I'd fallen for. The first, and the one that hurt the most. There'd been boys and girls since; Brian, Tracy, Alison. Some of us had gone farther, but none of us had gone all the way – even when one of us had wanted to. And none had lasted. It was high school.

And now, at least in my dreams, there was Maggie. Oh, Maggie.

John still had the same confident stride – I'd call it cocky now – and a physical grace despite having muscled up over the summer. His eyes were shadowed by the Canadiens ball cap he wore. But his teeth – so white – and the stubble making them shine all the brighter. His wingmen, Carter and Steve – now Thug One and Thug Two – flanked him, also wearing matching Habs hats. They'd all grown hard and mean, since we'd stopped being friends. The change had been slow. But matters had gotten much worse since Maggie had moved to town. Still, while they'd been mean, they'd never been violent before.

Worried, I kept quiet.

Thug Two snapped my book from my lap and regarded it the way I would calamari: as something foreign, incomprehensible, and vaguely frightening.

He grimaced, tossing the book over his shoulder. I winced as the spine hit the pavement. It was a library book.

He used to love to read – loved fantasy especially. I'd expected more respect for the book given the amount of Dungeons & Dragons we used to play. The game had brought me and John close in the first place. We were role-playing relationships we weren't ready to pursue. My greatest act of courage didn't come in some fictional kingdom, but in admitting how I'd felt.

They walked past Maggie, and Scat must've said something she didn't care for. She flicked her cigarette at him. The Thugs laughed, but stopped with a withering glare from Scat. He turned that look my way, and for the first time I was afraid of him.

I heard the loud click-clack of heels on the asphalt.

"How's ye keepin', then?" Maggie asked.

She leaned over me, examining a mark on my nose. Her red hair wet, as if she'd just stepped from the shower. I tried not to think about that. But I did. The top two buttons of her blouse were undone. I tried not to stare. But I did.

Maggie nudged my chin up. "I said, y'alright?"

"Yeah," I said.

"Yer book," she said, pausing to examine it.

Why couldn't I be reading something cool? Murakami. Or Gemma Files.

"Ye like fantasy?"

I nodded and took the book back from her.

"You talking to me is liable to get me killed 'round here."

She snorted a laugh and smiled a fey little smirk. "Tha so? Well, I'd hate tae see ye die on meself's account."

I laughed. "Me too."

She smiled, but I was still confused. I didn't know what she wanted. I know what *I* wanted. But the odds of kissing someone as hot as Maggie were about as likely as me killing a dragon. My level just wasn't high enough.

It would sure feel good though. I mean, she was talking to me. She'd told Scat to hit the road. Even if she didn't *like* me, she didn't hate me either.

Her lips brushed against my forehead, lingered, and left a moist imprint behind.

"There now, tha what ye wanted?"

"Maybe on the lips," I said hopefully.

"Early days yet, Chuck," Maggie said, smiling. "Early days."

∼≋∭∼ ∼≋∭∼ ∼≋∭∼

We walked and talked. Maggie stopped in front of an old stone building on a heavily treed lot.

"Why are we at the Old Courthouse?" I asked.

We all called it that, despite the fact there was no "new" Courthouse.

"Once, there were a gallows here," Maggie answered, breathless. "The Veil be thinner where men hae died."

I shuddered and wondered how she knew. Wondered what she had meant about "the Veil." A rising breeze set the naked branches of the yard's trees clattering together. Superstition, maybe. I concentrated on one tree in particular, a great old oak with a worn band on one of its limbs where the bark was gone. At some point someone had wrapped a chain around the tree, and it'd grown into the bark. A lock, orange with rust, linked the chain's ends. Town lore said a man had been hanged here. Said his ghost swung there still, keeping the bark from ever growing back.

It had probably been a tire swing.

Maggie led me to the tree, but didn't touch it either. "Break the chain," she said.

I didn't ask why. I wanted to impress her, but I didn't see how I could. The chain was old. Rusted.

I hunted for a suitable rock. And bashed away. The lock broke after a few hits. Maggie looked at me as if I weren't done. I took the bit of chain that dangled loose.

Remembering the thrilling scare racing through my body when my dad had told me the story, I took up the chain. I'd believed the story then. Dad wasn't a man for ghosts or goblins. He lived in the real world. A world of metal, pistons and oil. He had stories of the Stanley Cup, the World Series, the Super Bowl. An underdog's victory had been as close as any of his tales treaded to fantasy.

My great-great uncle Benny was another matter. He'd given me an old horseshoe, rusted to Hell. For luck, he'd said. His pa had brought it over from the old country. Triple G Gramps had been missing, gone months, the story went. They'd found him, wandering the bogs and clutching that horseshoe wide-eyed and white-knuckled.

Or so the story went.

Dad and Uncle Benny told stories in the same cadence, and I'd wondered if he'd been the one to tell Dad about the Hanging Tree. There was something in how he spoke… I'd avoided this tree as much as I'd been fascinated by it ever since. Riding my bike close enough to feel the echoes of the first thrill in one breath, wheeling around and declaring it stupid hokum in the next.

Now here I was, standing under that branch. A sunny fall day, but I couldn't see it, not where I was, standing in the shadow of the Hanging Tree. It was cold as a prairie January, there in that shadow. A breath misted passed my lips. The oak's worn branch creaked, and I looked up. A man's body swung from a rope, twisting gently in the breeze. Wind took the body in and out of shadow; it disappeared with the touch of the sun, like all ghost stories do.

But I had my feet firmly planted in shadow, and as I pulled, tearing a new scar in the bark, the hanged man never entirely left my vision. I shuddered, breath caught in my throat; afraid to inhale. It couldn't be real.

I suppose Maggie could've slipped me acid. She got along well enough with the school druggies. I wasn't a complete drug noob. I drank beers when I could sneak them, had a couple of tokes of a joint, ate some magic mushrooms – at least that's what I'd been told they were – but I didn't think I was high. I'd wished for something like this many times. Never imagined I'd get it. But now...

I think I believed.

The chain came free and I stumbled backward, tripping on a root, and landed on my ass. The hanged man stretched out his gaunt, skeletal arm toward the oak. A tall, narrow silver door twinkled like a star in the shadow.

"Ye comin', then?" Maggie flashed a 100-watt grin and pulled me up.

I touched the door and home was long, long gone.

〰〰〰 〰〰〰 〰〰〰

I stepped out under the same oak, but it wasn't fall. Snow had piled and blew on the wind. Maggie, beside me, growled.

"Autumn fer our people be long past," she said. "A winter's come tha spring'll ne'er wake from."

"What the hell?" I asked, showing a little anger of my own.

"Yer a Changeling."

My face screwed in confusion. "A Changeling?"

"Aye."

"What does that mean?"

"Yer form isn't solid."

I tapped my chest and smirked. "Feels solid."

"Enough cheek, yeah? That's nae what I be meanin'."

"Well, what then?"

"Ye appear as ye expect to. Ye feel ye dinnae fit in, and so ye dinnae. With yer family, friends, strangers."

"I don't fit in 'cause the first thing my mom said when she saw me was 'He's not mine.'"

Maggie shrugged. "She *were* right. Yer no belonging tae her. Or to *there*."

I grunted.

"Ye can be whate'er ye want tae be. Right now there be three boys wanting a hero. Hoping to be saved. Ye could be tha hero."

"What do you mean?"

"Yer old friend, with the hat."

"Why would I want to help *them*?"

Maggie smiled. "Prove ye can. Prove yer stronger."

"What, like a double-dog-dare?"

"If ye like," she said.

I had no idea how to do what she asked. "Why would they take Scat?" I said instead.

"Red Caps," Maggie said with a shrug. "Tae them, the way the lads bully ye, that *be* friendship. Yer all a tribe. They just happen tae be at the top and ye the bottom."

I shivered, from the cold, from the regret in her words. From my own fear. I could be whatever I wanted to be. And as sudden as the cold had come, I could no longer feel it. I looked at my arms – thick, black hair sprouted from them, from everywhere as they grew. As I grew. But the Wookiee suit I'd sprouted had brought a smile to Maggie's face, which helped with the last vestiges of the cold more than the hair.

There were no tracks in the snow. Nothing but trees and an icy white graveyard.

"How will we find them?"

"I dinnae know." Maggie said. "What d'ye suggest?"

I wanted to protest, but I also wanted to impress Maggie. Going all hairy from the cold had been instinct. Could I control the power?

"I'll track them," I said, sniffing at the air.

At first I smelled nothing. Only the cold sterility of winter. But gradually, individual scents trickled past my nose, and I understood what they were. The oaks were pungent, thick and heady. Maggie, rich and coppery. I could smell myself, which was oddly disconcerting. I smelled like me, no other way to put it. I also wished I'd taken a shower before we'd left.

I needed to probe beyond Maggie's proximity. She was distracting, in a good way. But I wasn't here to nose-stalk her. My head pounded as it grew used to processing the new stimuli.

There.

Unless faeries smelled like they'd bathed in Axe Body Wash, I'd found Scat.

"Let's go," I said and loped off, following Scat's trail.

Easy going for me proved harder for Maggie. My feet grew as I ran, splitting my runners and keeping me from breaking through the hard-crusted tops of the snowbanks.

I couldn't leave my only guide behind. I was already halfway between a wolf and a man. My nails turned black and hardened, sprouting long claws. My palms were thick pads with more dark hair peeking out from between them. I growled as my jaw lengthened. New teeth split my gums. It hurt. A lot. The pain ended in a moment and I was a wolf. A big one. I had done this. *I* had made this happen.

"Climb on," I said, amazed my voice still worked.

Maggie smiled and ran her hands through the thick fur covering my body.

"Proper forward, Charles," Maggie said. "Ye're a dab hand."

I tried to smile and my tongue lolled out of my mouth. Maggie hopped on my back and I took off like a bullet through the trees. They blurred as I rushed past them, like telephone poles by the highway. I ran. Hunted and ate as we went.

All the while, Maggie urged me on: "Full pelt."

The forest seemed to go on forever.

⁓ᶘᶙᶚ⁓ ⁓ᶘᶙᶚ⁓ ⁓ᶘᶙᶚ⁓

A gap split the trees ahead. I burst through, panting with exhilaration. Jagged spires of rock scraped at the clouds.

I knew our destination immediately.

Not as high as the wall of jagged rock separating it from the forest, it was squat and lumpy next to those snow-capped spires. But where winter buried everything else, this mountain was bare, black rock. Brown, dead grass surrounded it. Magma oozed from its pinnacle and other fissures along its broad cone, dripping down its sides like blood. Blobs of molten rock hissed and steamed, exploding in the cold air.

"Stop here," Maggie said.

"Why?" I asked. "We've still miles to walk."

"If ye set foot on their lands as ye be they'll know it."

"Oh." Then they'd kill Scat and the Thugs. "How should I fight them? As a giant? A dragon?"

I quivered with anticipation. If being a wolf had felt cool, I couldn't *wait* to be a dragon. Man, I hoped Maggie would tell me to be a dragon. They had the whole package. Flight, invulnerability, enhanced senses, flame breath. A guy could really cut loose as a dragon.

"Ye need tae be one o' them," Maggie said.

"One of them? A Red Cap?"

Maggie nodded.

"What are they? Goblins? How'll wearing a funny hat scare them?" I grimaced. "I think I should be a dragon."

"Red caps dinnae fear dragons," Maggie said. Either anger or cold lent a flush to her face. "They dinnae fear anything. Yerself'll only egg them on, hammer 'n' tongs. They'll empty the mountain tae bury ye under their dead if ye show yerself scaly. The only thing'll give them pause be a stronger, meaner Red Cap."

"How do I turn into a Red Cap?" I asked. "I don't know what they look like."

"Listen tae yer body," Maggie answered cryptically. She must've noticed the look on my face. "Yer a Changeling," she said by way of elaboration.

I shrugged. "And?"

"Yer body holds the possibility of all of Faerie."

I'd heard that from the hockey team too.

"Okay," I said, squinting my eyes shut. "Red Cap. Here goes."

I tried to silence my doubt. Doubt drifted to irritation, to anger. How dare she bring me here? And to rescue Scat? If anyone deserved to be left for dead, it was him. But we'd been friends once.

Something wet trickled down my forearms. I heard it spatter to the snow. I could smell it. I'd squeezed my hands so tightly, my fingernails had bit into my palms. I'd been given enough bloody noses and split lips over the years to know the scent of blood. Everyone said blood smelled like copper, but it'd always smelled more like pain to me. It had never smelled...*exciting*.

I opened my eyes and looked at Maggie. She'd always been taller than me. But a few inches had turned to a couple of feet. My senses were sharp as when I'd been a wolf. My short limbs were gnarled and distorted with muscle. I looked ridiculous.

And I was naked.

I should've been embarrassed. Instead, I stood there with my bits dangling in the cold air, seething, angry breaths gouged through clenched teeth. If Maggie said the wrong word I knew I'd try to tear her apart.

She didn't smell afraid, rather a mixture of pleasure and amusement.

I nodded. The form felt...right. Better than any I'd tried before. Better than the one I'd been born to.

"Two things missing," Maggie said. She pointed to a set of rusted iron boots, dusted with snow. Gingerly, she pulled a skeletal foot from each boot. "Ye'll need these."

I tapped them with a long, hard fingernail. The nail *tinked* loudly as it struck the iron. I stuffed one huge, hairy foot into a boot. The metal hissed against my flesh. *I can do this.* I groaned and stepped into the other. Those jerks had better appreciate this. The rust had flaked away from the boots and they were a hard, flat grey against my ruddy skin.

"Oh, and one more thing," Maggie said.

"Yeah?" I growled.

Maggie presented me with a ragged knit woollen cap. It was red, of course.

"Yer hat be dry."

She placed it on my head and pointed to a cavernous scar in the black mountain. Instinctively, I knew what she meant.

Blood. How Red Caps earned their name – soaking their hats in the blood of their victims. The gouges in my palms had already closed over. I couldn't use that blood anyway. I wasn't a victim. Not anymore. I licked my lips and looked at Maggie.

She sensed my intent. "Yer nae ready fer meself, Charles."

I don't know how she cowed me, how she smothered the building murderous rage, but she did.

"Soon," I said.

"Soon." Maggie nodded in agreement. "But in the meantime…"

Something broke in me and I ran toward the mountain, howling like a mad thing until I was inside. I blinked my eyes and I could see. My nose tasted the air.

Axe. Scat and the Thugs had been dragged this way.

"Who're ye, then?" a voice spat from above me.

Another Red Cap dropped from the ceiling, his iron boots fracturing the obsidian tunnel floor. I didn't see him, instead, smelling the blood pulsing in his arteries and veins. It pounded like a jackhammer, powered by a furious heart. The blood on his cap was dry too. I could smell it. He was spoiling for a fight.

Good.

I've been in lots of fights, but I wouldn't say I'd learned much from them, other than covering up. Here was different. *I* was different.

I charged.

Fists met flesh like two gnarled oaks ripped up in a tornado. He choked on a rock-like tooth as I throttled him. An iron boot slammed into my knee. The spikes on his boots dug into my flesh, twisting. I held his foot there with one hand and slammed my other fist into his gut. He folded and I snapped his face down, bashing it against his own iron boot, flattening his pickaxe nose. The Red Cap reeled and I fell atop him, pounding him with fist after fist.

I jerked the cap off my head and pushed it against the Red Cap's pulpy face. As his blood seeped into the cloth, I sighed. Relief. The feeling was short-lived.

I wasn't done.

My iron boots clinked loudly off the obsidian tunnels as we stalked deeper into the caverns. I rode a crescendo of violence through the Red Caps' warren-like home. I don't remember much of it. Just howling and raging. Seething and smashing. Maggie pointed, and I attacked.

*   *   *

"Charles, o'er here."

I followed Maggie's voice into a bone-filled room. Scat was there, and the Thugs.

I wanted to leave him there. Or kill him myself. But he hadn't always been bad. We'd been friends. He and the Thugs had introduced me to D&D before they thought it was uncool. My imagination was a boon then, before hockey became everything. Before they grew, and I didn't. Before I'd told John how I felt.

"It's me, Chuck," I said. I couldn't bring Scat and the Thugs home. But John…I could save John, Carter, and Steve. "C'mon, I'll take you home."

Scat eyed me suspiciously, but he nodded and his cronies dumbly lined up behind him.

*   *   *

I stayed a Red Cap. John, Carter, and Steve had been beaten and tortured by them. While I was glad they weren't dead, I had no desire to set their minds at ease. We reached the Hanging Tree; the gate took its sweet time opening. When it did, I made to step through.

"What're ye doing?" Maggie asked. "Shove their arses through and be done wit' 'em. Ye cannae go back."

"Why not?"

"Yer needed here."

"I'll come back," I said. "I'll visit all the time."

"No," Maggie demanded, her voice dangerously loud to my Red Cap ears. "Yer stayin'."

I didn't like the sound of that.

"No."

"We need ye," she said. "More'n they."

I scowled. "I need to at least say goodbye to my dad."

"I suppose," she said, and then smiled. "Yeah, I suppose tha be fer the best."

I stepped through the gate and willed myself to change.

⁓ ⁓ ⁓

The Hanging Tree didn't look right.

It had always seemed larger than life, but now, there was a hugeness to it that frightened me. The fear made me angry. Snow shrouded the ground here too. A faded poster with my face on it had been stapled to the tree. Missing. Reward. Dead, shrivelled flowers and burnt out LED candles ringed the tree. Someone had made a little shrine.

A branch crunched under my foot and I looked down. The iron boots. They still enveloped my feet. I was still a Red Cap.

"What did you do?" I yelled at Maggie. And I'd thought I'd been angry before. *"What did you do?"*

There was nothing cheerful in her too-large smile now. Her tall, lanky form shuddered and compressed to a height with mine. Her hair hung in tangles and knots to her ankles, wet and red with blood. Scat and Thugs One and Two laughed and moved to Maggie's side. They were Red Caps too.

"They're dead, aren't they?" I asked.

"Yer old friends?" Maggie smiled like a crocodile. "Nae. They'll be keeping our caps dripping fer a time."

I tried to change again. Nothing happened. I tore at the iron boots, trying to rip them from my feet. The metal sizzled against my fingers. My hands recoiled, and I hissed in pain. I screamed. Raged. My body hurt, like I was crammed into too small a place. I couldn't breathe in my anger. My skin itched and burned like I'd come down with a rash.

"Yer bound by iron," Maggie said. "One of us now. It be over…Boyo."

"I'll find a way." I spat the words through my rock-like teeth.

"There be no way," Maggie said. "Ye made the change in Faerie. Things done there cannae be undone."

"It was all a trick? You never liked me."

"Glad tae hae the power, sorry tae pay fer it." She smiled. "Of course it were a trick, foolish boy. But I liked ye well enough. Else I'd not've made ye one of us." A pause. "And a fetching Cap ye be."

I lunged at Maggie but her three goons buffeted me aside. I bounced off the Hanging Tree, tearing the missing poster free. It quavered in my hands. Three months. Three months I'd been gone. It'd felt like hours. Less. What would Dad think? That I'd run away? That I was dead? Would he be sad? Or happy to be rid of me?

"Change me back!"

Maggie smiled and licked her lips. "If ye kill all ye love, I'll turn ye back. No dodges."

I knew who she meant without her saying it. My dad. My friends. I didn't want to stay like this, but I didn't believe her. Not for a second. And what would the point be of getting my old life back without the people who'd made it worth a crap?

"No," I said.

"Fine." Maggie shrugged. "Lads, hit him sick." She smiled and I thought of the Joker. "Before ye do up yer caps."

I was going to die. And it was my fault for being a stupid jerk who'd trusted the surprise ally who offered me free powers. I'd always fallen for that trick in games. I hated not being any smarter in real life.

No.

Not my fault.

Theirs.

The Red Caps loped forward, tongues trailing from their mouths, and I ran at them. Snow squealed under my iron boots. I dove and tackled Thugs One and Two, arms wide. Scat was out of my reach. I wanted to punch and kick and bite the Thugs until only I stood. Scat circled behind me, laughing. I whirled about, hurling one Thug then the next as far as I could.

One landed on something and I heard a hiss, and then he wailed in pain. The chain that'd bound the tree. I could smell the iron in it. And something else. Behind the missing poster. Our family's lucky horseshoe had been nailed to the tree. I could use some luck. I struggled to remember the shoe as a good thing. Iron was a weapon against one of the Good Folk

– one of my kind. No, a Red Cap was a thug. A brute. A monster.

Not one of my kind.

I shook my head. I didn't know what – who – I was. I screamed and charged. I heard a triumphant whoop from Maggie. Scat grinned and licked his lips.

As I rushed forward, I couldn't say who I meant to harm. All I could sense was iron, blood and hate. The iron burned as it touched me. I jerked the horseshoe from the tree and pounded at my boots. Dimly, I heard a click. My pain and the fog of hate it fuelled diminished and I found myself atop Scat…as myself, a skinny kid struggling with a monster.

The snow was cold against my bare skin for a second and then hair sprouted. I could still change.

I could be whoever – whatever – I wanted.

Maggie had said Red Caps only feared a stronger, meaner Red Cap. The bigger you were, the more they wanted to tear you down. Good. My limbs stretched and bulged. Scat groaned beneath me as I added mass.

The Thugs and Maggie swarmed me like angry hornets, scratching, biting. But their stings didn't pierce my thick, scaled hide. Soon I had two in each of my giant dragon mitts. They kept worming, struggling. I gave them a good squeeze.

"You're going home," I said. My rumbling voice shook snow from the trees.

They may've tried to say something, but I wasn't about to listen to any arguments, nor compromise. I hurled them at the Hanging Tree. They disappeared past its bark and into Faerie. I imagined them tumbling through the snow on the other side. They'd come up spitting mad, charging back towards the gate.

I couldn't allow that. My dragon body didn't have any less rage than a Red Cap. I wanted to wrap my tail around the tree and wrench it from the ground. Tear roots and clods of frozen earth free to dirty the snow. I drew in a deep breath of air. I wanted to release a torrent of fire, to consume the Hanging Tree. But then my friends would be stuck on the other side. I couldn't strand them, I knew of no other way back to Faerie. I released my fire into the sky instead.

Panting, I picked up the chain and wrapped it around the tree. My mouth still felt hot. I bit down upon the chain's edges, melting it into a closed loop.

I flopped down before the tree and waited, but they didn't come back. I melted back into my small, weak body, staring dumbfounded at the churned snow. Uncle Benny's old horseshoe still burned me, but it was with cold, not the fiery pain I'd felt as a Red Cap.

A fire truck's siren wailed in the distance. There'd be a lot of questions to answer. Soon. For now, I was glad to be in my own skin. Glad to be home. Glad to be me.

PIED

Quinn McGlade-Ferentzy

Some of us take an awful lot of pride in our work. I take a lot
of pride in my work. This is a story about that. They say pride
is a sin, and, sure, I get that. But sin has no place whatsoever
in the world I'm telling you about. Because this story starts in
a nice little suburb where life is smooth and the roads get
repaved each spring without fail.

And then – there were rats. Rats going about their ratty
business and living ratty lives. This sort of business and life
is precisely what the nice people of the nice suburbs had
decided was *not at all* okay. But rats began popping up everywhere that the nice people of the nice suburbs had decided
that rats were *not at all* welcome.

Of course, they weren't, but good luck telling that to the
matted masses of hunchbacked vermin that began to line
the streets and swarm up through storm drains and toilets.
Try telling the beady-eyed army that picked over compost
heaps to stand down. Try not to be disgusted yet impressed
by feats of rodent ingenuity, as they knocked over trash
cans, disabled home security systems, and started small
fires. The first round of exterminators were unable to make
a dent.

Jeremy, a local malcontent, made several "best laid plans"
jokes that fell flat and caused him to lose his TV privileges.
Take note of the real, human, stories that underlie national
events. Jeremy missed the news report on the rats. It featured

many close-up shots of tiny, grabby paws and bald slithery tails.

These rats were the unexpected bane of everyone's existence. They gnawed foundations. They bit children. They tore up lawns. They needed to go.

The first sign of something beyond a garden-variety infestation was the zero-percent success rate of even the most hard-core poisons. Born and raised on the mean streets of Toronto and Hamilton, these rats were well accustomed to the old tricks. These rats, much like their human cohabitants, had left the city to try and find a nice, quiet, neighbourhood to raise their kids.

Which is what they did. They raised massive clouds of offspring that not even dogs wanted to deal with. Indeed, the country's best ratting terriers were brought in, and immediately decided that they were too old for this shit. They staged a coup and formed their own autonomous pack.

This is the state that I found the little suburb in. It was, may still be, a dreary sort of town. Neat, orderly streets and avenues that pointed right at the massive mall that squatted in the heart of the city. Not the sort of place that usually requires my services. I could tell that this wasn't the sort of place where *things* happened. *Things* happened to other people. Other places. Here, the myth that misfortune only plagued the lazy reigned supreme and no one wanted to admit their hand in the current state of affairs.

When I first pulled into the civic centre, I got sidelong looks. You know the kinds I mean. Some people gape. Some sneer, but all turn away far too quickly. Of course, rats are my territory, but this town wasn't my turf. This cookie-cutter little suburb wanted order and easy, ready-made, pre-packaged life in bulk. Here, eccentricity was deemed synonymous with bad.

So, of course, they didn't like the way I dress, the way I walk, talk, and hell, I'm sure they'd object to my breathing if they could. I knew it would take desperation on their part and long tedious, minutes on my end to get this job done.

I received an audience with the various grounds-keepers and caretakers. And then their supervisor, and their supervisor's supervisor, until I was *finally* referred to the head of the Neighbourhood Association. They were a nice, normal couple who told their son, Jeremy, to be polite to me. This, despite their frosty reception of my job offer. I met them in their home, as it wouldn't do to have me loitering about on the porch where any schmuck could see me.

"So, can you really do it? Get rid of all of them?" one of them asks me.

"*Can I do it?* Can Houdini escape cuffs? Can Mussolini dangle from a hook? CAN I DO IT! Sure, I can fix your itty-bitty ratty insurrection issue. Like it never happened."

The nice couple gave me a look from my custom-made, gen-u-ine, one-of-a-kind pink, lavender, and fuchsia John Fluevog work boots to the tip-top of my newly shorn scalp. I roll my eyes and produce certificates, contracts and testimonials by the dozens. Hell, I'd have contacted my first ever clients via séance if I had thought it was necessary to convince them. These people were at their wits' end and, despite their extreme distrust of me, they agreed to sign. They never used the word "rat" during our negotiations. The husband nodded. The wife gave me a strained sort of smile. We shook on it, pretending a "r-word" hadn't just skittered through our conversation.

"So which payment plan can I get you on?"

I assure them that they won't pay a cent until after the problem has been resolved. I shoot a glance at a rat scrambling up the silk drapes. She peers over her shoulder and slinks off, suitably cowed. The nice thing about nice people is that they're more than happy to write it off as if it hadn't happened.

Have you ever seen a snake charmer? Have you ever seen a singer shatter crystal? If you combine these two simple principles, you'll have no trouble at all understanding what happens next. The nice people of the suburbs were more than happy to dream up any old explanation in between episodes of *The Bachelor* as to why the rats started streaming out along the main street.

And *I* was more than happy to lead the rats to the river.

Don't make that face. Rats are excellent swimmers. Nature is cruel, but I am not. Despite what you may hear.

The rats were ferried safely away; the traditional fee of a single coin, waived.

Instead, I took their secrets.

How else could I charge such a low sum for ridding an entire town of their vermin? I took away the rats, and everything they had heard while lurking about the town. I learnt of affairs and debt and shame. I learnt a few truly horrific things that the nice people pretended they didn't know. I catalogued their petty deviances and dalliances. The nice folk could sleep easier and tread lighter, though they'd assume the lack of rats was what eased their collective malaise. Just like that, my job was done.

Not that I haven't tried, but I cannot live on secrets alone. So, I went back to collect my fee. It was, if I recall, a rather modest sum, considering the rats beyond number I had removed from the picture. And any idiot can kill a rat: stamp on their skulls, set them on fire. You all know the drill. Most creatures die easily, don't they? But it takes a true artist, a master of the craft, to get the rats to clean up after themselves. Sealing up their holes, sewing chewed fabric, replanting destroyed lettuce. Rats can be very accommodating creatures. They're social animals, after all.

But, as is the nature of nice people, they were all too quick to forget the extent of their rat problem. They were more than willing to look between me, the dozens of other rat catchers, killers, and trappers, and decide that they simply *couldn't possibly* decide who had done the job.

I am not greedy. My fee is reasonable. But the secrets of vermin don't buy bread and booze and lipstick. Money greases the wheels that spin this world, like it or not.

I explained myself very calmly. I spoke slowly, and let my words sink in. The reaction? I was denied payment. Worse, I was chased out of town.

This has happened before and the logical solution of bringing the rats back is a no-go. Secrets are non-refundable. Once told, a secret becomes a statement and, slowly, that statement turns into useless, verifiable evidence. As long as I keep a firm lid on my secrets, they stay fresh. There's power in mysteries, more than you find in evidence. Evidence tells you what you know, secrets show what you don't.

Plus, as the squeaking matriarch of the rat clan reminded me, "No backsies."

So, I went back to the nice couple who had hired and so rudely dismissed me. They acted as though they couldn't see me, as if avoiding my eyes would hide them from sight.

"Since you hired me to remove an undesirable infestation, and I have done so, and you have refused to pay, all I can do is assume the job is not yet done. I will come back, and I will finish the job."

Of course, it would take every ounce of cunning I had to pull it off. I made my hair look neat, orderly, and respectable. I made my face look clean, orderly, and respectable. My clothes, too, became sober, orderly, and respectable.

And then, I applied for a loan.

Homecoming is a North American tradition dating back to this one time a human mother witnessed an animal physically forcing her spawn from the nest. Though exactly what kind of animal has been lost to the annals of history, everyone agreed that said animal had the right idea.

For anyone paying close attention, this first mother was, of course, a rat.

Homecoming is when formerly kicked-out spawn are welcomed back, victorious, to the nest.

Jeremy was nearly unique in his little nest, his colony, his suburb. He had two pet rats. This wasn't ever discussed, as most of the adults who had dealt with the prior infestation were reluctant to even mention the word. But really, why shouldn't an almost-man have two small pets to keep him, and each other, company?

They were, as anyone with eyes could see, very nice rats. Anyone with a sense of touch could feel that they were very nice rats. Both had soft coats and were in the habit of grasping new fingers with their forepaws and shaking said finger. And it was a nice, friendly handshake at that, not business-like or brusque, and not prolonged and awkward. They were sleek and black and were just as happy scurrying around his room as they were hiding in the hood of the sweatshirt Jeremy wore nearly every day. If humans had a rat standard, they would recognize them as exceptional rats.

Jeremy, Artemis and Apollo had decided to sulk about the downtown. He was one of the first of his high school group to come backinto town from a more or less successful year at Queens. And he felt unanchored, nothing he had just spent the past eight months caring so much about mattered here. He had been "away" and now he was "home."

Jeremy is going for a walk. Times past, he'd skip through a ravine and end up in his friends' backyard. Now, his friends were still away, basements and poster-plastered bedrooms cold, empty and waiting. So, he's mostly going for a walk to get out of the house. It's not that his parents were awful people, but they were overly concerned with all the things Jeremy didn't care about. In fact, the more Jeremy cared about something, the less his parents were concerned.

Jeremy stops in front of a brand-new bar. The paint on the sign had barely dried. He heard a rustle inside the dim bar and leapt backwards when a newly bald yet still respectable looking human steps out.

"Did I frighten you?"

"No—" Jeremy answered far too quickly; not yet comfortable with new places, least of all new bars.

The bartender, owner, or whoever, smirks and went back to plastering the façade with large, rainbow posters. One appears to be advertising an old-fashioned circus; the other had bright neon lettering commonly associated with only the cheesiest techno. The last poster to go up showed several large, hairy men in small, leather shorts. It's daytime and people are watching. The posterer hummed happily, ensuring the leather asses were affixed firmly, the crotches at precisely eye-level.

"Is this a gay bar?" Jeremy ejaculated, in spite of himself. He tried to sound interested, but not too eager, curious but unconcerned.

He failed miserably, of course. He was both eager and concerned. The bartender paused.

"Yes. And no. Here, find out for yourself." The bartender smiled, and with an unnecessarily grand sweeping gesture, produced a bright flyer reading, "Admit one"

"Bring your friends." Jeremy had a feeling he was being dismissed. He left, hurrying, and not looking back. Artemis poked her head out for one last look.

His friends, had all gone to Ottawa for school. Or at least the bulk of them had all gone to the same school and lived in the same dorn and now seemed to only exist as faces in pictures having way more fun than Jeremy. And now they all conspired to take the same bus home after exams. And while he hadn't exactly wanted to go to that school or live that life, he couldn't help but feel a tad bitter about it all. This was one of the first times his actions had real consequences. So, he could (and did) mock their "precious little group bus adventure" because the group didn't include him.

Getting ready to go out is another ritual that cannot be easily traced to any one origin. However, it can be noted that getting ready en masse raises the collective expectation to a fever pitch that no reality could ever meet. Jeremy burst right into this hive, sniffling a little but trying his best. He has been summoned, by text, to the suburban basement all his friends have gathered in. He breathed easy for a second. This is the basement, after all, where he spent most of his teenage years stoned, drunk, and a mess but otherwise accepted. Art and

Ap sniffed the air, but felt no real attachment to the smell of recycled, climate-control dust. They were young, as far as rats go. Jeremy teetered. He waited. He felt the crumpled flyer in his pocket, a little torn now, having been snatched from his father's stubby forepaws right before he left the house.

This was his argument; this was his answer to the question of where to go and what to do.

As soon as it was the exact right time to go out, the group formed a loose procession. Figuring out the exact right time to go out on the town was the main reason to take advanced math. Take last call, subtract cover fees, factor the probability of who you're Facebook stalking, divide by number of flaky people and the remainder is when you should leave your house if you want to have fun at all. This was the second wave of student coming back, a strange swarm of sequins and rolled ankles. Poorly fitted collared shirts and embarrassing jeans.

And then there's Jeremy. In the back. With rats in his hood. For a moment, he thought he must be the loneliest, prettiest, most special, and (most importantly) most alone boy in the whole wide world.

Of course, Jeremy was dead wrong. And while he was walking down a road unmapped by his predecessors, he didn't walk it alone.

Tonight, the children would leave.

Some of them, like Jeremy, were following a map I drew up.

The night was full of the victorious whoops and jeers of those returned, and the troupe swelled, stalled, smoked, and getting there was about as easy as herding cats. Which was much more difficult than herding rats. But they made their way gradually to "Jeremy's Bar."

Because it's what the whole group was calling it, and Jeremy couldn't help but think it too.

"Well, it's about time I get something." He tried to make light of it. The first thing the group noticed when they entered the bar was how dark and narrow the passageway was. The only light was from a small window beside which a bored-looking girl no one has ever seen before sat waiting for them to either pass the test or get out already. Unwillingly, she approved their ID's. But she did all this with a heavy dose of scorn and suspicion. The look she gave them was less about official laws and more of a searching, pulling look. She was, after all, looking for secrets. Several of the group noticed a schism between the bar's elegant veneer and the coat-check girl's grubby gutter punk ways.

"All right. You guys are good to go in." She squeaked them through the second set of doors and into a room that was somehow darker than the first. Jeremy realized that the flyer hadn't been advertising this place as "the place to be" but as "A place to be." The source of light was undetermined and, at first listen, the music was just a throbbing bass. Either a promise or a threat, no one could tell. Jeremy was so engrossed in his conversation with the bartender about rats, that he didn't notice the vast majority of his friends depart for the usual haunts their older brothers and sisters had been complaining about for years. And then, Jeremy realized he was surrounded by a group of strangers. People he had gone to elementary school with, but never talked to. And he had the further realization that they were all here for the same reason he was.

They were wrong about what the reason was though. The reason was that I had called them all here. And then, it was last call. And the lights went up. And everyone was gone.

Sunday was a day of rest. A day of brunch. Sunday was also the day that Jeremy's father decided that maybe he should look for his son. He didn't give the boarded-up storefront that had been a throbbing, pulsing nightclub just one day before any more recognition than that.

"Good riddance. We've given them a damn parade. We gave them marriage. Why the fuck do they still need bars?" he scoffed to Jeremy's mother.

Some of you will read this story and wonder. Wonder what on earth happened to all those poor, dear, sweet little children.

You'd best ignore the dark shadows skittering along your baseboards, the gnawing in your cupboards and the echo of soft little paws and sharp little claws as you try to sleep.

I can easily tell you but really, is it any of your concern? I only took those who wanted to leave your world and enter mine. It's not a story about kidnapping. It's not a story about rats.

Once upon a time, I came to a town with a problem. The townspeople had decided that certain undesirable elements were incongruous with the image of themselves that they wished to maintain.

In short, *you* wanted me to clean up what you thought were vermin.

And yet you ask about what happened to the children?

I come away as the villain in this story. But know this:

I only ever did what you asked.

LA BÊTE SAUVAGE

KARIN LOWACHEE

The prince watched Beau sleep. Beau's skin was the colour of paper in the moonlight and if Petrus touched one pale cheek he fancied that he could read the other man somehow, the handsome features a language that would tell him the spells and incantations of his consort's heart.

⚜ ⚜ ⚜

The six sisters trapped in statues lined the front courtyard, their skirts made of draped indigo shadow, their white lips parted half in mockery and half in scream. They were Beau's sisters, who had laughed at him until enchantment shut them up. In the prince's night wandering he'd begun to bid them good greetings. Perhaps it was the kindred regard of mutually cursed souls, though he walked the world in flesh like any man now.

On this, his third night outside of the castle while Beau slept, he thought the sisters gazed down upon him with reproach. As if they knew he shouldn't have been inviting the darkness in by going out to meet it. But they were made of stone now and he ignored their silent judgment.

The forest beyond the castle stood tall and thick enough to block even moonlight. Shadow played with shadow here, indistinguishable silent siblings beneath the straddling trees and squatting bushes. Late winter still touched the ground in frost kisses and tongued its way up through the soles of his boots. Though his man's sight struggled in the night, some other remembered instinct guided him through the grasp of chill air and the sound of little feet in the undergrowth. He smelled dead leaves and cracked pebble berries, and animals too long starved through the months. Wolves, deer, crows. And very faintly on the breeze, human. A traveller, a brigand. A lost or abandoned child. Whoever it had been, they were long enough dead to leave behind only the faintest scent of decay.

Maybe one of them he had killed long ago.

He made his way through the layers of leaves, arms wrapped around his middle, not because he felt the cold, clad only in shirt and trousers, but just so the branches and brambles didn't sink their spines into him and hinder his progress. Once, in the previous two nights, he'd crawled beneath a bed of twigs and leaves, and lay until dawn eked through the upper turrets of the forest. Once, he'd chased an owl through the winding staircase of boulders embedded against the side of a cluttered green hill. And once, he'd crouched by a stream and drank the black water, blurry stars behind his own reflection, and looked up to meet the golden eyes of a fox on the opposite side of the embankment.

Tonight, he heard footsteps following him through the well-trodden path.

They came to him in a shamble, a slide and step and slide, some off-beat parlor dance. When he stopped, the sound stopped. When he began to walk again, the slide and step trailed after him. Finally, he turned to stare into the deep shadows. Not even the nocturnal animals spoke, and the air sat motionless. He barely felt its touch along the fine hairs of his forearms or across his jaw. Yet, when in that stillness, the dislodged gait took up again, a tendril of his hair lifted and grazed across his cheek, as if some whirling couple passed by him in a ghostly waltz.

"Show yourself!"

Sound died. His voice didn't echo in the cathedral height of the forest.

"Show yourself, whoever you are!"

The shadows at the funnel end of the path tore apart. He heard the voice before he saw the twinkle of eyes. "As my prince commands."

The voice was smooth and lighter than the night. The face emerged next, its angles and curves apparently lit by the glow of two pale eyes. It was an austere but beautiful face, the colour of cinnamon. Vaguely female, not wholly male. It stood crooked, legs like wishbones, chin lowered and eyes raised. Long black hair fell in sheets across its shoulders, blending with its loose, formless clothes.

As the creature approached, it brought with it the scents of nutmeg and saffron and salt water.

"What are you?" he asked it, standing his ground. This misshapen thing with the pretty face seemed to bear no threat and moved at that same ungainly shuffle.

"A follower, nothing more." It smiled. Its teeth were white against the rich flavour of its skin.

"How do you know I'm the prince?"

"This is the third night you've come into the forest. You come from the direction of the enchanted castle, do you not?" It pointed down the path.

"There is no enchantment in that castle, not any longer." He didn't know why he confessed that. It wasn't a thing one ought to have confessed.

But the creature laughed. "No enchantment in your consort's sisters locked in stone? No enchantment in the perpetual sun and blooming flowers in your court? No enchantment in the invisible servants at your hearth and airy music at your harp? Magic does not so easily wilt, my prince."

As the creature spoke its voice grew louder, its bow spine straightened. Petrus took a step backward.

"You've come to curse me again?"

"It wasn't I who had cursed you in the first place, my prince."

"Then what do you want?"

"To bless you." The creature made a gesture, like a young page tipping his cap in welcome. The scent of sharp spices rolled out on the air.

"I seek no blessings from a thing like you."

It laughed again, high and bell-wrought. "A thing! Very well. Go back to your castle, dear prince. But think of this: I would give you all that your heart desires. The *thing* that you seek here in the dark of night, in the depths of this forest."

"I seek nothing but the air."

"You seek to *breathe*. Such could be your blessing." The pale eyes disappeared as the creature blinked, once and twice. Then a third time. It began to retreat down the path. An awkward gait, a stir of leaves. "Farewell. Until tomorrow night."

He watched it disappear, and not even its scent remained.

⟿ ⟿ ⟿

The long length of the decorated table separated them, he and his Beau. No flowers or greenery stood tall enough to obscure their mutual images, only a regiment of candlesticks set at precise intervals, their fire glow creating the only warmth between him and this man. Beau perched on the velvet chair like a painting, nothing moving but his hands as they sliced and stabbed the roasted fowl on his plate. He ate delicately, reflected movements of the fineness of his features, from eyebrows to full petal lips. He wielded the knife with strength, though, the marble anvil of his wrist surrounded by black leather. The expanse of polished wood and shining silver allowed for words to skate toward the prince.

"You left again last night," Beau said.

He hadn't stirred when Petrus returned to the bed, but that didn't mean he hadn't been awake. The prince had known from the first time he'd laid eyes on his consort that the other man's beauty did not stand in the way of his intelligence.

"You've ventured out the past three nights now," Beau continued. "What draws you to the woods, my dear prince?"

"Only the air."

"Is the air of your castle not pleasing? Are your gardens not warm and sweet to smell?"

Somehow, such inquiries over the years had become insults. It was nearly imperceptible, but the shadows shifted just a little on his consort's features and exposed a twist of lips. Subtle derision. Many times, he had hurled these questions to Petrus with the bluntness of a cudgel. *Is this life not well with you? Am I no longer pleasing to your eyes?*

The prince didn't respond. By now he knew that infuriated his consort more than any words.

They were both trapped portraits in the gilt frames of this once-enchanted castle. He would say it had begun the day Beau's father had died six years ago; one of the horses had kicked the old man for no apparent reason and his frail body had been crushed immediately. The prince thought perhaps his consort blamed him, as it had been *his* horse, *his* stables that the father had loved to frequent, but Beau never accused him out loud. It had been his choice to live here, after all, as companion.

The mourning had brought Beau's four brothers back from the seas, and the fifth, the youngest, from his wanderings. He'd embraced their company for a month before even they were forced to abandon him to tend to their worlds and the family's regained merchant riches.

It was impossible to console him now. Beau had not shed such tears when his sisters had been encased in stone, though his heart had been open to them despite their mocking treatment of him. Once upon a time, he had been the light even in the midst of a dark forest and a darker castle. He had come to Petrus on a promise, and remained out of his own will.

But something had died that day with the father. Something the prince thought might have been both that promise, and the will.

His own solitary years alone in this castle had not provided him any kind of magic to help it. He could not breach the silence.

⚜   ⚜   ⚜

The wolves howled that night, past the outer courtyard and its iron gate, deep inside the forest. Petrus stood by the tall glass of their bedchamber, opened it and looked out. The torches had been snuffed, yet through the shadows he saw the amber eyes of the beasts, flickers of life even from a far distance. Something stirred them. Something called to him to come out and meet them in the tangle of branch and shadow.

He felt it like a tug in his blood, as if what flowed through his veins was for the sole purpose of sweeping him toward the night and the freedom to run.

"What transfixes you?" Beau asked, still abed but facing him.

He didn't turn. Perhaps in darkness it was easier to speak without recrimination.

"Don't you feel it?" he wondered aloud, listening to the wolves. "They're restless and hungry."

"They're dangerous." A pause. He heard the layers of covers shift as his consort's body moved. "Is it them, those animals, that you go to see?"

A real curiosity edged his tone. He'd known Petrus when such wildness was as kin to him as the frozen sisters were to Beau.

"I told you," he said, "I go for the air." Could he admit to him that the open forest, even in its enclosed march of trunk and bramble, was more kindness than the polished stone and stately columns in his own castle grounds? Could he say that a man's flesh was no barrier to creature dreams? "Don't you wonder," he said instead, turning now toward the shadowed angles that created Beau's form out of the dark, "what it would be like to live out there?"

"No," came the immediate answer, like the stoppering on the mouth of a bottle. "I've lived out there, don't you remember? It's from out there that I came to you, and it was a place of ostracism when my family lost their fortune, and poverty when we came to live in the woods. And a man such as I am…as we both are…"

He didn't finish it. He didn't have to. Early in their togetherness, Beau had told him of the stones and curses that had followed his footsteps in the town. This castle protected them from the outside world.

His memories were as strong as the prince's continued to be, though both their states had changed. Petrus looked back out again, past the leaded glass, his attention pulled to the sounds of the wolves. "But that's not all there is."

Through the howling rose a whiplash note, snapping the air between the soulful call of more familiar four-legged denizens.

"What is that?" his consort demanded, now sweeping from the bed to stand behind his shoulder. Startled breath grazed the side of the prince's neck and he shivered.

He squinted into the shadows at the edges of the forest, beyond the castle grounds. The keen hurled above the night in long curves, stopped, and started again. Staggered waves. He gripped the stone sill of the window and leaned forward. Through the rustle of underbrush in the distance, among the amber sparks of wolven stares, a pair of moonlight blue eyes emerged.

"Foul thing," he murmured. The cold of the stone beneath his palms bit through his skin.

"What do you see?" Beau's hand found his shoulder and held on. His human sight did not extend so far, but he knew the prince's did. Even in this form.

The faint musk of nutmeg and saffron and salt water drifted up toward their tower, captured by the warmer spring breeze that forever blew through the castle and its grounds.

"Stay here." He pulled away from the touch. He knew the protest even before Beau voiced it. "Stay here!"

The growl set the other man at bay and the prince went out to the night alone.

⁂

The gazes of the stone sisters followed his flight toward the woods. He glanced up at them by habit and the shadows fell across their faces to lock their features in knowing shapes of warning. Hesitant, terrified, even frozen in such dire rapture, their emotions grew from the play of light and dark. At some angles they so closely resembled Beau that he matched their expressions in what he saw across from him at supper. His consort could be as flawless as marble, carved out of a cold regard.

He felt Beau watching from the tower as he made his way past the gate to the edge of the woods. The wolves had silenced but that keening still split the air, echoing among the vaulted trees like an operatic soprano in the opulent theatres of the cities he refused to visit.

"Show yourself!"

The cold slid through his sleep shirt, up the wide legs of his lounge pants. He was bootless but barely felt the spike and tickle of undergrowth. The dirt grew warm between his toes and filled his nostrils with pure nature.

The keening ceased.

From the wrought-iron pattern of branches and gloom in front of him, the jerk and slide of uneven steps surfaced. Soon the bow-bent, cinnamon-skin creature faced him, its pale eyes alight, its mouth in a wide smile.

"You've come, my prince."

"You disturbed my sleep and you skulk by my home. I've come to tell you to go away."

It shook its head once. "You were not asleep. Do not begin a blessing on a lie."

"I seek no blessing from you, I told you."

"How fares your Beau? Is he still shrouded in mourning?"

He wished for his sword, or his dagger, some instrument of killing to wield against this persistent menace. Though the creature spoke in mild tones and kept its distance, there stirred an urge in him to wreak some violence upon its body.

"Do not speak of him." The prince took a step and loomed above the thing. "Now return from whence you came. If you are indeed a creature of magic, then I tell you thrice tonight: *Go away!*"

It laughed, the sound of a death knell. "I am a servant of the power, my prince, not a creature of it. Your declarations hold no sway. But here, I'll grant you a premise upon which you may ponder. I was a servant also to the one who had changed you and your castle all those years ago. She, too, had sought to bless you, though the gift was taken with ignorance." It seemed to hunch its shoulders even more to peer up at him from a lower height. "After all this time, do you not yearn for the gift again? Why else this roaming of the woods in the dead of night?"

Petrus held his breath to rid his air of this creature's scent. He couldn't move his limbs, recalling as through a dark glass all the murky features of that night when he'd fallen asleep a man and awakened something else. Through all the many nights since his hidden marriage, he went to bed with the dreams and the fear of opening his eyes to the crimson and gold cast of a beast's nocturnal vision. But such senses were dimmed now. And beyond the regard of his consort, on the opposite sides of an echoing room, he had begun to miss that red sight.

"You hadn't wanted the arranged love of a political bride," the crooked stranger continued. "You hadn't desired a *bride* at all. You hadn't wanted the gilt of epaulets, and sabres that had never touched a battlefield. You used to sit in your mother the Queen's grand library and find more comfort in the dusty realm of fantasy than in the parties surrounded by preening, would-be princesses and their fawning, powdered parents. Tell me that what you once called a curse was not a blessing in disguise? – as *you* became, in disguise. As your consort peeled away this disguise with his love and clear sight."

Now it was his turn to laugh, his shoulders straightening back, his hand cutting the air between himself and this low form bent at the waist like the servant it claimed to be.

"If it were such a blessing, then why this life now? My Beau resents me and this perpetual paradise wherein we now exist." He couldn't say the word for perfection without a small snarl of his lips, the same expression that greeted him every morning and heralded him to bed every night. "If it were such a blessing, then it was given only to be taken away."

"As all things must be." The creature shuffled closer. Its brown fingers drifted out to grasp lightly at his wrist. He almost pulled back but there was only a strange benevolence now in its upward stare. "Blessings, too, have consequence, my prince. And you have learned, have you not? You may only know what your heart truly desires when it has been given...then taken away."

The forest growth beneath his feet seemed to pull him down. He knelt there now, at eye level to the creature, his hands curled into the dead leaves and tossed twigs, the marred imprints of where the wolves had tread. The stirred scents were well-remembered, just as the texture of all that earth between his fingers.

"My mistress," the creature said, "bade me find your castle once the spell was broken. Ask your consort what it is that *he* desires."

"Not this." Petrus raised his chin to the shadows of the trees above. "He's afraid of the wild things."

"As once he feared you," the servant said. "But he fears you no longer."

"What he feels for me now is worse than fear." In such quiet hours he felt it like the touch of an icicle. If he held too tightly it would only melt and leave him with its absence. Beau was such an element, as changing as emotion, or some result of nature no man could hope to harness.

"Ask him," said the creature, "as you had asked him so long ago…if he could love you. Ask him what it is he now desires."

When the prince dropped his gaze from the necks of the trees, the servant was gone. The touch of its long fingers was a breath across his wrist that he chased with his opposite hand. Warmth resided on the surface of his skin, but deep beneath that murmured his own acute fear and a sick persistent chill.

Perhaps it was he who feared Beau now. They had lived these past years since the old man's death without word of true desire, as if the speaking of it would cast a new curse upon their routine household – one from which there would be no recovery.

⚬⚬⚬   ⚬⚬⚬   ⚬⚬⚬

"You've dirt beneath your fingernails," Beau said, upon seeing him in their bedchamber once again. The window remained shut and latched. His consort sat on the end of the high bed amidst rolling velvet covers and shining silk pillows. The candles were lit but breathed too distant and inconsistent in the walls to cast much light or warmth. Yet Beau had spied his dirty hands.

He moved to the side of the bed, numb from the transition between winter and spring.

"What did you find out there, Petrus?" The voice followed his every step.

In a fit of cavalier need, some dim reminder of those first few weeks when they'd chased each other around his aviary with teasing discovery, he said, "A servant of dark magic. A servant of the one who'd draped this castle in the spell your father stumbled upon."

The mention of the old man did him no kindness, but he didn't seek it. Sometimes any reaction out of Beau was better than the lifeless alternative.

His consort's displeasure coated the brittle tone of the inevitable question, though it was only a practical wondering. "What did this servant want?"

Petrus sat on the bed and Beau turned enough to look him in the eyes. "He wants to know what you desire," the prince told him. "Should you come to some conclusion, I would caution you to keep it to yourself. Wishes have a way of twisting one's fate into something unrecognizable."

Beau said nothing for the space of many heartbeats. They watched each other like animals. "This servant," he said finally, "sought nothing from you?"

"It knows already what I desire." He yanked the heavy covers aside and slipped beneath them to turn his back to the other man. "As do you, I think."

Their intimacy had transformed, like the chimera he had once been and still felt beyond the continuous rally of creature dreams. Something more beast than beauty shaped their love now, and there would be no paternal catalyst for the healing of it.

⌒⑄⑄⏝⌒ ⌒⑄⑄⏝⌒ ⌒⑄⑄⏝⌒

In the morning his brother-in-law, the youngest of the six, showed up in the grand foyer. The boy had long been peripatetic, sometimes sailing aboard his older brothers' vessels, but mostly relying on the strength of his boots and the accuracy of his star readings as he traversed the land. It had been three years since his last visit and the prince was glad to greet him – some other face to fill this castle with warm smiles and open arms than was readily exchanged by its regular occupants. They embraced and kissed each other's cheeks, and the boy asked after Beau.

"Still abed," the prince replied. "Come and eat something and let's share the world until he rises."

Restless even after leagues of travel, the boy gnawed on a hunk of bread and wandered out to the courtyard and the statues. The prince trailed him, stepping on his shadow.

"They're so constant." The boy gazed up with analytical eyes into the frozen suffering of the sisters he'd barely known, as crumbs dropped in specks to the marble landing. The dribbled enchantment of the castle had never bothered the boy; he claimed to have seen far stranger things in his travels. "For some reason," he said, "I had thought it would fade over time. That perhaps these six would begin to melt their stone and in my next visit they would be as Beau remembered: full of complaining and persecution. But the weaver of your magic has somehow sustained these grounds and every living thing in it, hasn't she?"

The prince glanced away from the statues toward the waving, laden branches of the orange trees in the grove nearby. "There's a punishment in its specificity. I've only begun to see it as of late. These of your kin were made stone because of their attitudes toward my consort. And now my consort is as a stone to me, even if he walks from court to courtyard like a living thing. What runs this household isn't the imperfection of the natural world."

His brother-in-law was silent upon the words. He finished his bread and dusted his sun-darkened hands on faded leather breeches. "Then leave it."

The prince touched the boy's shoulder, held on. "And leave him? No. My love yet abides, despite the thorns."

"Both of you, then. There are better enchantments in the world, ones you earn from plowing through the grit." The boy gestured up at the towers of the castle, at the peeping of the birds. "Not this falsity."

"And live as a wanderer, like you? He wouldn't care for that. Hadn't he and your brothers told me long ago of the wan circumstances of living in the woods? Of the misery and hardship from an unsteady future? Not to mention the hatred of strangers for what we are. This castle is enchanted but it provides."

"But provides what?" In wide daylight and through the burnished colour of his skin, this boy resembled Beau. His mind moved with the speed of flipped pages in a stiff breeze. "Have you asked him if he would wander with you?"

"No, he has not." The deep voice drifted to them, accompanied by the harder steps of black boots across the flagstone. The prince watched Beau approach, take his brother's arm, and kiss his cheeks. The boy likewise embraced him and for a minute they remarked upon each other's features in that way of long remembrances. "What of this wandering now?" Beau said. "What fanciful ideas dare to mar this façade?"

The prince couldn't help but look above his consort's head at the sisters. "No more fanciful than anything else. I was telling our brother that leaving this place has never been an option."

"You leave it quite often at night," Beau replied.

So they sparred even now, and he was too sick of it to curb his words. "My purpose isn't to see the world, but to hunt it."

Both brothers stared at him, as if they had just come upon him in his enchanted form. He remembered that first meeting and how Beau had appeared through his creature's eyes: like spun glass, like silk. One touch and this man would shatter or tear.

How wrong he had been.

⚜ ⚜ ⚜

The keening awakened him and Beau was gone from their bed. That witch's servant called to the stars, called to *him*, and it had managed not to rouse him from his racing sleep. Soon Petrus found himself barefoot in the woods once again, the gates of his castle lost in night behind him and the path before him wrecked by the passing stride of wolves and the cold dance of air.

Before him crouched the servant creature, and beside him stood a second *thing*.

It was a cousin visage of the chimera he'd once been, eyes rimmed red, fangs long and claws like diamonds. It paced the forest floor like some great desert Goliath thrown wide from its natural surroundings, dwarfing all but the oldest trees. Its coat was golden; its mane black. It shone beneath the moonlight and he saw his hand reach out to touch its glory before any thought of fear or caution.

"Beautiful," he murmured, just as it raised its eyes and stared back at him.

He knew those eyes.

"His desire," the servant creature said, and all around the prince was the scent of nutmeg and saffron and salt water. And this beast, the earthy musk rising from the soft mane as he ran his fingers through it. "Had you not known? It was you, in this form, that he always loved."

Loved for pity, the prince had thought. And then loved for grace, he'd assumed. All of his actions through the years responded to those assumptions, building a barrier between them more sustaining than any magic. Never had he considered that it had been simply love. That Beau would have lived his days with an enchanted beast and forsaken every other magical consequence – not for him, but for them both.

Had Beau known all along that he would miss it? Had he seen through death and despair to what *he*, the prince, had mourned – and mourned still?

"Here he stands," said the servant, as if it read his mind. "Are you in the forest, my prince, only for the air?"

He shook his head. He tried to speak but the beast was close to him now, eye to eye, its muzzle pushed insistently against his cheek with such playful force that it nearly cast him off his feet.

Behind him approached slow, cautious steps and he turned to see their brother, rendered motionless now upon the path.

"Brother," the prince said. "Bear witness and then…do with the castle what you will." He would not wait. He couldn't doubt. And what had he to fear when Beau had led the way before him? This headstrong man that had borne the weight of a spell through all transformations.

He turned back to the servant, where it crouched all twisted-limbed and cinnamon-skinned. It curved a smile up at him, hand moving to its head as if to tip a hat.

It began to draw upon the ground. It began to speak. The words rang familiar in the prince's human ears, but as he fell to the ground and the shivers of change wracked his body, what had sounded like gibberish now trickled like song into his mind. A voice singing, no longer a soulless keen. A chant of magic, pushing all stagnant will from his pores, so when he opened his eyes again he saw the fire of the night in all of its splendour.

He saw Beau's brother kneeling upon the path, as if in prayer or thanks.

And he saw the red wildness of his consort, his beauty, coiled to hunt by his side.

MARTINIS, MY DEAR, ARE DANGEROUS

KATE STORY

Or:

*A Fantastical Fragment of a Memoir by a Legless Ex-Oil Exec
on Encountering the Fabled Rapture of the Deep*

*Comprised of journal entries, definitions wrested from the
interweb, writings after the fact, and unexpected bursts of
poetry (the latter due to an undergraduate degree in English
Literature attained during the author's Younger Years)*

*Note: all errors, in fact or judgment, are author's own

*I have heard the mermaids singing, each to each.
I do not think that they will sing to me.*
    "The Love Song of J. Alfred Prufrock" —*T.S. Eliot*

Underwater, everybody is "disabled." Everybody needs adaptive equipment to dive: to breathe, to swim. So making further adaptations is just one extra step.

That's what I was saying to myself as I wheeled into my first diving instruction session at the pool.

I'd taken to stubbornly refusing to tell people in advance about my disability. Maybe this is an angrily defiant phase all people who suddenly find themselves using a wheelchair go through; I don't know. I just know I started doing it. Restaurants, for example. I'd make a reservation, arrive in my chair, and then make a big deal about not being able to get into the goddamn place (or, as is often the case, to the bathroom). Useful? Probably not. Satisfying? To me, yes, somewhat. In those moments people didn't look at me with pity. But they fucking looked at me, oh yes, they did. Some of them hated me. Good.

So I showed up to this lesson all ready for a fight. Instead, I get this sweet young woman with long, red curly hair, just like my sister, just like my mother, just like. Except I think she really *is* pretty, doesn't just look that way (to invoke that terrible song). And she says, Oh, I'm so sorry ma'am, I don't have my HSA certification. Would you like to train with Petrov?

There's special scuba-diving training for the disabled?

Reader, there is.

⚬ᘒᕫᐧ ⚬ᘒᕫᐧ ⚬ᘒᕫᐧ

Let's fast-forward a year to my first real outside-the-swimming-pool scuba session. Tobermory, Bruce Peninsula, Lake Huron. Serious shit. Tobermory, Ontario wears a borrowed name. The original town lurks in Scotland, on the Isle of Mull.

The town's name is derived from the Gaelic *Tobar Mhoire: "Mary's well." Legend has it that the wreck of a Spanish galleon, laden with gold, lies somewhere in the mud at the bottom of Tobermory Bay: a member of the defeated Spanish Armada fleeing the English fleet. A local witch Dòideag cast a spell, the ship caught fire, and the gunpowder magazine exploded, sinking the vessel. No one has ever managed to find any significant treasure.*

Why did Dòideag do it? Nobody knows. The lesson here: don't piss off a witch.

Ontario's Tobermory is maggoty (as my Newfoundland grandmother used to say) with wrecks as well. That's why the dive shop is here, that's why the Magical Mermaids are here, that's why we're here.

Reader, we are here for treasure.

There's a group of us, a rag-tag bunch who all "graduated" with water wings from dive instruction in Toronto. With us is Petrov, our dive instructor; he organized this trip, 300 kilometres north-west of Toronto, hired an accessible minivan and everything. We arrive, meet the local dive master, Petrov checks our gear, and we waltz onto a hired boat which is going to take us out to a shipwreck, one shallow enough that even we beginners can dive down to it. I am the only gimp in the group.

"Hey, teach?" It isn't a lesson, but I have taken to bugging Petrov because he acts as if every goddamn thing one does in life is a test. "Hey, teach? What do we have to do to pass?"

"Come back," Petrov says.

⟳⟳⟳ ⟳⟳⟳ ⟳⟳⟳

As we leave shore I spot a row of girls on a beach. They talk and laugh; they have long hair, they are effortlessly girly. They appear to be making some kind of craft project with beads and, instead of lower limbs, they have brightly coloured tails, like fish tails. These look suspiciously to be made of the same material as a wetsuit. I point them out to the boat pilot and he says, "It's the Magical Mermaid Camp." He says this as if

I will, of course, have heard all about the Tobermory Magical Mermaid Camp and he is slightly embarrassed on my behalf at this obvious lapse in memory.

"Magical Mermaid Camp?"

"It's a summer camp. They do stand-up paddleboarding and crafts and shit." He realizes he has said *shit* and turns red.

"How can they do stand-up paddleboarding?"

"Huh?"

"They stand on their tails, or what?"

He laughs uncertainly and squints out across the water like he is very, very concerned about where the boat is going.

Behind us, across the water, even over the noise of the boat engine, I hear the mermaids laughing, each to each.

⁓))⟫⟫⟫∽ ⁓))⟫⟫⟫∽ ⁓))⟫⟫⟫∽

Diving in a pool is all about the learning curve: equipment, safety procedures, checks.

Diving in a Great Lake is something else.

I am tricked out in my Darkfin gloves (there are webs between the fingers to give me more push-pull), along with the standard Self Contained Underwater Breathing Apparatus gear every scuba diver needs: mask, regulator, air tanks, fins, buoyancy control systems. It's heavy. I have additional weights on my legs to keep them from floating once I'm in the water. Petrov is my dive buddy and I am his. We will, once in, hold on to opposite ends of a towline. We will check in at regular intervals. If we are all right we will give the OK sign (not a thumbs-up: that means, "I want to go up"). I've done this in pools, over and over. But…

I haul my carcass out of my chair, weighed down with all my gear and I perch on the edge of the boat, knowing that the next thing is to make myself fall backwards, head-first, into the water, arms wrapped around my gear like Ripley in that terrible third *Aliens* movie, falling backward into the fire...

It's a beautiful day. I haven't mentioned that. It's sunny and the water is insanely turquoise, and the wreck we are here to see isn't from the Spanish Armada, but it's a wreck all the same, a steamer called the *Wetmore,* which strikes me as just the name you'd give a ship if you wanted to doom it to sinking, that or it should be the World Lesbian Flagship, and the *Wetmore* is so close that it almost feels like I will dash my skull open on its enormous boiler when I fall...

"What is taking you so long?" Every sentence sounds like you could append the word *asshole* when it is said in a Russian accent.

"My entrance," I say.

"Entrance?"

"I'm getting into the water."

"No, you are not. You are shifting around like weird."

"It's hard, okay?"

"Just get in the water. It doesn't matter." *Asshole.*

I glare at Petrov through my mask, twist sideways, and flop into the water like a dead carp.

༺༻ ༺༻ ༺༻

It's cold.

There are bubbles streaming behind me. No, that's above me. That way is up.

I am suspended inside the turquoise.

I let myself sink through the water, find a point where I can be suspended. Neutral buoyancy. This is better. No hurry, not right now. Just this. Just waiting for Petrov.

There are no sides in a Great Lake. No painted stripes and numbers on the bottom.

It's a Great Lake.

The steamer is right there, just like in the pictures we've studied. I reach out toward the huge boiler, but don't touch it; it might be sharp. A fish swims out and I almost flinch – almost, but not quite. My Darkfin gloves make my hands look like those of a super-villain. BatGimp.

I wave my BatGimp TM hand in front of my face and want to laugh. It is so quiet down here, so lovely. I can see the others spread out along the wreck, can see a school of pale unidentified fish, the bottom of our tour boat. There's a big splash and I know it's Petrov. I wait for him to settle into the water, then swim for the end of the towline. He gives me the OK sign, a question, and like I'm supposed to I give the OK sign back.

I feel amazing. Tranquil, suspended. Held.

And then I let go of the tow, and spin, turning around and around in the water, making myself dizzy, like I used to do when I was a little kid. Flashes of colour whirl around me. It is the Magical Mermaids. They have left their beaded crafts, they have dived into the water and swum out to greet me, and now they swim around me and laugh.

One of them leaves her sisters and comes to twine around my legs. I can't feel her, of course, but I can see her. She is smiling. She has long, curly red hair, like my sister. She takes hold of one of my ankles and pulls me down, down onto the lake's floor, and holds me there. I can't shake off her grasp. She holds me, trapped. I will die. I look into her laughing face. I am happy.

⚓ ⚓ ⚓

That night, back in Toronto, Petrov tells me off about letting go of the tow. I apologize and promise I'll never do it again, and then he and I get destroyed on vodka.

Something he does after Drink Number Three – a sort of wave of his hand as he orders another round – makes me suddenly realize that Petrov is playing for the team. Or the other team. Not my team, but…you know what I mean.

"Petrov, you're gay," I say with my typical tact. I am flabbergasted. Until this moment, my gaydar had not pinged at all.

"Ya."

His Russian accent has become thicker with each drink, like we are sinking slowly through the strata of his linguistic accomplishments.

"Me, too."

He snorts vodka out of his nose, which makes his eyes stream. This is Petrov laughing. "Ya, no kidding, never would I guess that. You are so feminine, so dainty."

"Shaddap."

"Is why I come here – came here. Russia isn't so good for people like us."

"Here's to people like us."

A vodka or two later:

"What the hell's your first name? You must have a first name, right?"

"Petrov."

"Fuck off."

I laugh and the world slides sideways a bit.

I tell him about the red-haired mermaid, although I don't tell him about my sister.

"Rusalka."

"Rusky what?"

"Rusalka. We have these. Red-haired girls who are murdered, or end their own lives, before their wedding day. They live in water and lure men in and drown them."

Jesus.

"Sounds like the collectively guilty conscience of a violently patriarchal culture to me."

"Sure. Did she say your name?"

"What?"

"Did she say your name? They know your name."

She hadn't said my name, and I am suddenly filled with sadness.

No, not sadness. I am filled with a sense of strangeness on earth. How will I ever feel at home here?

"You will be okay. You have animal helper." He points at his own chest.

"Petrov, what the hell are you talking about?"

"In fairy tales. As long as you have an animal helper, you are okay."

"You are not an animal, Petrov. You are a human being!"

Blank look.

"*The Elephant Man*?"

"I am not an elephant, I am bear!" he yells.

As Don Marquis would say, reader, sometimes I think our friend Petrov is a trifle *too* gay.

∼⁂∼　∼⁂∼　∼⁂∼

When I wake up in the morning and do my daily lower-body check, I find a bruise shaped like a handprint on my ankle. Like the bruise I found long ago on my sister's throat.

∼⁂∼　∼⁂∼　∼⁂∼

Dad can't even speak. We called the police but they aren't doing anything and anyway, I think the chief's son is one of the ones who did it to her

I tried to take Miranda with me when I left the field party but she kept saying, "Get away from me, freak!" and the jocks stood around and laughed

The doctor said there's no damage and she'll be able to have babies later on when she wants to, like that's the fucking main point of life

Mom's useless, of course, just drinking. Then she went off and she's with HIM. She thinks she's so clever and secret, but you'd have to be a fucking idiot not to know about IT

I want to fucking kill those guys

I'm so fucking mad at her for not coming home with me. Why didn't I make her?

—journal entry, age 15

There's a culture in scuba diving, as in any obsession – for these fuckers are obsessed, make no mistake about it. Addicted. Insane. But of all the kinds of divers and diving, the absolute craziest, the most extreme, the ones the other divers look on with a sort of head-shaking grudging respect, are the cave divers.

They say creepy shit like, "The cave tried to keep us today," and you know, if something goes wrong, they can't swim up. They have to go out the way they came in. That's a long way, sometimes.

You've really got to be insane to be one of those.

So I've decided I'll become the world's first legless cave diver.

(Of course I have my legs. They just aren't any use to me at present. So I call myself legless. Reminds me of the old days, the field parties before field parties became a war zone, when we'd drink ourselves – you've got it – legless. It cheers me up.)

(No, I don't Google "disabled cave divers" to find out if some fucker has already beat me to the title. I don't want to know.)

⁀⁙⁀   ⁀⁙⁀   ⁀⁙⁀

Slept on the flight; Gravol and gin. Hallucinatory dream of M – wearing a silver sequined dress – a man picking her up like a bride and the dress grew long, longer, until it swirled behind her like a silver tail. She was laughing or terrified, I couldn't tell which. They disappeared through a doorway, into the water. The house was underwater. I tried to go after them; then remembered I couldn't walk.

My first dream where I can't. Five years.

She Who Will Not Be Named sent another poison text – wants to be maintained in the lifestyle to which she has very much become fucking accustomed...

—journal entry, present day, written on the tarmac in St. John's, Newfoundland, while awaiting deplaning as they call it. As in, for most people and in my own days of yore, walking off the plane and now, for me, consisting of waiting to have my titanium travel chair brought to me, thank you very much.

⁀⁙⁀   ⁀⁙⁀   ⁀⁙⁀

We won't continue with all the filthy things I then go on writing about my ex. (She just couldn't *handle* it, wiping my ass in hospital just wasn't *sexy*. Yes, I think I married a version of my own *mother*, God help me)…

I've left my father at his Toronto condo, under excellent care. I am on my way to Bell Island. I have told my father I am on a business trip – lots of those in my previous life, the life he doesn't know I've left behind, and so it's believable.

I am on my way to Bell Island because Bell Island, Newfoundland, just a short ferry ride from a place that wears its history on its sleeve by being named Portugal Cove, has abandoned mines, lots of them. And they are flooded, and one can dive in them.

⁓⁓⁓⁓⁓ ⁓⁓⁓⁓⁓ ⁓⁓⁓⁓⁓

Background information:

My mother is less relevant to the present story than the others. She still floats in and out of my father's life, I gather; less, now, since his diagnosis. Care-giving never really was her bag. So, less about her then, and more about the others. My beautiful sister, Miranda, recovered physically from the attack and her teenaged wildness turned into the kind of political extremism that is never satisfied. Anti-poverty activism led to vandalism led to jail time led to more extremism; work for various environmental groups, always ending in a dramatic exit; and last I heard she was setting off bombs beneath oil pipelines. Yes, I take that personally.

My father is very ill: pancreatic cancer. Right now we're spending my future, he and I. He doesn't know that. For the first time since I came out at the age of twenty-one, I have a secret from my father. He doesn't know that right around the time I began my diving lessons I quit my job, and ever since have been living – and paying for his full-time care – from my ill-gotten oil-exec investments.

The paraplegia? Yes, people always want to know "what happened." Five years ago, I was in a car accident. When my sister visited me at the hospital – first time I'd seen her in a very long time – she couldn't resist pointing out that a car had almost killed me. The *irony* of it, she said. Because…yes, you get it immediately. Because I am an *oil executive*.

But I am not. Between jobs? What it feels like is this: I am between lives.

Five years.

I wait to wake up.

∼⟨⟨⟩⟩∽   ∼⟨⟨⟩⟩∽   ∼⟨⟨⟩⟩∽

Over sixteen square kilometres with 100 of kms of mine tunnels plunge beneath Bell Island and under the sea floor of Conception Bay where WWII wrecks reside. Abandoned decades ago, these mine passages are now flooded. Exploration of these passages revealed a trove of artefacts and the cultural history of mining. The tunnels contain mining relics, pipes, heavy equipment and remarkable graffiti that tell the story of miners who died during their work on Bell Island…

—National Geographic Society of Canada

∼⟨⟨⟩⟩∽   ∼⟨⟨⟩⟩∽   ∼⟨⟨⟩⟩∽

Reader, when I researched cave dives that I could physically GET to, there weren't very many fucking goddamn options. But it transpires that the ferry from Portugal Cove to Bell Island is accessible, the entrance to the mines is through an accessible museum, and while there is a short flight of stairs leading into the mines proper, the nice lady on the phone assured me that some stout fellas would get me down the stairs, *me love*.

"I'm pretty big," I said. Miranda got the petite-and-pretty genes in the family.

The woman laughed. "So am I, me love. We'll get you down."

⁕⁕⁕

My mother is from Newfoundland. This may surprise you, although I have already referred to my "Newfoundland grand-mother." Many people have a notion of all Newfoundlanders being these fuzzy, happy, friendly people. My mother is a brittle, brilliant, narcissistic asshole. But we did make the occasional foray "home" in the "summers" (a.k.a. the brief two weeks on that awful island when you might actually see the sun). Her parents were originally from Bell Island. Her father was an iron ore miner before they closed the last of the mines in 1966. Typical in the history of Newfoundland, the mines had never been owned and run by Newfoundlanders so when it got expensive to extract the ore, the outside interests simply closed things down.

Just like the offshore oil fields in more recent history.

My grandparents moved to a place called Paradise. It isn't.

I don't remember much about them except a rather exquisite sense that they embarrassed my mother.

But in all those trips home we never visited Bell Island itself.

Here's to you, Ma and Poppy.

⁕⁕⁕

Three words about drinking and diving.

Don't do it.

Nitrogen Narcosis: a reversible alteration in consciousness that occurs while diving at depth.

—Wikipedia, the free encyclopedia

＊＊＊

If you are drunk – or even hung-over – it gets worse. Except – it feels really fucking good. To me, anyway – other people get anxious or have trouble seeing. Me, it makes me feel tranquil and powerful. Master-of-the-universe powerful. It occurs because of breathing gases under elevated pressure. You won't experience it in shallow dives. But as soon as you go deep, there it is. Every single person who dives experiences it. You do not become immune.

Petrov called it Martini's Law. Narcosis, he said, results in impairment more or less equivalent to the feeling you get after drinking one martini for every ten metres you descend below a twenty-metre depth.

> *Martinis, my dear, are dangerous.*
> *Have two at the very most.*
> *Three and you're under the table.*
> *Four and you're under the host.*

http://www.slate.com/articles/life/drink/features/2013/martini_madness_tournament/sweet_16/dorothy_parker_martini_poem_why_the_attribution_is_spurious.html Too bad. The idea of her writing it is so appealing. And wouldn't you like to sit and drink four martinis with Dorothy Parker?

The mines have been explored to a depth of seventy metres.

That's five martinis. Five martinis are too many martinis.

I am staying at a new hotel across from an old Methodist church just up from the harbour. It could be anywhere in the world. There are large portraits of rock stars on the walls, and the restaurant and bar are fully accessible with fully-accessible washrooms; take note, disabled travellers. There is an excellent wine list and martini menu. There is an excellent if very young staff. The rooms are everything a hotel room should be. I celebrate my arrival in St. John's. I drink five martinis. Even while wildly drunk, I am able to empty my urostomy bag without spilling a drop.

Another legless dream. Driving the car with Dad. The accident. Him passing out suddenly in the passenger seat, just like it happened and I'm yelling DAD DAD but this time, I remember that I can't use my legs any more. What the hell am I doing driving? And I'm drunk, too? We drive into a wall, but it's a wall of water. Green as poison.

—journal entry, present day

Thought I was drunk enough to avoid dreams.

I meet up with Petrov at the ferry terminal in Portugal Cove. I am late, because the accessible taxi I booked weeks ago to get me from St. John's to the ferry terminal failed to materialize. I tore the ear off the dispatcher and got myself a ride, but not fast enough to prevent me from being the last one to the ferry.

Petrov is standing on the wharf. He's been here for a week already, now. Told me he's always wanted to check out the mines; a buddy of his was part of the Geographic Society's initial explorations and studies in decompression sickness. I suspect he feels sorry for me. But no. One thing I've learned is, divers all just want the dive. If it takes hauling a dead carp around, so be it.

He is looking for me, and looking worried. It's almost heartwarming. I've never seen Petrov look worried before; the man's got a face like a cliff wall.

I am hungover. I should call the dive. There's no shame in calling the dive.

You must abort if something is wrong. That moment when you have almost reached the treasure – but you know you have to abort – and do? That is what separates the ones who come back from the ones who do not. (Asshole.)
—Petrov

I do not call the dive.

Everything takes time when you use a wheelchair. The door to the taxi opens slowly. The ramp lowers slowly. I don't wheel down the ramp fucking slowly, however. I shoot out like a round from an AK-47, yelling at the taxi driver that his company is paying him not me, by God, and if he doesn't like it...

I hurtle down the steeply sloped road to the wharf and, as filled with rage as I am, I almost hope the driver doesn't hear the filthy rest of what I say.

The ferry operators are literally beginning to raise the on-ramp.

"Lower that ramp, you sons of bitches!"

They lower the ramp.

Petrov does not offer to push me onto the ferry and I am glad. Personally – not speaking for all and sundry in a chair, just for myself here, although I'd be surprised if anybody would disagree – I hate it when people manhandle my chair without asking. This happens more than you would expect.

The ferry lurches toward the red, red island rising out of the slate-coloured waters of Conception Bay.

It's humiliating being carried down the stairs, and some brawny local whacks my titanium chair off the side of the huge, corrugated metal tube that leads us to the mines, a terrible clatter. It takes three men to haul me down. Petrov takes my feet. I am glad – he knows I can't feel down there, will be careful.

It's a relief to settle back into my chair.

The dive master is trying her best not to be uncomfortable with the reality of me. "We've explored the mines down to a depth of seventy metres," she says. "But there's lots more to explore! The mine itself is 1800 feet deep. It's a maze of tunnels." She's my generation and freely mixes metric and imperial. We've already had an extensive overview of diving in the mines, a safety protocol review, and been read the riot act about straying from the yellow lines that mark explored territory. We aren't to stir up the fine dust that coats the mine face ("face" is what the miners called the floor); it will obscure our vision and fuck with our equipment.

This mine closed in 1949, same year Newfoundland, broken by World War II, gave up nationhood and joined Canada. After that, the mines flooded with fresh water. The ocean presses above us, above this blood-red rock.

It's dark down here. The dive leader turns off her light and encourages us to do the same. Dark. Totally, completely dark. The early miners used candles on their hats, for Christ's sake. Candles, or seal-oil lamps. Boys worked down here. Ponies.

We all have three lights on us – one to use, and two back-ups.

We all know the rule of thirds – a third of our air to get to our destination, a third to get back. Because the final third is for if anything goes wrong.

⚓ ⚓ ⚓

The water is very cold, colder than Tobermory. Graveyard cold.

Over a hundred miners died here over the years. Explosions, runaway carts. And one diver, on the very first cave dive expedition back in 2007. Embolism.

It's true. You can feel them.

We swim by an overturned mining cart. See an ancient headlamp on the ground. Vast pumps that used to keep this place dry. We are not to touch anything. Nothing is labelled. I am glad. Petrov turns to me from his end of the tow line and gives me the OK sign, and I OK him back. We are moving slowly. The other divers disappear around a corner. The darkness sweeps around us, excepting the small, warm, wavering obloids of our headlamps.

The miners painted numbers on the walls to tell them what level they were on, for they feared getting lost. Me, I fear that I won't.

38. Red columns, red dust. Edges of pillars, broken metal that can tear into our suits. It's cold.

39. I am not feeling it, not yet – that tranquillity, that power.

40. A glimpse of the other divers up ahead, swimming down a long, tilting slope.

Petrov checks in with me. He waves – *Isn't this amazing?* – and I nod. It *is* amazing. It is so cold. I'm feeling narked, I know it, but…it feels so good.

And that's when I see it out of the corner of my eye, behind us. A trailing russet mane, like kelp, like hair. A pale oval beneath it.

We are catching up to the others. They turn a corner. Petrov turns after them.

I let go of the tow rope. The thing turns its face toward me.

She is and is not my sister. My sister as she was that morning when I found her drowned under grass, half-naked and cold as a fish in a ditch, my beautiful nasty sister, muddy and bloodied. Like she'd gone over the top in the wars, and hadn't she? One fucker left his handprint in bruises on her neck. Every one of them left his print on her.

The mermaid with the red hair; did my sister have these long, needle teeth? She has traded her pink neoprene tail for one silver and poisonous as mercury.

She swims away from me, away from the others. I follow. I've left the trail of yellow nylon rope crumbs.

Where is she? I almost panic. But after a few more turns, into darkness – utter darkness – I hear her.

She sings.

You can't sing under water.

I check my air. I am near half into it. I should, according to every rule, turn back.

I am pretty sure I want to come back. But not absolutely positive.

And there's the singing.

Petrov will be beside himself. I am a very bad person for letting go of that tow rope. He deserves a better dive buddy. He always says: *You must be willing to turn around, leave the feelings behind. You can go back to them later. The feelings will wait for you.* (Asshole.)

If you don't chase fear you will spend the rest of your life running from it.

Yeah. That's what I'm afraid of.

I have heard the mermaids singing...

She whispers it then. My name.

⚬⚬⚬

What did she do to me?

Mermaids don't *do* anything.

This is the treasure, they say. This is what you long for, long for with an ache that fills your body like water.

They make you *feel*.

And if that doesn't frighten you, reader, then you are not aware, not awake.

Or you don't have feelings like I have feelings.
And that, reader, I find hard to believe.

I have seen them riding seaward on the waves
Combing the white hair of the waves blown back
When the wind blows the water white and black.
We have lingered in the chambers of the sea
By sea-girls wreathed with seaweed red and brown
Till human voices wake us, and we drown.
"The Love Song of J. Alfred Prufrock" —T.S. Eliot

DAUGHTER CATCHER

URSULA PFLUG

The witch Siena lived at the bottom of the gardens on Vine Street where there were woods, mostly cedar and willow for it was damp. Nature's natural cycle seemed altered there, for the ground was in places knee-deep in broken sticks and littered with the arms of dead trees. It was March, and Siena piled sticks and some old, half-rotten clothes into a big heap; the village teenagers might come one day to have a bonfire. No one else came down much, so that the few paths were often overgrown, too brambly to struggle through, and decorated with takeout containers, beer bottles both whole and dangerously broken, and Styrofoam, both in cup and slab and pellet form.

The streets and driveways of the village were swept clean often, the lawns sprayed and weeded and raked and mowed, but no one cleaned up the ownerless woods, unless the witch did it. Siena didn't actually hear what people said about her, but she could guess: they thought she was stupid enough to think if she cleaned up after them they might give her daughter back. Noelle wasn't dead, Sienna was sure of that. She'd have felt it if the girl was dead, just as she'd have felt it if her men had died. But her entire family was still alive, Siena knew it for a fact. She just didn't have them near her anymore, the way they were supposed to be.

Early spring runoff filled the lowland gully beyond the fallen trees and piles of sticks. While she gathered bottles, disconcerted as ever by how many there were that once contained hard liquor of all sorts, Siena talked to herself. When had she begun? She knew it didn't help her reputation much, that she'd spent too much time alone in the raggedy woods. She rarely entered the village proper anymore except to fill recycling bins before anyone else was up, as she was doing now. It was very early on Thursday morning, and Siena was fulfilling her weekly ritual of carrying sacks of pop cans and bottles up the disused lane from the woods to the street. Surreptitiously, she tipped the sacks into the big, blue plastic boxes, otherwise woefully empty. Why, Siena often wondered, was it better to dump garbage off the bridge at night than to sort it into bins? Why was that so hard? But the villagers couldn't, wouldn't, didn't.

Siena knew that even before dawn on Sundays the towns-folk made an opposite trek to her own: they went out, also with sacks, but they went to the bridge and tossed in their old pillows, used condoms, empty pill bottles, pornography, vomit-stained sleeping bags, single shoes and sometimes even used toilet paper. They treated the gully beneath the bridge as an impromptu landfill in the middle of town. Yellow, green, orange and clear garbage bags hurled on top of one another made such a nice sound: a kind of sliding squishing ker-thunk. The witch, they seemed to think, would deal with it. She always had.

And the morning after their midnight purges, Siena thought bitterly, they could go to church and talk about how disgusting she was: now so solitary, and untrustworthy because of it, and because she wove things she found out of old string she gathered; she knitted spiderwebs out of the dirty old string, and hung them from the trees. They were frightening, like things spiders on LSD might have made, and there were more each year. Siena made them painstak-ingly; each intricate piece of webbing took at least a month to make. It was especially because of the spiderwebs, Siena thought, that they could face the day pretending they were clean nice decent people. But she couldn't have stopped making them even if she'd tried. They were a compulsion, like her paranoid and vengeful thoughts: she was sure the villagers looked the other way when their boys bent to reach for stones, even though they knew not one would ever make its mark; Siena knew how to deflect stones even before they flew.

Aside from taciturn little boys, the only other person the witch saw early on Thursdays was a woman who combed the streets looking for things others had thrown away that she might drag home to sell at her weekend yard sales. "Looks like rain," the woman said this morning.

"Yes. Have much luck today?" Siena asked.

"Some old shirts, and two nice lamp stands." She gestured at the lamps, missing shades. Siena had hailed from the city once, and knew the lamps would sell for a hundred dollars each at a trendy retro boutique. But how would the woman get to the city? And how much would the store owner give her for the lamps? And so, she just smiled and nodded, and only said, "The lamps are nice." They'd already spoken more than they ever had. Speaking to a real person was actually quite hard.

"Do you want to buy them?" the woman asked, startling Siena out of her reverie.

"No."

"I guessed not," the woman laughed.

Was there a touch of derision in her laugh? Siena couldn't be sure. "Why's that?" she asked, a little belligerently.

"They say you sleep under a heap of odds and ends, other people's garbage and sticks."

It seemed hard to believe she'd survived winter doing that, but maybe she'd been so damaged by trauma Siena didn't even know where she slept anymore. The ragpicker looked at her, and Siena waited for the verbal spasm of hatred she knew must be coming, either from herself or from the woman. But they just looked at each other, and finally Siena pointed at the lamps and said, "You'll get twenty dollars for them when the cottagers come to open up."

The woman looked immensely pleased. Siena looked at the black, hooded sweatshirt draped over her arm. "My son would've liked that," she said, suddenly not wanting to end the conversation, challenging as it was. She thought it might be the first one she'd had in years.

The woman stared. "You used to have a family once, didn't you?" she asked.

"Yes," Siena said.

"Your daughter was very bad. She sold drugs at the high school and was killed by the bikers who supplied her when she didn't pay. They cut up her body and distributed it in many places, so they could never be caught."

Siena figured then the woman had been so poor for so long it had driven her crazy, and forgave her this new assault. Besides, Noelle had been loud and unkempt and never did anything anyone asked, laughing at them instead, or crying, but that had been the extent of it. "That was Paul Hubert," she said. "I heard that story too. It wasn't Noelle, not at all. And even with Paul, why didn't someone help him, teach him to love himself enough he wouldn't have to turn to drugs?"

This last line she knew came out of the witch wisdom her own mother had taught her. She hadn't said anything like that in years, was surprised at herself. After Noelle's disappearance, what had any of it mattered? She couldn't believe in it anymore. If her magic hadn't been able to protect Noelle, it was worse than useless.

The woman looked startled. "They said you couldn't even really talk anymore."

"I couldn't. But I had to defend Noelle. Usually I don't hear the rumours. No one says them to my face."

"That was so long ago," the woman said, memory dawning like daybreak on her creased face. But she didn't continue, and Siena didn't know whether she was referring to Noelle, or to Paul Hubert, or to her own demise. "We're not any of us as young as we used to be," she continued, peering into Siena's face. She looked familiar, as if they'd once sat on committees together. They'd baked for the same fundraisers, surely. "Sally," the woman said, stretching out her hand. "Sally Fish."

Ah, the minister's wife. What had happened to her? Siena must've heard, and then forgotten, just as Sally had mistaken Noelle's story for Paul Hubert's. Even in a village, memory was fickle. And what about Siena herself? Did she really sleep under sticks? The village had watched her lose everything, and grow prematurely old because of it. Whatever her life had become, it sure wasn't what she'd planned. Siena shook Sally's hand. "Siena Straw."

"I know who you are, Siena. You had the most beautiful gardens, flowers and vegetables both. You were a really good herbalist and you always looked elegant."

"I was just born with skinny genes, is all. And I was good at putting together outfits from thrift stores. If I had money for new clothes I gave it to the kids."

"It was always so important to them," Sally said, "the right kind of sneakers and jeans at school."

"Yes."

They parted, and the next Thursday Sally wasn't out, nor the next. Siena went back to piling sticks and talking to herself. "The paths through the cedars all grown over with brambles and garbage. The slabs of Styrofoam and piles of old shoes replicating each night so that in the morning there were even more. Why always this bleak, black badness, inconsolable beyond hope at the core, at the bottom, collecting at the fallen logs. The beads of dirty Styrofoam, disintegrating. They make me feel so ashamed." Siena thought she might die under the weight of it. But she couldn't; what if her daughter came back and her mother wasn't there? Siena knew at one time or another she'd felt a little of what Noelle might've felt when she'd run through town shouting obscenities at the minister and the principal and the constable. Perhaps what Siena could not speak, the girl had. And so, the stones they threw at Noelle had in their way been meant for her.

"Maybe they'll give Noelle back if I take their garbage as well as my own. Heaping it into a higher and higher mound each night after spending hours and hours and hours collecting it. And then burrowing beneath it to sleep, in spite of it smelling rather badly. There, I've just admitted it, even to myself. I'm looking for my daughter's body," Siena muttered, piling sticks. She'd misplaced it somewhere, she knew. "My daughter isn't dead, only mad or missing. Maybe she's not out here at all. I bet they've got her in a basement somewhere."

The week after that the geese were flying overhead in pairs, looking for nesting spots, just as Siena and her husband had come here from the city, looking for a quiet pretty place to raise their brood. The geese flew over her piles and honked derisively, and Siena built herself an actual lean-to out of deadfall and Styrofoam instead of burrowing under her shame pile that night, and tried not to talk to herself so much. Her conversation with Sally had been so short, and now weeks old, but still it had reminded her of the difference. Her husband had often made fun of her constant mumbling. She'd done it even then, when he was still around. But that too had been different. Mumbling to a person didn't get you called crazy; it was just a little rude.

She unwound string from a tangle of sticks and sat down on a pile of other sticks and began to make a spiderweb, part God's eye, part dream catcher. It was obsessive, but she couldn't help herself; when Siena found string, she had to make something out of it. Something more or less circular to hang in a tree. Siena told herself she was making magic; it was a witchy thing, not a dream catcher but a daughter catcher. Still, the objects never seemed beautiful and powerful as she'd intended when she was done but rather sad and lonely as she felt, and possibly mad. And yet consciousness glimmered on, and Siena survived the spring's windiest gale in her makeshift lean-to. Her shelter looked a little like an igloo from a distance, the water-rounded, white slabs piled into circular walls. The Styrofoam had good insulation value.

Two geese flew overhead several times each day, and at last Siena broke down and cried, missing her husband so badly she couldn't give the pain a name. Geese mated for life, as she'd always felt she and her husband would. As the years passed, and Siena outgrew her youthful restlessness, the boredom that came after the first thrill of marriage was replaced each year by joy at discovering its yet undiscovered riches: for each year there were more. She should've gone with him. Then they could've still had a kind of happiness, if not the ridiculous happiness they'd had before. Now she was alone without any of them, cleaning up after people who scorned her.

But he'd left, and their son had gone with him, although the young man was old enough to go out on his own now, seek a wife and a fortune. But he and the old man got along well; any wife the lad found would have to make herself part of their life more than they'd ever make themselves part of hers. She could do the books and mind the clutter: they had never been high on organizational skills, Siena's men hadn't. They liked the same things: military history and beer. They worked together now, she'd heard back when she still spoke to people, in some faraway town, setting up a shop selling memorabilia of oh, so many wars. But between them, they knew most of their facts, would be able to back up each piece of begged or borrowed or stolen or scavenged bit of merchandise with a story, quite likely to be true. Siena missed them desperately. Twice in the woods she had found old, old guns, and saved them for her men, should they ever pass back through. But why would they?

And so she talked to herself and performed her forest cleaning tasks, even though there was always more to do; it was an obscenely endless job. Sometimes she realized she'd thought she was talking to her daughter, and then Siena would start to cry again. She and Noelle had been as close as the old man and the young man, in their way. They'd liked the same things: poetry and painting and witching. It got you every time, that witching. They should've chosen different professions. A witch would always have stones thrown at her, at one time or another in her life, it was true. Her own mother, a witch also, had told Siena that, trying to herd her to a gentler occupation. But for Siena, the witching was the gentlest task she knew, and the most necessary. And so she'd turned her back on her own mother's words, her own mother's tears, sure she and her daughter could change things together; change the world's view of what a witch was. She longed for the days her mother had told her about: the days when witches were well paid and cared for with kindness and invited to good parties, and not forgotten but necessary and ostracized in the ragged woods at the bottom of the gardens. Her mother had been right, of course, except that Siena herself had avoided the stoning her entire life; and she'd inured herself against the gossip. It was her daughter who hadn't found the strength of will to turn the stones back in mid-air or, as Siena herself was able to do, before they even flew. She'd been too young, the girl had, and too full of fun and too full of love; that had bothered people.

Siena herself had always been a quiet unassuming sort and so people had largely left her alone even though they knew what she was. And if anyone ever pointed a finger right at her and began to speak of what was wrong with her witchery, how ungodly it was, she knew how to deflect them with a joke, or flattery, or a spoonful of hope for their poor, little broken-hearted souls – and so they put down their pebbles and unkind words. But all that had been before they'd stoned her daughter, and Noelle had gone mad or missing or maybe both, and the mildly, as most everyone's are, broken hearts of her men had broken further, and they'd left. They'd asked Siena to go with them, but she hadn't.

If she moved and her daughter returned to find her, Siena had to be there, didn't she?

She knitted, wondering as always why her burrowing and her knitting didn't coerce the villagers to give her daughter back. It was witchy magic, after all. It was supposed to work. Her mother had taught her that, taught her how clear intent poured into the creation of an object would amplify its power to heal.

But they hadn't worked, not one of them, and there were thirty or forty spiderwebs now, strung here and there in the woods. No wonder no one came down here much anymore, not even the dog walkers. Siena's daughter catchers were disturbing, never mind unsuccessful. Perhaps she'd take them all down. And so, she wandered the woods with a new purpose, ostensibly to find and detach and burn all her creepy hanging things. She found and detached and bagged six, and where she'd thought she'd hung the seventh, she instead found a tall boy with wild red hair, stuffing it into his pocket.

"Why do you want that?" Siena asked.

"Want what?" he asked, his hand covering the bulge in his pocket.

"My spiderwebs. I made them."

"Oh!" he said. "We thought Noelle made them. They bring luck in love."

"How could Noelle make them if she's gone?"

"Maybe she's a ghost," the young man offered. How old was he? Had he known Noelle, or did they just talk about her, like everyone else? How old would Noelle be now, if she were here?

Siena began to stare and stutter, as if to prove everything he'd heard about her was true.

"You look cold," he said. "Come to the fire for tea?"

"Okay," Siena said, surprised. And she did. There were four or five of them, sitting on logs and stumps and one broken chair arranged around one of her stick piles, which they'd set alight. They made tea and gave her some., and when they poured a little rum in their own and asked her if she wanted any she didn't refuse.

"Just don't break the bottles, okay? I cut my fingers when I clean up down here."

"I wouldn't," the boy said. "What's your name?"

"Siena. You?"

"Peter."

"Hello, Peter. Why aren't you afraid of me?"

"Because you're Noelle's mother."

"Maybe. But I'm evil. And she must've been evil too, or they wouldn't have stoned her." It was only saying it aloud that made Siena realize some small part of her believed it to be true.

"You're not evil, you just went crazy because you lost Noelle. That would happen to anyone. But don't stop making those weird string things. They're magic. They're infallible."

"Who do you love?" Siena asked.

"I don't like anyone in that way, and no one likes me. Although Liz has been my best friend since kindergarten, so I'm not exactly alone either."

One of the girls in the circle smiled at Siena. She had black braids and wore a little skirt that in better light Siena would've known wasn't made of leaves, and striped knee socks and sneakers. "But they've worked for lots of us," the girl said.

Siena smiled to herself, and fell asleep, the fire and the rum so warm. When she woke, the moon had risen and the youngsters had gone home to their families. Siena walked back to her igloo, too, but on the way she saw a glimmer of water beneath a heap of deadfall. She investigated further, stepping in it, and was shocked; the icy water came almost to her hips. Siena would've fallen as if she'd stepped off of the creek bank, which was precisely what she'd done, except the mounds of deadfall and garbage prevented it.

She hauled herself out before her muscles could seize up from the cold.

Had there always been a creek here? It was as if she'd forgotten it even existed, but how could that be so? It was so full of garbage it was obliterated from sight, but that didn't account for its absence from her mind.

Siena saw another daughter catcher then, hanging just out of reach as if blown by the wind. She didn't care what the young people said, to Siena it radiated evil. Her thoughts, after all, were full of malice. When she made them, some tiny secret part of her wished terrible things upon the townsfolk because of what had happened to Noelle. But by the old laws of mirrors, Siena knew this was a dangerous thing to do, that she brought judgement upon herself when she wove malice into her magic. People would talk about her even more than before, and she'd grow even more bitter and solitary because of it, and weave even more hate into her webs, and the villagers, sensing her hate, would call her an evil witch, and so on, in an unending circle of fear and hate.

Still, she hiked her skirt and shinnied up the tree and pulled it down. There was love in the webs too, the yearning she felt for Noelle, or they wouldn't work to find the kids the love they so craved. She took it home to her stick and Styrofoam shelter. Peter was right, she had gone mad. The villagers were right about her. How could she not have seen it? Still, the shelter was a step up from the stick piles she used to burrow beneath. When had she built it? After she'd talked to Sally, she thought. And after she realized birds took better care of themselves than she did.

In the morning she hoped the youngsters would invite her for tea again, but they would be in school. The same two geese flew overhead; they took a long time to make

their decision about where to build their nest, or else they
just wanted to drag out their weeks of dinners out and movies
and sex, before the long work of raising a family began. Seeing
them, Siena wished again that her men hadn't left. She
wished her husband had stayed behind and helped her dig for
her daughter's body.

She wished he'd believed, as she'd believed, that they
could still find Noelle, that their love could find a way. Siena
allowed herself a little resentment then, toward her missing
husband. There was a streak of weakness in him, she'd always
secretly felt, an inability to hold on, hold out. If he'd stood
beside her it would've been easier to say, "You shouldn't have
stoned Noelle. She was just letting her hair down, letting off
a little steam. Things would've felt better for you if you'd done
it a little more yourselves." She could've spoken before it even
happened, but when she already felt it coming, said something like, "Noelle's a little frisky, it's true, but great care must
be taken of the free-spirited; they teach us all that joy is still
possible. To judge them is to judge ourselves. We'd do better
to imitate than to decry."

But she hadn't. Or if she had, she hadn't done it enough.
Or if she'd done it enough, it hadn't made enough of a difference. They'd still stoned Noelle. She'd still gone mad or
missing or both.

Siena went to investigate the missing creek, had a memory then, of a time when the creek had been beautiful. One
spring it had flooded its banks so that when she and her
daughter and her son, maybe nine and eleven then, had sat
on the swing at the edge, their feet dangling in the risen water.
The current was fierce that spring, and they had slipped into
the water and been pulled with huge force around two bends
until the place where several fallen trees slowed the stream.

Screaming and laughing, the three of them, laughing because of the speed of the current, screaming because the water was still icy with melt-off. Everything so green. Each spring it felt like that, as if a winter of starvation was being assuaged. Siena remembered how that day had been so much better than the expensive asphalt-paved fair. A better thrill, and free. She and her children had looked into one another's eyes, wide with excitement, barely believing anything could be so wonderful. And then done it again.

How could she have forgotten the creek? It must have been the trauma.

But it seemed not only she but everyone in the village had forgotten.

Siena's heart could not break any more than it had already broken; it had calcified, scarred over. The truth was, she no longer had the strength or hope even to leave and try and find the men. But what was there to stay for? She'd never find Noelle. Noelle was mad or missing or both.

"They don't have her in a basement," the girl with black braids said. She was sitting beside the dead fire.

Siena stared at her.

"I heard you say they did one time," Peter's friend said. "You were walking, talking, didn't notice I was here."

"Just like now. So how do you know?"

"It's a feeling mostly, not that that's much help, I'm sure. But it's pretty strong. I'm Liz, by the way." Siena stared at Liz. Was she a witch? Witches were always taught to pay great attention to their intuition. "Do you have another?" Liz asked.

"What?"

"Spiderweb. The others took the others, and there weren't any left that I could find."

"Is that why you're not in school? You came down here looking for a spiderweb?"

The girl nodded.

"What's his name?" Siena asked.

"I've known him since kindergarten, but he acts like my brother. I can't get him to see me as potential girlfriend material. Noelle's spiderwebs are a charm. She's the patron saint of love."

"But I make them, not Noelle."

"You make them for her," Liz said. "So she'll feel your love and come back. So in that way they're still hers. And I bet she makes them work for us, from wherever she is."

"Did you know Noelle?" Siena asked.

"We all knew her," Liz said. "We used to come down here and party. She was a little older. It was a few years ago, back when you still lived in the..." the girl's voice trailed off, as if she were embarrassed for Siena.

"House?"

"Yes," Liz said.

"Who lives in my house now?" Siena asked.

"It's empty. No one will buy it or rent it."

"Maybe if I stop hating them they'll give her back. I just can't figure it."

"What did your mother say?" Liz asked.

"Don't beat yourself up so much." Siena laughed at the memory. She'd always been hard on herself, and her mother had always told her to love herself. But then her mother had died, and Noelle had disappeared, and then the men had left. Since then Siena had been hard on herself for pretty well every minute of every day.

"Here. I have one in my pocket. If I give it to you will you go back to class?"

"Yes." The girl held her hand out for Siena's gift.

"Did you know there's a creek under all that garbage?" Siena asked as Liz got up to go.

"Really? They're connected, the missing creek, missing Noelle. I'll get the others and we'll clean it."

"Thanks," Siena said.

But what did she mean? Thanks for helping clean the creek or thanks for believing Noelle was still alive?

Liz was as good as her word. Over the ensuing weeks, the teenagers came and built igloos out of Styrofoam they could stay in when their parents kicked them out for being lippy. They made stick piles and burned them. They carted bags and bags of bottles to the recycling bins on Thursday mornings until every blue box in the village was full. Even Sally Fish came to help; occasionally she found an object she could sell at her weekend sale.

"It was time to clean the place up," Sally said. "I had to help, after what they did to Noelle."

So, she'd heard the truth at last. Siena was glad, but she didn't make a big deal out of it. After weeks of burning and recycling and land-filling garbage, there was a creek. It was still a little murky, so they planted cattails along the edges. By early fall it ran crystal clear, and there were little brown trout in it, and geese flying in screaming V's overhead. At first, they weren't very good at it, their V's misshapen; it reminded Siena of when her son had first learned to drive. She missed him terribly and started to cry all over again, even though the creek cleanup had distracted her all summer, the youngsters and their bonfires and tea had kept her warm. So many of them had found love, and all, they insisted, although Siena still wasn't sure, because of her magic spiderwebs. They brought glue guns and glued the walls of her hut together, so it would be less drafty in the coming winter. Peter brought a little window to set into the side.

But Siena cried, missing her husband. She'd always called him her husband even though they'd never married in a church, but the witch figured God wouldn't have noticed the difference; what he'd have noticed instead, if he'd been looking or cared, which was doubtful, was how she'd poured everything into her family: scrubbing and cleaning and working and growing vegetables and cooking and canning and washing and hanging clothes until she was so exhausted she couldn't even remember what her own dreams had been for herself, or if she'd ever even had any. She hadn't minded; she'd loved them all so much; it had been worth it. And while the family was on the poor side and complained a lot because of it, they were largely happier and more content than they knew. Isn't it always so? Although there were days Siena had noticed how lucky they were, that a tiny bit of heaven had come unglued from the sky to land at their feet, astonishing them, allowing them to live in it. It was like a secret, and she'd taken the best care of it she knew how. Remembering her lost happiness, Siena began to shake her head then, and muttered, "I tried not to talk about it too much, lest someone notice and try and take it away. They were always doing that, weren't they?" She dug, first haphazardly and then with more frenzy, in her pockets where she thought she'd once put away a little string.

But a hand touched her shoulder then, making her turn and take a cup of tea. It was Liz. "Maybe they'll return one day, as geese. Remember that story? They'll land and shed their feathers and put on clothes," and again Siena wondered whether Liz might be a witch, whether one could be born into it, and not just trained by one's own mother.

"Why would they do that?" Siena asked.

"Well, if we found Noelle they'd have no reason to stay away," Liz said, and with a sudden abstracted look on her face got up and wandered away.

"I know you won't make them anymore, but you brought so much love into the world making spiderwebs for her and giving them away," Peter said. "Maybe Noelle's supposed to just be the patron saint of love."

"You can't say that to a mother," Sally Fish said, and again Siena wondered what had happened to the minister's wife. One day she'd have to ask.

"Come here!" Liz called. "I found the most amazing feet!" Peter got up, and when he and Siena got to the creek where Liz was pointing he put his arm around the girl and she smiled, a cat in pyjamas, suddenly.

There were two dead trees lying across the creek, too big and heavy to move. But beneath them in the now sparkling clear water, there were two elegant feet. And the toes, it was undeniable, were wiggling not just with the current but with life. Siena stepped into the shallows at the edge and leaned over to peer under the tree. A young woman was lying on the soft sand at the bottom of the creek, her arms folded across her chest, a fraying daughter catcher held over her heart. Her eyes were closed. Sienna reached in and stroked Noelle's feet.

"How do we get her out?" Siena asked the gathered teenagers. "So she can be loved too and not just always create it in other's people's lives?"

"By teaching her to love herself, like you did for us," Liz said.

"I didn't know that's what I did," Siena said.

AS NEVER BIRD
SANG BEFORE

SEAN MORELAND

For my mother, Carol Caskey Moreland (1948-2018),
giver of life and saver of stories

I

The sirens outside like cries of a prehistoric predatory bird. Winter tensed, afraid they were coming here, for her mother, but the sirens soon passed, a hush hanging in their wake.

They had been closely side-by-side for countless hours now. Winter in the chair, leaning in a low brood, her mother in the bed, pressed there by pain, both held in a puddle of sickly yellow light, its edges draining into the dark around them. The chair wedged in against the bed, like there'd been a collision.

The chair was sprung-backed and badly seat-worn. Her mother's card-table favourite, it sagged now with the weight of so many meals, games, conversations. Winter's left arm squeezed knees to chest, her right rested on the bed, touching the nubby blanket over her mother's shoulder.

The bed sagged too, the middle mattress more concave than it had a right to be, given how little weight her mother's withered body placed on it. Her mother's head, with its cloud of once-dark hair, her shoulders with their too-protruding bones, were propped on a heap of pillows, folded below her like broken wings. Her thin legs were raised, feet pillowed too, the blanket-tent they shaped moving in little waves as the toes below curled and uncurled rhythmically, a reflex-ritual against pain.

Finally, the bulb of the bedside lamp went out with a sizzle, pool of light draining instantly. Winter blinked rapidly, bringing forth phairies. Frenetic and incandescent, they fluttered around the room in a bright fit before flickering out. Then she and her mother were left, side-by-side, in a darkness that stood and stretched, languid as a cat. As it spread, Winter felt a little bird take shelter in her palm. Warm, trembling, her mother's papery hand curled in hers.

Winter's heart quickened with her mother's shallow breaths.

Winter knew she should go, look for a replacement bulb, but she stayed, cupping the brittle bird now between both her own hands. Her hands were long-fingered, strong, and helpless. Winter spoke, breath breaking into words before she knew what they were.

"When you are gone, what will I do? How can I still be *me*?" came the question. She felt a vague shame that this was what she had to say, what she needed so badly to know.

"You are so much stronger than you know. No matter what happens, you will always be you, my beautiful. My wonderful daughter," her mother whispered back. It was quiet then, so close to silence that the sound of their breath was painful, as was the hiss of precious time slipping unstoppably away.

Winter blinked phairies back into being, watched them line up along the felt outline of her mother's hand in hers, turning it into electric origami. Then nervous feet shuffled up outside the door. The shuffling gathered itself into an interrogative knock.

"Everything all right?" Aunt Ellis's muffled question dangled in mid-air, a wire hanger in an empty closet, waiting to be clothed. Unanswered, she offered, "The doctor will be back any minute." The shuffling receded.

The darkness yawned impatiently, bored by their breathing.

Winter's mother gasped, shaped the pained sound into words; "May God's bright wings lift you through this world, my beautiful Winter." Winter watched electric origami crumble, phairies dancing off, drawn instead to those laborious exhales.

Those were Winter's mother's last words. Winter laced them into her heart and lungs, wrote them in luminescent paint inside her skull, taught them to the phairies so they could flash them back to her when summoned by finger or thumb. Her mother's breath continued for two hours, the warmth of her hand in Winter's for an hour after that. For Winter, that time was a trackless fraction of infinity, but the hours counted, hungrily.

Silence hung heavy. Even cupped in Winter's palms, her mother's hand grew cool, began to leech her heat. Winter sat with the dark, with the feasting hours and with her mother's sagging shell. Winter sat with the phairies, watched them limn her mother's still form with dancing light.

Muffled voices, the shuffle of many feet, and "Winter? The doctor is here," called Aunt Ellis.

Ellis changed the dead bulb, driving out darkness and phairies alike. The doctor's glasses flashed in the awful whitish light, his face slid into a too-familiar mask of clinical sympathy. He inspected and prodded while Ellis led Winter from the room. Documents were shuffled and signed while the doctor and Ellis took turns showering Winter with words as if they could wash her loss away.

It wasn't until Aunt Ellis said, "Your father will be here soon" that Winter finally began to weep. Her eyes screwed tight, hot tears streaking her cheeks. She knuckled her burning eyes, bringing the phairies in a luminous flood, and she held tight to their flashing with every shred of herself.

Winter's father came a little later, two large, empty suitcases and a new chill coming with him. After pressing Winter in a painful hug, he told her to pack her clothes. Winter lay on her bed, brokenly imagining the antiseptic place awaiting her mother's body, the suffocating place awaiting herself. She pressed her fists against her eyes. There was a transient flicker, but with her father there, the phairies didn't want to come, and Winter didn't blame them.

"Stop it, Will – you'll hurt yourself." Winter's eyes snapped open as her father seized her shoulders, a failed attempt at gentleness, and pulled her to a sitting position.

She wanted to scream, but her voice was elsewhere, her mouth a silent, stale cavity.

"We have to pack your things, Will. I'll help you."

He opened Winter's closet, scanned the cluster of dresses, blouses, sweaters hanging there.

"The dresses stay here, Will. You know how Shannon and I feel about all that."

Her father wouldn't stuff her dresses, her costume jewels, her favourite shoes into plastic bags that day, to take to Goodwill. Not on the same day they stuffed her mother's body into a plastic bag, with Winter watching, tear-streaked. No, he'd come back three days later, after the funeral. He wanted to be gentle with his prodigal son.

II

On the drive to her father's, the city sneering by, Winter felt the hours watching. She rubbed her eyes, dusting the dashboard and her father's sombre profile with the faintest spray of phairie-light.

"Will—" He reached over with his right hand, left angled on the wheel, and tried to pull her hands from her face, "stop that, you're only going to–" Winter snatched her hand away violently. Startled, her father jerked the wheel and the car pitched with a squeal.

Winter didn't need to speak. Her eyes screamed louder than her voice could have, warning him back. Blinking down a hurt that with him always neighboured on rage, her father cleared his throat, promised himself patience. He tried for a few more minutes to talk to Winter during the drive, but found her silence unassailable. He felt tears prickling behind his eyes, but he kept them in, used them instead to water his resolve. He knew it wouldn't be easy, but he would finally have his son back. That was what mattered.

"Will, I love you more than anything in the world. I think you know that. You'll always be my son, no matter what."

His love was a hunting knife, his daughter a shot-crippled deer.

Winter had long known this, though, and she became an empty forest, her face a fall of unbroken snow. Her father's sidelong glances at her, searching for legible prints, found nothing to track.

"You know I love you, Will, and I want what's best, don't you?"

Winter's silence finally stoppered her father's throat too, and the rest of the drive offered only the hum of the engine and the rush of grief-wet streets.

⁓⁓ ⁓⁓ ⁓⁓

Her father's house, where she'd spent her childhood, hadn't felt like home to Winter even before her parents separated, and it never felt less so than now. Like her father, it was large, cold, uncompromising. Its walls simulated safety and comfort, but Winter knew it was a prison, where she would have to wear another's uniform and bear a stranger's name.

"Will, I'm so, so sorry for your loss, love. But it is so good to see you, to have you with us," said Shannon, hands on Winter's shoulders, cheeks. Winter mumbled an equally meaningless response. The house was less stark now than when Winter had last been here; surely Shannon's influence. It had become a parody of warm hospitality. Welcome mats, throw rugs, stuffed sofa pillows, pictures of people, other people's pets. The worst were the pictures they'd placed on the mantle above the gas fireplace. Pictures that were somewhere between pleas and threats, pictures of Winter as Will, as her father's Will…Winter with a baseball jersey, a stunned smile for the camera her mother had held. A smile smeared there for her father, beside her in the picture, his muscled forearm jovially over her shoulders, half around her neck in affection, protection and threat.

Winter went to her room, said she needed to sleep, sure she'd never be able to sleep here, in a shrine to the little boy her father had always wanted and that she could never be.

She lay in that haunted room and stared while the hours counted, until, to her surprise, exhaustion dragged her down to sleep.

Winter slept and she dreamt. She dreamt of her mother's laughter, of playing cards, clubs and hearts, of spades digging graves. Of playing charades, of the dance she did to show "winter," which became her name. That laughter became the rush of waters, and she dreamt of a deep river muttering secrets beneath the gaze of green woods. She dreamt of the blazing grin of a giddy sun, and the silvery glisten of a dead fish drying on stony shores.

She dreamt of a beautiful girl, swaying leaves for hair, rich bark for skin, whose kiss made that fish into a storm of silver butterflies. She dreamt, and waking was painful when it came.

Two days later, Winter was stuffed into a stiff suit, her feet shod in square black shoes, her neck noosed into a dark red tie. The funeral a wreck of ironies, Winter mired beside her father, strangers shaking her hand, so sorry for your loss, how handsome you've become. Strangers offering her father condolences, clasping his shoulder, so proud now, your son so grown, Shannon dabbing at mascara-inky tears. Winter's face a fall of unbroken snow, grief blazing below.

Grief in a mask, a demented clown, seizing her organs, twisting them into balloon animals, here, her stomach a balloon monkey, her lungs the wings of a balloon swan, sadclown mad-twisting them until they burst…

Father Mark Something from St. Brigid's. The graveside service, clustered mourning of doves, pecking wet grass. A murder of birds merged in Winter, chattering. Well good, she didn't have to hear Father Mark's measured, empty words, rod and thy staff they, what? And where was her mother's God, with her bright wings, in all this? Later, the ashes were scattered in the woods near Green's Creek. Her mother had loved that spot, the wooded, reedy crook where the broad river sent a gentle tendril inland. They had gone there often before the divorce.

The birds, the squirrels, the phairie-play of sunlight and breeze in the leaves; that was what mattered, for both Winter and her mother. The rest of the tired ceremony, the priest, the brassy plaque, Shannon's brassy hair, the strangers' stones and markers, the plastic faux-gravestone of her father's face, all irrelevant.

With the comfortless ritual over, Winter was driven back to her father's house, head low, while he and Shannon splattered her with platitudes and promises of help. There, amidst talk of therapy, medication and faith, Winter radiated resignation. But inside she felt freer, for when she breathed deeply, she could already taste her escape.

III

She waited in the dark in dead Will's room, lightly brushing her closed eyelids now and again to bring the phairies and make the waiting bearable. She waited until Shannon and her father's muffled talk sank into silence, and then she waited longer, clustered phairies over the stippled ceiling like river-waves under moonlight. She breathed, watched the phairies pirouette, until a shift in the cricket song provided her cue. Winter slid into a hoodie, closest she had to an inky cloak, and watched her shadowed reflection in the mirror. She'd become anonymous, a rogue, a digger of skulls! She smiled at her shadow-self, smiled wider at not seeing herself smile.

She grabbed her backpack from beneath the bed, slipped her arms into it. She went to the open window, inhaled starlight and shadow. A familiar feeling – she'd crept from this window many times as a little kid, gone out to stare at the stars, to soak the night in through her skin. She popped the screen, scraped through the window, crept from ledge, to trellis, to tree. Then Winter was off, a thief in the night, taking only some clothes, a toothbrush and a towel, stealing only herself.

She kept to the edges of houses and lawns, away from the incandescent pools of the street lights, until she was out of her father's neighbourhood. She relaxed a little then, knowing she was unlikely to be recognized, but kept her pace quick, hood up, head down, just in case. She cut across Jeanne d'Arc, through Hiawatha Park, and toward the bike path. The path followed the course of the river past Green's Creek, followed it all the way downtown, and was sure to be quiet this time of night. Before she made her escape, Winter needed to see the Creek again. Not stuffed in a suit, not choked by a tie, not flattened beneath her father and a stranger's version of God. She ducked onto the path near the Bruystruck still with that stream of oil-blackness and silvery glitter, its rippling surface mirroring moonlight and stars. She saw a knobby log a few feet from her on the shore, bare patches of smooth, beaver-stripped wood glowing from the rough bark.

She stopped, breathed deeply, slid out of her backpack, set it gently on the log, shed her hoodie next. Her bare arms pimpled with chill as she hung the hoodie from a nearby branch. It swung there, a legless spectre, watching. She slid off her sneakers, placed them beside the log, then skimmed down her jeans, folded them neatly over it, covering a pale patch of bare wood with their warmth. Shirt next, socks on top of the tidy pile, and Winter shivered in the panties she'd smuggled into her father's house. How cold the water would feel; how cold the world felt, without her mother.

She slipped over sharp stones, the dark water swallowing her feet first, her ankles and calves, swallowing her knees, her thighs, and she gasped at the cold her blood brought to her brain. She thrust forward, arms straight before her, legs kicking hard, and dove down.

She came up, spluttering, spitting sour water, blinking fiercely, soundless fireworks of phairies bursting in the air, and that's when she struck the thing. Swollen, cold, strangely giving against the clumsy thrust of her hands, the body bobbed there, languidly. Winter wasn't sure why she hadn't seen it before, so white did it glare in the moonlight now, its pallor drawing the phairies. They flickered curiously at its edges.

The body was belly-down, the great wings, half-extended, drifting lily-white and lily-limp. No longer riding high on the water, the swan sagged, formerly glossy feathers now soaking and frayed. Its swollen body tapered into a once-elegant neck, so badly broken that now it made a skewed V. The head had sunk below the water, but the blow from Winter's arms brought it up, slack beak and marble-blank eyes breaking the surface, staring at her, expectantly.

Coughing, shocked, Winter splashed and kicked back toward the shore. The dead swan did not follow. It bobbed there, anchored against a sunken log, wings stirring in her wake. Its head, so small and fragile next to those great wings, sank back below the water in disappointment. Winter clambered back to shore and stood, shivering, staring at the swan, at the small swarm of phairies that continued to attend it.

Still shivering, Winter searched the scrubby shoreline until she found a long, sturdy stick. When she did, she waded back into the water, walking in until the river coldly clasped her neck. Then she stretched out her arm until the end of the stick met the body of the swan. She could see the tip of the branch that anchored it now, dug into the feathers where the right wing met the body. She leaned further, shuffling to keep balance, until she could push the pale form free of the clutching branch.

She felt something delicate break, and then the swan began to drift away. The little head breached again, dead eyes electric with moonlight, phairie-glow and gratitude. Those eyes made a promise to Winter, and then the dead swan receded, drawn out to the river. Winter waded back to shore. Though her body was frigid, her eyes still burned, and she felt warmth in her right hand, trembling like a little bird.

She fumbled with her backpack and pulled out the big, nubby towel. She shut her eyes as she roughly scrubbed her face, and when she opened them again, a stream of phairies cascaded out into the dark. Drawn to the dance of moonlight on the water, they wove themselves gracefully into those silver ripples, and the river danced with them. Winter, now dried, dressed again and blanketed herself in the damp towel. Lying awkwardly on the large log, pillowing her head on her backpack, she watched the dance for a little lifetime until it ended, unexpectedly, in sleep.

IV

By ten in the morning, Winter's father had noticed the empty bed, the empty room, the open window. By ten-thirty, he had called the police, crying, "My son, my Will, he's missing." Ten hours later, Will was missing still, although the police insisted that technically he wasn't missing yet, wouldn't be until the following morning. "Richard," Shannon said, doing her best to soothe, nervous at the dark knot tightening behind her husband's face, "they'll find him, he'll be fine, I mean, he'll be home soon, he—"

Richard's gravestone face caused her words to catch in her throat, and she fell quiet. Shannon prayed for her dear husband, prayed for his poor son, too, prayed God would help him back to himself, and help him home safe, soon. She prayed Will would find his true path, would understand the pain he caused his father, caused her.

Richard prayed too, in his own quiet way. He prayed that Will would make it home, prayed this Winter business would finally be outgrown, prayed God would make his son the man he should have been.

Having his son back, that was what mattered. They prayed, they waited. They checked with the police again, learned nothing. They waited, they ate without tasting, they worried, they watched TV unseeingly.

Finally, nothing to do but wait, they went to bed.

A curious numbness settled over Richard. A resignation, really, that Will was gone into the wide world, would have to make his own way, somehow, by whatever name he hid himself behind.

Despite his resignation, Richard was sure sleep would keep its distance tonight. "He'll come home safe, honey. I just know he will," Shannon murmured, stroking his back. To his surprise, sleep began to steal over Richard in a stilling mist.

Then the doorbell broke the night, both of them shooting upright in bed. Richard rose with a clear picture in his head; police, arms crossed, sombre, "Sir, we found your…" And his son, head hung, in a skirt, face smeared with makeup, probably stolen, having been caught doing God knows what…

Richard raced down the stairs, Shannon close behind, and he paused when he reached the door. He took a deep breath, tried to cool the crucible of love and disappointment, relief and rage that his son brought bubbling up. He took another breath, preparing a face that suitably mixed sympathy with apology, something he could offer both his son and the officers. He felt Shannon's hand on his back and resisted the urge to shrug it off.

As he pushed the door open, porch-light pouring into the dark living room, he felt that mask slip. The boy, his son, stood there, naked, dead-white, a ghost risen inside a circle of light, a halo of moths milling about him. The boy's large, dark eyes stared through him.

"Will...?" Richard said, uncertain, staring at his son's hairless, narrow body, glistening wet, striped with mud.

"Oh, my God, Will, are you alright? You're naked, you—" Shannon pushed past Richard, reached out to touch the boy's shoulder.

"You're...You're soaked to the bone, and freezing!" Her hand leapt back, and she shook it, as though trying to dislodge some clinging insect that might be about to bite. She stepped back inside the house, beckoning the boy with her hand.

"Come in here, come in, I'll get some towels, some blankets..." Shannon turned and rushed back up the stairs. Will (*it* is *Will, isn't it, Shannon?* Richard wished he could ask – *it is Will* behind those black-marble eyes, behind that so-pale face?) stepped slowly forward, his feet slapping on the tiling of the hall. Each footfall left a muddy puddle, and a filthy pond had formed on the porch where the boy had stood and rung the bell.

Richard knew he should say something to his son, should embrace him, should tell him how good it was to see him, but he couldn't, somehow. He couldn't bring himself to get too close to the boy, something turning him away. His son was home, though. His prayers were answered. Wasn't that all that mattered? The boy stepped past Richard with an awkward, waddling gait, and that's when Richard saw the folded, wet wings, their bent feathers shedding muddy water on the living room floor. As Shannon's bare feet thumped back down the stairs, her arms laden with towels, Richard said, "Will... What... What's happened to..."

The boy's head turned, turned, on its too-long neck, an impossible torsion, to face him. Shiny black marbles fixed, uplifting hard, sharp lips, Will said, "I made a promise, Father, and have come here as an answer to your prayers."

A scream went up from the stairs, and a flock of white towels flapped down, settling over the living room like snow.

ABOUT THE AUTHORS

Lisa Cai was born in Toronto. She graduated from York University with an Honours BA in History and a Masters of Library and Information Science from Western University. She currently works in the tech field. She has been published in *Young Voices* and *Existere: Journal of Arts and Literature*. *Incompatible*, her first novella, was self-published in 2018.

www.tinyurl.com/ybxngmyz

Robert Dawson teaches mathematics at Saint Mary's University in Nova Scotia. When not teaching, doing research, or writing, he enjoys fencing, hiking, and cycling. His stories have appeared in *AE: The Canadian Science Fiction Review*, *Compostela: Tesseracts Twenty*, *Nature Futures*, and numerous other periodicals and anthologies. He is an alumnus of the Sage Hill and Viable Paradise writing workshops.

Evelyn Deshane has had creative and non-fiction works appear in *Plenitude Magazine*, *Briarpatch*, *Strange Horizons*, *Lackington's* and *Bitch* magazine, among other publications. She received an MA from Trent University and is currently completing a Ph.D. at the University of Waterloo. Evelyn's most recent project *#Trans* is an edited collection about transgender and nonbinary identity online.

www.evedeshane.wordpress.com

Nathan Caro Fréchette is a queer transgender man, a sequential artist, publisher, and author. He has published over a dozen graphic and prose short stories, as well as five novels, three graphic novels, two works of non-fiction, and the online comic *Some Assembly Required* (www.tapas.io/series/Some-Assembly-Required1). He has taught creative writing for over a decade, has a degree in Film Studies and another in Sequential Art. He was the founder and director of the French-Canadian literary magazine, *Histoires à Boire Debout*, was an editor for the French-Canadian graphic novel publisher, Premières Lignes, and is the co-founder of the Ottawa-based publisher, Renaissance.

Chadwick Ginther is the Prix Aurora Award-nominated author of the *Thunder Road Trilogy,* and *Graveyard Mind.* His short fiction has appeared recently in *Abyss & Apex, Fire: Demons, Dragons and Djinns, Parallel Prairies,* and Exile's *Those Who Make Us: Canadian Creature, Myth, and Monster Stories.* He lives and writes in Winnipeg, spinning sagas set in the wild spaces of Canada's western wilderness where surely monsters must exist.

@chadwickginther   www.chadwickginther.com

Kate Heartfield is a former newspaper journalist living on the outskirts of Ottawa. Her first novel, a historical fantasy called *Armed in Her Fashion,* was published in 2018. Her short fiction has appeared in magazines including *Strange Horizons, Lackington's, Podcastle* and 2018 National Magazine Awards Gold Medal winner *EXILE/ELQ,* and in anthologies including *Clockwork Canada, Blood and Water,* and *Monstrous Little Voices: New Tales from Shakespeare's Fantasy World.* She has written an interactive novel for Choice of Games based on the *Canterbury Tales.*

@kateheartfield   www.kateheartfield.com

Ace Jordyn of Calgary has a passion for telling folk tales, fairy tales, and fantasy with a historical twist. Her folktale *When Phakack Came to Steal Papa, A Ti-Jean Story* was a finalist in the 2017 Prix Aurora Awards. Ace was also a finalist for a Prix Aurora Award for editing *Shanghai Steam Anthology*, which is recommended reading in Orson Scott Card's *Writing Fantasy & Science Fiction*. *Painted Problems*, her independently published book, is read in elementary schools across Canada. Ace is a proud member of the Imaginative Fiction Writer's Association and a founding member of the blog group Fictorians (www.fictorians.com).   www.acejordyn.com

Richard Keelan is a writer and programmer living in Ottawa. He writes fantasy, science fiction, and software for medical devices. His work has appeared in *AE: The Canadian Science Fiction Review*, *Daily Science Fiction*, *The Arcanist*, and hospitals all over the world.   @R_Keelan www.rkeelan.com

Nicole Lavigne has a BA in English and Theatre from the University of Ottawa. She still lives in Ottawa but considers all of Canada her home after bouncing across the country as a military brat during her childhood. She is a writer and oral storyteller, and daylights as a (mostly) mild-mannered government employee. Her stories have appeared in anthologies by Witty Bard Publishing, Visual Adjectives, and Bundoran Press, and she has recently been translated into Chinese by *Science Fiction World* magazine.

@nl_lavigne   www.nllavigne.wordpress.com

Karin Lowachee was born in South America, grew up in Canada, and worked in the Arctic. Her first novel *Warchild*

won the 2001 Warner Aspect First Novel Contest. Both *Warchild* and her third novel *Cagebird* were finalists for the Philip K. Dick Award. *Cagebird* won the Prix Aurora Award in 2006 for Best Long-Form Work in English and the Spectrum Award, also in 2006. Her other novels are *Burndrive* and *The Gaslight Dogs*. Her books have been translated into French, Hebrew, and Japanese, and her short stories have appeared in anthologies edited by Nalo Hopkinson, John Joseph Adams, Jonathan Strahan and Ann VanderMeer.

@karinlow   www.karinlowachee.com

Quinn McGlade-Ferentzy is an angry li'l queer. She collects tattoos and cats and her parents are very proud. She's currently studying Philosophy at Guelph University.

Rati Mehrotra lives and writes in Toronto. Her short stories have appeared in *AE: The Canadian Science Fiction Review*, *Apex Magazine*, *Urban Fantasy Magazine*, *Podcastle*, *Cast of Wonders*, *EXILE/ELQ*, *Clockwork Canada*, and many more. Her debut novel, *Markswoman*, was published in January 2018.   @Rati_Mehrotra   www.ratiwrites.com

Sean Moreland lives and teaches in Ottawa. He created *Postscripts to Darkness* (www.pstdarkness.com) and his short fiction and award-winning poetry has most recently appeared in *Lackington's*, *Black Treacle*, *Acidic Fiction*, and *Dissections*. He has published essays in many collections and journals, and recently edited *The Lovecraftian Poe: Essays on Influence, Reception, Interpretation and Transformation* (2017), and *New Directions in Supernatural Horror Literature: The Critical Influence of H. P. Lovecraft* (2018).

Fiona Patton was born in Calgary, Alberta, and now lives in rural Ontario with her wife, Tanya Huff, and a menagerie of dogs and cats. She is the author of seven heroic fantasy novels, as well as nearly 40 short stories. She has been interested in robots since 1977, because, of course: *Star Wars*.

Ursula Pflug of Peterborough, Ontario, is the author or editor of three novels, two story collections, two novellas and two anthologies. She is working on a new Exile's anthology, *The Food of My People*, with Candas Jane Dorsey, due for publication in 2019. Her latest book is the novella *Down From*, published in the U.K. in 2018. She has appeared in *Lightspeed*, *Fantasy*, *Strange Horizons*, *PostScripts*, *Leviathan*, *Lady Churchill's Rosebud Wristlet* (*LCRW*), *EXILE/ELQ* and elsewhere. Her books have been endorsed by Tim Wynne-Jones, Candas Jane Dorsey, Charles de Lint, Matthew Cheney, Heather Spears, Leanne Betasamosake Simpson and Jeff VanderMeer, and her award-winning short stories have been taught in universities in Canada and India.

@UrsulaPflug   www.ursulapflug.ca

Kate Story of Peterborough is a writer and performer, and a Newfoundlander living in Ontario. Her first novel *Blasted* received the 2009 Sunburst Award's honourable mention, and she is the 2015 recipient of the Ontario Arts Foundation's K.M. Hunter Award for her work in theatre. Her short stories have been published in *World Fantasy*-nominated and Aurora Award-winning collections, and *EXILE/ELQ*. Her third novel, *This Insubstantial Pageant*, was published in 2017; the *Toronto Star* named it a "top science-fiction read…exotic, funny and very sexy." Her first young adult fantasy novel *Antilia: Sword and Song* came out this year.

Liz Westbrook-Trenholm lives in Ottawa with her husband, writer and publisher Hayden Trenholm. She has published or broadcast mainstream and speculative short fiction, most recently in *Neo-opsis*, the Prix Aurora Award-winning anthologies *Second Contacts* and *The Sum of Us*, and and in Aurora-nominated *49th Parallels*. Her story, *Gone Flying*, won the 2018 Prix Aurora Award for best short fiction.

Tamara Vardomskaya is a Canadian writer, a Clarion 2014 graduate, and a Ph.D candidate at the University of Chicago. Her fiction has appeared at *Tor.com, GigaNotoSaurus,* and *Beneath Ceaseless Skies.*

COVER ARTIST

Arthur Rackham was an English book illustrator. He is recognized as one of the leading literary figures during the Golden Age of British book illustration. His work is noted for its robust pen and ink drawings, which were combined with the use of watercolour.

ABOUT THE EDITOR

Derek Newman-Stille is a queer, nonbinary (preferring they/ them for pronouns), disabled author, editor, artist, academic, and activist living in Peterborough, Ontario. Derek is a Ph.D (ABD) candidate, and the eight-time Prix Aurora Award-winning creator of the digital humanities site Speculating Canada and associated radio show. They are also the creator of the digital humanities site Dis(Abled) Embodiment, and co-creator of the sites QueerPop and the fairy tale site Through the Twisted Woods. Derek teaches at Trent University in the English Department and Women's and Gender Studies Department. They have been published in fora such as *Quill & Quire, The Playground of Lost Toys, Accessing The Future, Disabled People Destroy Science Fiction, The Canadian Fantastic in Focus, Mosaic: An Interdisciplinary Critical Journal*, and *Misfit Children: An Inquiry Into Childhood Belongings.*

www.speculatingcanada.ca
www.disabledbodiment@wordpress.com
queerpopblog@wordpress.com
www.throughthetwistedwoods@wordpress.com
@DNewmanStille
www.dereknewmanstille.com

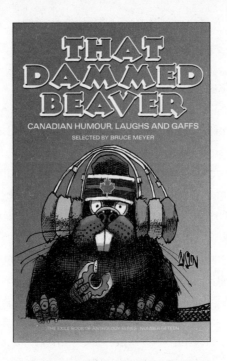

THAT DAMMED BEAVER:
CANADIAN HUMOUR, LAUGHS AND GAFFS

EDITED BY BRUCE MEYER

"What exactly makes Canadians funny? This effort from long-standing independent press Exile Editions takes a wry look at what makes us laugh and what makes us laughable." —*Toronto Star*

Margaret Atwood, Austin Clarke, Leon Rooke, Priscila Uppal, Jonathan Goldstein, Paul Quarrington, Morley Callaghan, Jacques Ferron, Marsha Boulton, Joe Rosenblatt, Barry Callaghan, Linda Rogers, Steven Hayward, Andrew Borkowski, Helen Marshall, Gloria Sawai, David McFadden, Myna Wallin, Gail Prussky, Louise Maheux-Forcher, Shannon Bramer, James Dewar, Bob Armstrong, Jamie Feldman, Claire Dé, Christine Miscione, Larry Zolf, Anne Dandurand, Julie Roorda, Mark Paterson, Karen Lee White, Heather J. Wood, Marty Gervais, Matt Shaw, Alexandre Amprimoz, Darren Gluckman, Gustave Morin, and the country's greatest cartoonist, Aislin.

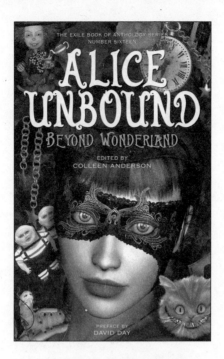

ALICE UNBOUND:
BEYOND WONDERLAND

EDITED BY COLLEEN ANDERSON

"This tremendously entertaining anthology…will delight both lovers of Carroll's works and fans of inventive genre fiction." —*Publishers Weekly*, starred review

A collection of twenty-first century speculative fiction stories that is inspired by *Alice's Adventures in Wonderland, Alice Through the Looking Glass, The Hunting of the Snark,* and to some degree, aspects of the life of the author, Charles Dodgson (Lewis Carroll), and the real-life Alice (Liddell). Enjoy a wonderful and wild ride down and back up out of the rabbit hole!

Patrick Bollivar, Mark Charke, Christine Daigle, Robert Dawson, Linda DeMeulemeester, Pat Flewwelling, Geoff Gander and Fiona Plunkett, Cait Gordon, Costi Gurgu, Kate Heartfield, Elizabeth Hosang, Nicole Iversen, J.Y.T. Kennedy, Danica Lorer, Catherine MacLeod, Bruce Meyer, Dominik Parisien, Alexandra Renwick, Andrew Robertson, Lisa Smedman, Sara C. Walker and James Wood.

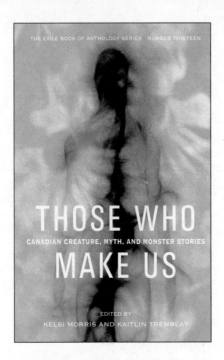

THOSE WHO MAKE US: CANADIAN CREATURE, MYTH, AND MONSTER STORIES

EDITED BY KELSI MORRIS AND KAITLIN TREMBLAY

What resides beneath the blankets of snow, under the ripples of water, within the whispers of the wind, and between the husks of trees all across Canada? Creatures, myths and monsters are everywhere…even if we don't always see them.

Canadians from all backgrounds and cultures look to identify with their surroundings through stories. Herein, speculative and literary fiction provides unique takes on what being Canadian is about.

"Kelsi Morris and Kaitlin Tremblay did not set out to create a traditional anthology of monster stories… This unconventional anthology lives up to the challenge, the stories show tremendous openness and compassion in the face of the world's darkness, unfairness, and indifference." —*Quill & Quire*

Featuring stories by Helen Marshall, Renée Sarojini Saklikar, Nathan Adler, Kate Story, Braydon Beaulieu, Chadwick Ginther, Dominik Parisien, Stephen Michell, Andrew Wilmot, Rati Mehrotra, Rebecca Schaeffer, Delani Valin, Corey Redekop, Angeline Woon, Michal Wojcik, Andrea Bradley, Andrew F. Sullivan and Alexandra Camille Renwick.

CLI FI:
CANADIAN TALES OF CLIMATE CHANGE

EDITED BY BRUCE MEYER

In his introduction to this all-original set of (at times barely) futuristic tales, Meyer warns readers, "[The] imaginings of today could well become the cold, hard facts of tomorrow." Meyer (Testing the Elements) has gathered an eclectic variety of eco-fictions from some of Canada's top genre writers, each of which, he writes, reminds readers that "the world is speaking to us and that it is our duty, if not a covenant, to listen to what it has to say." In these pages, scientists work desperately against human ignorance, pockets of civilization fight to balance morality and survival, and corporations cruelly control access to basic needs such as water.... The anthology may be inescapably dark, but it is a necessary read, a clarion call to take action rather than, as a character in Seán Virgo's "My Atlantis" describes it, "waiting unknowingly for the plague, the hive collapse, the entropic thunderbolt." Luckily, it's also vastly entertaining. It appears there's nothing like catastrophe to bring the best out in authors in describing the worst of humankind. —*Publishers Weekly*

George McWhirter, Richard Van Camp, Holly Schofield, Linda Rogers, Sean Virgo, Rati Mehrotra, Geoffrey W. Cole, Phil Dwyer, Kate Story, Leslie Goodreid, Nina Munteanu, Halli Villegas, John Oughton, Frank Westcott, Wendy Bone, Peter Timmerman, Lynn Hutchinson Lee, with an afterword by internationally acclaimed writer and filmmaker, Dan Bloom.

The Exile Book of Anthology Series
Number Eleven

playground
of
LOST
toys

Edited by Colleen Anderson and Ursula Pflug

PLAYGROUND OF LOST TOYS

EDITED BY COLLEEN ANDERSON AND URSULA PFLUG

A dynamic collection of stories that explore the mystery, awe and dread that we may have felt as children when encountering a special toy. But it goes further, to the edges of space, where games are for keeps and where the mind plays its own games. We enter a world where the magic may not have been lost, where a toy or computers or gods vie for the upper hand. Wooden games of skill, ancient artifacts misinterpreted, dolls, stuffed animals, wand items that seek a life or even revenge – these lost toys and games bring tales of companionship, loss, revenge, hope, murder, cunning, and love, to be unearthed in the sandbox.

Featuring stories by Chris Kuriata, Joe Davies, Catherine MacLeod, Kate Story, Meagan Whan, Candas Jane Dorsey, Rati Mehrotra, Nathan Adler, Rhonda Eikamp, Robert Runté, Linda DeMeulemeester, Kevin Cockle, Claude Lalumière, Dominik Parisien, dvsduncan, Christine Daigle, Melissa Yuan-Innes, Shane Simmons, Lisa Carreiro, Karen Abrahamson, Geoffrey W. Cole and Alexandra Camille Renwick. Afterword by Derek Newman-Stille.

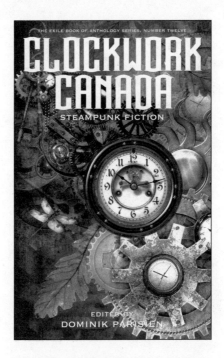

CLOCKWORK CANADA:
STEAMPUNK FICTION

EDITED BY DOMINIK PARISIEN

Welcome to an alternate Canada, where steam technology and the wonders and horrors of the mechanical age have reshaped the past into something both wholly familiar yet compellingly different.

"These stories of clockworks, airships, mechanical limbs, automata, and steam are, overall, an unfettered delight to read." —*Quill & Quire*

"[*Clockwork Canada*] is a true delight that hits on my favorite things in fiction – curious worldbuilding, magic, and tough women taking charge. It's a carefully curated adventure in short fiction that stays true to a particular vision while seeking and achieving nuance."
                                                                                    —*Tor.com*

"…inventive and transgressive…these stories rethink even the fundamentals of what we usually mean by steampunk." —*The Toronto Star*

Featuring stories by Colleen Anderson, Karin Lowachee, Brent Nichols, Charlotte Ashley, Chantal Boudreau, Rhea Rose, Kate Story, Terri Favro, Kate Heartfield, Claire Humphrey, Rati Mehrotra, Tony Pi, Holly Schofield, Harold R. Thompson and Michal Wojcik.

FRACTURED:
TALES OF THE CANADIAN POST-APOCALYPSE

EDITED BY SILVIA MORENO-GARCIA

"The 23 stories in *Fractured* cover incredible breadth, from the last man alive in Haida Gwaii to a dying Matthew waiting for his Anne in PEI. All the usual apocalyptic suspects are here – climate change, disease, alien invasion – alongside less familiar scenarios such as a ghost apocalypse and an invasion of shadows. Stories range from the immediate aftermath of society's collapse to distant futures in which humanity has been significantly reduced, but the same sense of struggle and survival against the odds permeates most of the pieces in the collection… What *Fractured* really drives home is how perfect Canada is as a setting for the post-apocalypse. Vast tracts of wilderness, intense weather, and the potentially sinister consequences of environmental devastation provide ample inspiration for imagining both humanity's destruction and its rugged survival." —*Quill & Quire*

Featuring stories by T.S. Bazelli, GMB Chomichuk, A.M. Dellamonica, dvsduncan, Geoff Gander, Orrin Grey, David Huebert, John Jantunen, H.N. Janzen, Arun Jiwa, Claude Lalumière, Jamie Mason, Michael Matheson, Christine Ottoni, Miriam Oudin, Michael S. Pack, Morgan M. Page, Steve Stanton, Amanda M. Taylor, E. Catherine Tobler, Jean-Louis Trudel, Frank Westcott and A.C. Wise.

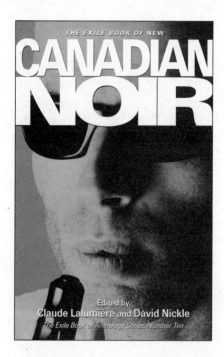

NEW CANADIAN NOIR

EDITED BY CLAUDE LALUMIÈRE AND DAVID NICKLE

"Everything is in the title. These are all new stories – no novel extracts – selected by Claude Lalumière and David Nickle from an open call. They're Canadian-authored, but this is not an invitation for national introspection. Some Canadian locales get the noir treatment, which is fun, since, as Nickle notes in his afterword, noir, with its regard for the underbelly, seems like an un-Canadian thing to write. But the main question *New Canadian Noir* asks isn't "Where is here?" it's "What can noir be?" These stories push past the formulaic to explore noir's far reaches as a mood and aesthetic. In Nickle's words, "Noir is a state of mind – an exploration of corruptibility, ultimately an expression of humanity in all its terrible frailty." The resulting literary alchemy – from horror to fantasy, science fiction to literary realism, romance to, yes, crime – spanning the darkly funny to the stomach-queasy horrific, provides consistently entertaining rewards." —*Globe and Mail*

Featuring stories by Corey Redekop, Joel Thomas Hynes, Silvia Moreno-Garcia, Chadwick Ginther, Michael Mirolla, Simon Strantzas, Steve Vernon, Kevin Cockle, Colleen Anderson, Shane Simmons, Laird Long, Dale L. Sproule, Alex C. Renwick, Ada Hoffmann, Kieth Cadieux, Michael S. Chong, Rich Larson, Kelly Robson, Edward McDermott, Hermine Robinson, David Menear and Patrick Fleming.

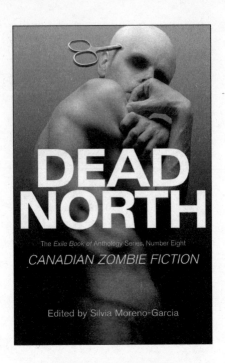

DEAD NORTH:
CANADIAN ZOMBIE FICTION

EDITED BY SILVIA MORENO-GARCIA

"*Dead North* suggests zombies may be thought of as native to this country, their presence going back to Aboriginal myths and legends…we see deadheads, shamblers, jiang shi, and Shark Throats invading such home and native settings as the Bay of Fundy's Hopewell Rocks, Alberta's tar sands, Toronto's Mount Pleasant Cemetery, and a Vancouver Island grow-op. Throw in the last poutine truck on Earth driving across Saskatchewan and some "mutant demon zombie cows devouring Montreal" (honest!) and what you've got is a fun and eclectic mix of zombie fiction…" —*Toronto Star*

"Every time I listen to the yearly edition of *Canada Reads* on CBC, so much attention seems to be drawn to the fact that the author is Canadian, that being Canadian becomes a gimmick. *Dead North*, a collection of zombie short stories by exclusively Canadian authors, is the first of its kind that I've seen to buck this trend, using the diverse cultural mythology of the Great White North to put a number of unique spins on an otherwise over-saturated genre."—*Bookshelf Reviews*

Featuring stories by Chantal Boudreau, Tessa J. Brown, Richard Van Camp, Kevin Cockle, Jacques L. Condor, Carrie-Lea Côté, Linda DeMeulemeester, Brian Dolton, Gemma Files, Ada Hoffmann, Tyler Keevil, Claude Lalumière, Jamie Mason, Michael Matheson, Ursula Pflug, Rhea Rose, Simon Strantzas, E. Catherine Tobler, Beth Wodzinski and Melissa Yuan-Ines.

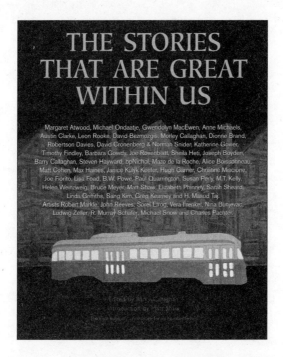

THE STORIES THAT ARE GREAT WITHIN US

Margaret Atwood, Michael Ondaatje, Gwendolyn MacEwen, Anne Michaels, Austin Clarke, Leon Rooke, David Bezmozgis, Morley Callaghan, Dionne Brand, Robertson Davies, David Cronenberg & Norman Snider, Katherine Govier, Timothy Findley, Barbara Gowdy, Joe Rosenblatt, Sheila Heti, Joseph Boyden, Barry Callaghan, Steven Hayward, bpNichol, Mazo de la Roche, Alice Boissonneau, Matt Cohen, Max Haines, Janice Kulyk Keefer, Hugh Garner, Christine Miscione, Joe Fiorito, Lisa Foad, B.W. Powe, Paul Quarrington, Susan Perly, M.T. Kelly, Helen Weinzweig, Bruce Meyer, Matt Shaw, Elizabeth Phinney, Sarah Sheard, Linda Griffiths, Sang Kim, Greg Kearney and H. Masud Taj. Artists Robert Markle, John Reeves, Sorel Etrog, Vera Frenkel, Nina Bunjevac, Ludwig Zeller, R. Murray Schafer, Michael Snow and Charles Pachter.

THE STORIES THAT ARE GREAT WITHIN US

EDITED BY BARRY CALLAGHAN

"[This is a] large book, one to be sat on the lap and not held up, one to be savoured piece by piece and heard as much as read as the great sidewalk rolls out...This is the infrastructure of Toronto, its deep language and various truths." —*Pacific Rim Review of Books*

Among the 50-plus contributors are Margaret Atwood, Michael Ondaatje, Gwendolyn MacEwen, Anne Michaels, Austin Clarke, Leon Rooke, David Bezmozgis, Morley Callaghan, Dionne Brand, Robertson Davies, Katherine Govier, Timothy Findley, Barbara Gowdy, Joseph Boyden, bpNichol, Hugh Garner, Joe Fiorito and Paul Quarrington, Janice Kulyk Keefer, along with artists Sorel Etrog, Vera Frenkel, Nina Bunjevac, Michael Snow, and Charles Pachter.

"Bringing together an ensemble of Canada's best-known, mid-career, and emerging writers...this anthology stands as the perfect gateway to discovering the city of Toronto. With a diverse range of content, the book focuses on the stories that have taken the city, in just six decades, from a narrow wryly praised as a city of churches to a brassy, gauche, imposing metropolis that is the fourth largest in North America. With an introduction from award-winning author Matt Shaw, this blends a cacophony of voices to encapsulate the vibrant city of Toronto." —*Toronto Star*

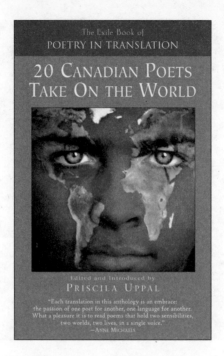

The Exile Book of
POETRY IN TRANSLATION

20 CANADIAN POETS
TAKE ON THE WORLD

Edited and Introduced by
PRISCILA UPPAL

"Each translation in this anthology is an embrace:
the passion of one poet for another, one language for another.
What a pleasure it is to read poems that hold two sensibilities,
two worlds, two lives, in a single voice."
—ANNE MICHAELS

20 CANADIAN POETS TAKE ON THE WORLD

EDITED BY PRISCILA UPPAL

A groundbreaking multilingual collection promoting a global poetic consciousness, thisvolume presents the works of 20 international poets, all in their original languages, alongside English translations by some of Canada's most esteemed poets. Spanning several time periods and more than a dozen nations, this compendium paints a truly unique portrait of cultures, nationalities, and eras."

Canadian poets featured are Oana Avasilichioaei, Ken Babstock, Christian Bök, Dionne Brand, Nicole Brossard, Barry Callaghan, George Elliott Clarke, Geoffrey Cook, Rishma Dunlop, Steven Heighton, Christopher Doda, Andréa Jarmai, Evan Jones, Sonnet L'Abbé, A.F. Moritz, Erín Moure, Goran Simic, Priscila Uppal, Paul Vermeersch, and Darren Wershler, translating the works of Nobel laureates, classic favourites, and more, including Jan-Willem Anker, Her-man de Coninck, María Elena Cruz Varela, Kiki Dimoula, George Faludy, Horace, Juan Ramón Jiménez, Pablo Neruda, Chus Pato, Ezra Pound, Alexander Pushkin, Rainer Maria Rilke, Arthur Rimbaud, Elisa Sampedrín, Leopold Staff, Nichita St̆anescu, Stevan Tonti´c, Ko Un, and Andrei Voznesensky. Each translating poet provides an introduction to their work.

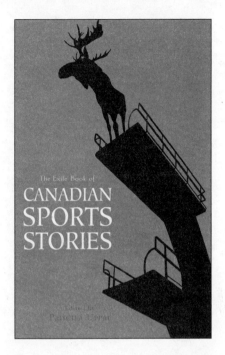

CANADIAN SPORTS STORIES

EDITED BY PRISCILA UPPAL

"This anthology collects a wide range of Canada's literary imaginations, telling great stories about the wild and fascinating world of sport... Written by both men and women, the generations of insights provided in this collection expose some of the most intimate details of sports and sporting life – the hard-earned victories, and the sometimes inevitable tragedies. You will get to know those who play the game, as well as those who watch it, coach it, write about it, dream about it, live and die by it."

"Most of the stories weren't so much about sports per se than they were a study of personalities and how they react to or deal with extreme situations...all were worth reading"
—goodreads.com

Clarke Blaise, George Bowering, Dionne Brand, Barry Callaghan, Morley Callaghan, Roch Carrier, Matt Cohen, Craig Davidson, Brian Fawcett, Katherine Govier, Steven Heighton, Mark Jarman, W.P. Kinsella, Stephen Leacock, L.M. Montgomery, Susanna Moodie, Margaret Pigeon, Mordecai Richler, Priscila Uppal, Guy Vanderhaeghe, and more.

CANADIAN DOG STORIES

EDITED BY RICHARD TELEKY

Spanning from the 1800s to 2005, and featuring exceptional short stories from 28 of Canada's most prominent fiction writers, this unique anthology explores the nature of the human-dog bond through writing from both the nation's earliest storytellerssuch as Ernest Thompson Seton, L. M. Montgomery, and Stephen Leacockand a younger generation that includes Lynn Coady and Matt Shaw. Not simply sentimental tales about noble dogs doing heroic deeds, these stories represent the rich, complex, and mysterious bond between dogs and humans. Adventure and drama, heartfelt encounters and nostalgia, sharp-edged satire, and even fantasy make up the genres in this memorable collection.

"Twenty-eight exceptional dog tales by some of Canada's most notable fiction writers... The stories run the breadth of adventure, drama, satire, and even fantasy, and will appeal to dog lovers on both sides of the [Canada/U.S.] border." —*Modern Dog Magazine*

Marie-Claire Blais, Barry Callaghan, Morley Callaghan, Lynn Coady, Mazo de la Roche, Jacques Ferron, Mavis Gallant, Douglas Glover, Katherine Govier, Kenneth J. Harvey, E. Pauline Johnson, Janice Kulyk Keefer, Alistair Macleod, L.M. Montgomery, P.K. Page, Charles G.D. Roberts, Leon Rooke, Jane Rule, Duncan Campbell Scott, Timothy Taylor, Sheila Watson, Ethel Wilson, and more.

The Exile Book of
NATIVE CANADIAN
FICTION AND DRAMA
Edited by
DANIEL DAVID MOSES AND BARRY CALLAGHAN

NATIVE CANADIAN FICTION AND DRAMA

EDITED BY DANIEL DAVID MOSES

The work of men and women of many tribal affiliations, this collection is a wide-ranging anthology of contemporary Native Canadian literature. Deep emotions and life-shaking crises converge and display the Aboriginal concerns regarding various topics, including identity, family, community, caste, gender, nature, betrayal, and war. A fascinating compilation of stories and plays, this account fosters cross-cultural understanding and presents the Native Canadian writers reinvention of traditional material and their invention of a modern life that is authentic. It is perfect for courses on short fiction or general symposium teaching material.

Tomson Highway, Lauren B. Davis, Niigonwedom James Sinclair, Joseph Boyden, Joseph A. Dandurand, Alootook Ipellie, Thomas King, Yvette Nolan, Richard Van Camp, Floyd Favel, Robert Arthur Alexie, Daniel David Moses, Katharina Vermette.

"A strong addition to the ever shifting Canadian literary canon, effectively presenting the depth and artistry of the work by Aboriginal writers in Canada today."

—*Canadian Journal of Native Studies*

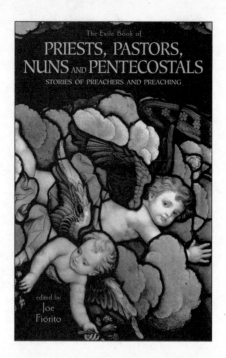

PRIESTS, PASTORS,
NUNS AND PENTECOSTALS

EDITED BY JOE FIORITO

A literary approach to the Word of the Lord, this collection of short fiction deals within one way or another the overarching concept of redemption. This anthology demonstrates how God appears again and again in the lives of priest, pastors, nuns, and Pentecostals. However He appears, He appears again and again in the lives of priests, nuns, and Pentecostals in these great stories of a kind never collected before

Mary Frances Coady, Barry Callaghan, Leon Rooke, Roch Carrier, Jacques Ferron, Seán Virgo, Marie-Claire Blais, Hugh Hood, Morley Callaghan, Hugh Garner, Diane Keating, Alexandre Amprimoz, Gloria Sawai, Eric McCormack, Yves Thériault, Margaret Laurence, Alice Munro.

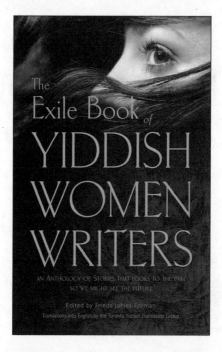

YIDDISH WOMEN WRITERS

EDITED BY FRIEDA JOHLES FOREMAN

Presenting a comprehensive collection of influential Yiddish women writers with new translations, this anthology explores the major transformations and upheavals of the 20th century. Short stories, excerpts, and personal essays are included from 13 writers, and focus on such subjects as family life; sexual awakening; longings for independence, education, and creative expression; the life in Europe surrounding the Holocaust and its aftermath; immigration; and the conflicted entry of Jewish women into the modern world with the restrictions of traditional life and roles. These powerful accounts provide a vital link to understanding the Jewish experience at a time of conflict and tumultuous change.

"This continuity…of Yiddish, of women, and of Canadian writers does not simply add a missing piece to an existing puzzle; instead it invites us to rethink the narrative of Yiddish literary history at large… Even for Yiddish readers, the anthology is a site of discovery, offering harder-to-find works that the translators collected from the Canadian Yiddish press and published books from Israel, France, Canada, and the U.S."

—*Studies in American Jewish Literature*, Volume 33, Number 2, 2014

"Yiddish Women Writers did what a small percentage of events at a good literary festival [Blue Metropolis] should: it exposed the curious to a corner of history, both literary and social, that they might never have otherwise considered." —*Montreal Gazette*